DREAM YOUR PROBLEMS AWAY

HEAL YOURSELF WHILE YOU SLEEP

By
Dr. Bruce Goldberg

NEW PAGE BOOKS
A division of The Career Press, Inc.
Franklin Lakes, NJ

DREAM YOUR PROBLEMS AWAY
EDITED AND TYPESET BY NICOLE DEFELICE
Cover design by Cheryl Cohan Finbow
Printed in the U.S.A. by Book-mart Press

To order this title, please call toll-free 1-800-CAREER-1 (NJ and Canada: 201-848-0310) to order using VISA or MasterCard, or for further information on books from Career Press.

The Career Press, Inc., 3 Tice Road, PO Box 687,
Franklin Lakes, NJ 07417
www.careerpress.com
www.newpagebooks.com

Library of Congress Cataloging-in-Publication Data

Goldberg, Bruce, 1948-
  Dream your problems away : heal yourself while you sleep / by Bruce Goldberg.
    p. cm.
  Includes bibliographical references and index.
  ISBN 1-56414-634-0 (pbk.)
    1. Dreams. 2. Dream interpretation. I. Title.

BF1091 .G64 2003
135'.3—dc21

                                    2002071925

Dedication

This book is dedicated to my thousands of patients who have been kind enough to use self-hypnosis in their dream therapy, without which this book would not have been possible. I also dedicate this book to the Universe, whose many wonders never cease to both amaze and instruct me in the art and science of self-hypnosis.

Acknowledgments

I would like to thank Michael Lewis, Acquisitions Editor of New Page Books, for his interest and assistance in bringing this book to the public. In addition, my heartfelt gratitude goes out to my editor Nicole DeFelice. Without her experience and detailed supervision, this book's final form would be quite different.

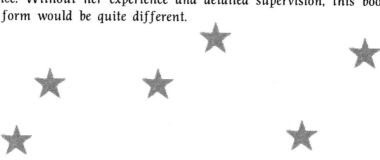

Contents

Introduction

The main purpose of this book is to teach you how to utilize your dreams to take charge of your life. This includes using these nightly visualizations in your mind to:

☆ Explore and remove the origins of current-day problems. I refer to these efforts to sabotage your growth as "self-defeating sequences."[1]

☆ Develop more love and understanding.

☆ Improve creativity at all levels.

☆ Facilitate the quality of personal and professional relationships.

☆ Initiate healing of physical, emotional, mental, and spiritual issues. Establish a harmony of body, mind, and spirit (soul).

☆ Master your psychic abilities, such as telepathy, clairvoyance, precognition, and telekinesis.

☆ Gain spiritual insights that accelerate your spiritual growth and psychic empowerment.

It is important to practice the exercises I present. Reading a book can be most enlightening and entertaining, but you must apply the techniques to actually benefit from this fascinating discipline.

You will learn that dreams are far more than just a symbolic representation of communication from your subconscious. Our subconscious never really sleeps, and when our physical body is unconscious and resting, our soul is traveling to other dimensions under the guidance of our Higher Self and Spiritual Masters. The memories of fragments of this tutoring appear as a dream.

Dreams are as valid and relevant to our lives as our waking state. The only real difference is that our dreams take place on a different plane of existence. This is why it is so difficult to understand and decode our dreams based on conventional paradigms.

I will present some of the conventional interpretations of dream elements, but only for background purposes. My premise is quite metaphysical. One of the reasons there is so much disagreement among the dream "experts" (and resulting misunderstandings of the general population concerning the meaning of dreams), is the censoring of this data experienced by our Higher Self and Masters and Guides before we finally receive it in the conscious state.

Some brain researchers feel that one dream may represent as many as 30 different dream scenarios that we experience throughout the night. It is our lack of understanding and inability to deal with the truth that creates this form of nocturnal camouflage. No wonder we are confused by the content of a typical dream and write it off as a fantasy meandering!

More therapists today are coming to the realization that ultimately, individuals must decipher their own dreams to understand the complexities of their own inner nature. This is just part of the new paradigm of the universe: Take responsibility for your own relationship with reality.

To use this book effectively, you must be prepared to take control of your own self-analysis, self-exploration, and self-discovery. Be prepared to chart your own course of psychic empowerment, and solve the mystery that is your self.

Think of the concept of solid matter for a moment. A table leg is solid, is it not? Yet when we take a subatomic particle and fire it at this same table leg, it passes through easily. The solidity of all physical objects is merely an illusion.

Our universe is composed of energy and matter. They may be transformed into each other, according to Einstein's famous $E=MC^2$ equation. Matter is composed of molecules, molecules of atoms, atoms of subatomic particles, and subatomic particles of quanta of energy.

Don't let the illusion of the physical world fool you. We can only perceive what our five senses can detect, unless we have highly developed psychic abilities. There are several forms of energy outside our normal sense detection spectrum. Ultraviolet rays, radio waves, X-rays, and cosmic radiation are among those energies we cannot detect without the aid of sophisticated scientific instruments.

Dreams exist in an environment that is also composed of energy. This energy is of a different order from that which we are able to measure physically. Our scientific instruments can't portray them, except for the alpha brain waves registered on an electroencephalograph (EEG). We can't see our dreams on a television monitor, or capture them in a test tube. Yet those things called dreams most certainly do exist.

The chapters on the dream world, dream lovers, and lucid dreaming will discuss the astral plane, which is precisely where our dreams originate. The nonphysical counterpart of our physical body takes on a new life while we dream. For those of you concerned about life after death, dreams of your life on this astral plane are among the most impressive forms of suggestive evidence of both the soul and its survival following the death of the physical body.

Our dream world is quite real. I cannot offer hard scientific evidence to support my hypothesis. Just as science cannot absolutely prove that the physical world is real, we have not found a manner to measure the existence of the world of dreams. Reality is an elusive concept and it is hard to quantify and define.

One of the great benefits of dreaming is a total freedom to create whatever we wish. This dream environment changes shape according to the will and imagination of the dreamer. This is due to the energy structure and less rigid nature of its environment. This is why this world of dreams is so subjective.

This dream environment, because it represents another form of reality, allows us to incorporate certain techniques to heal ourselves. I will present many simple and time-tested exercises to train you to master your dreams and dream your problems away.

We will also discuss keeping a dream journal. Most of us will quickly forget a dream if it isn't documented. This diary allows us to verify the accuracy of precognitive dreams, and note patterns in the appearance of symbols and recurrent subplots. It stimulates us to synthesize, understand, and eliminate experiences that tend to hold us back in life. Removing this "baggage" allows a fuller understanding of ourselves and more accentuated spiritual growth.

The dangers of "waking sleep" or robotic behavior will also be presented to illustrate how this dysfunctional paradigm retards our spiritual growth. Finally, I will thoroughly demonstrate how we can all use our dreams to see into the future or custom-design our own destiny.

How to Use This Book

This book contains dozens of exercises specifically designed to train you to experience self-hypnosis. It doesn't matter what your background is.

You can accept or reject any of the principles and concepts presented here. Empowerment is vital. I stress that in my Los Angeles hypnotherapy practice and in my personal life as well. If you become rigid and stuck in your views, you become trapped by your beliefs. You are no longer empowered because you are no longer free.

Always use your judgment and free will in trying these exercises. Use the ones you feel comfortable with and ignore the others. These exercises are all perfectly safe and have been tested for more than 25 years. You may create your own exercises from these models.

Read each exercise through to become familiar with it. Use the relaxation techniques given or your own. You may practice alone or with others. I strongly suggest that you make tapes of these exercises. Read the scripts slowly and leave enough space on your tape to experience each part of the procedure.

Practice once or twice a day, in 15- to 20-minute sessions. In general, it is considered more efficient to practice in the morning, as it may provide a relaxing start for the entire day. The more specific and realistic your schedule, the better the chances that you will succeed.

You should choose a part of your day when you are at your best. If you wait to practice until long after you get home from a hard day at work, you might only practice going to sleep. Self-hypnosis is more efficient if practiced when you are reasonably alert. Begin by picking a good time to practice.

If you wake up alert and rested first thing in the morning, practice then, before getting out of bed. Take into account whether or not you will be disturbed by spouse, lover, kids, pets, and so forth. Choose a time when you are not likely to be interrupted. Other popular times are before lunch or dinner.

Four components of successful self-hypnosis are:

☆ A quiet environment.
☆ A mental device.
☆ A passive attitude.
☆ A comfortable position.

When you enter into a self-hypnotic trance, you will observe the following:

☆ A positive mood (tranquility, peace of mind).
☆ An experience of unity or oneness with the environment.
☆ An inability to describe the experience in words.
☆ An alteration in time/space relationships.
☆ An enhanced sense of reality and meaning.

If you experience difficulty with an exercise, do not become frustrated. Some techniques are quite advanced and you may not be ready for all of them. Return to the ones you could not successfully work with at another time.

Practice these trance states when you have time and are relaxed. Be patient. It takes time to master trance states and to become accustomed to this new and wonderful world. No one way is the right way to experience a trance. Your body may feel light, or it may feel heavy; you may feel as if you are dreaming; your eyelids may flutter; or your body can become cooler or warmer. All these possible responses are perfectly safe.

Because you will be unfamiliar with the techniques at first, your initial practice sessions should run as long as you need. As you become more proficient, you will be able to shorten these sessions. Some days nothing may seem to work. Try not to become discouraged. Remember that other days will be more fruitful. Always work at your own pace and with an open mind.

Note to the Reader

This book is the result of the professional experiences accumulated by the author since 1974, working individually with more than 13,000 patients. The material included herein is intended to complement, not replace, the advice of your own physician, psychotherapist, or other healthcare professional, whom you should always consult about your circumstances before starting or stopping any medication or any other course of treatment, exercise regimen, or diet.

At times, the masculine pronoun has been used as a convenience. It is intended to indicate both male and female genders where this is applicable. All names and identifying references, except those of celebrities, have been altered to protect the privacy of my patients. All other facts are accurate and have not been altered.

—Dr. Bruce Goldberg

Woodland Hills, California

1

What Are Dreams
Really Made of?

We all dream nightly. Scientific research has firmly established that we dream for approximately three hours every night.[1] Some people never recall their dreams and state with certainty that they never dream. Others have nearly a complete recall of their nightly movies. Most of us fall somewhere in between, with recall of a few components of our dreams. Certain especially important dreams are remembered in great detail.

If the study of your own dreams is a new undertaking, be prepared for a fascinating journey into your mind. This trip will teach you a great deal about your psychological motivations and your subconscious mind. Your true innermost attitude toward problems of which you may not be aware can be revealed by your dreams.

It is difficult to describe the immense beauty obtained by your dream pictures and events. The practical aspect of my approach is to instruct you on how to use these dreams to solve problems. The subconscious affords us with the perfect opportunity to dream our problems away.

A dream is a certain series of images that appear to us on the private screen of our mind. When we are exposed to these plots, they usually seem real to us. Sometimes, the images of a dream relate to each other in a fantastically unreal way. They may surface as disconnected snatches of scenes entirely unrelated to one another or our waking lives.

Carl Jung described dreams as a type of hidden door in the innermost and most secret recesses of the psyche.[2] A hypnagogic dream occurs at the very beginning of sleep, and represents the borderline between consciousness and sleep. It is quite fragmentary, and often related to our last waking thought.

Displacement dreams are characterized by objects appearing where they don't belong. For instance, rather large doughnuts may be substituted for the tires on your car. Other objects may be seen sideways, upside down, or in other odd formations.

There appear to be four major sources of dreams. Our own subconscious; the subconscious of another person with whom we may be in contact; our superconscious, or Higher Self; and God all represent the origin of our dreams. We essentially meet ourselves in our dreams in several different types of very clever disguises. The basic types of dreams seem to be physical, mental, emotional, and spiritual in nature. We can more specifically list the different forms dreams take as follows:

1. Anxiety dreams deal with our fears and worries about life and death.
2. Event dreams concern themselves with actual circumstances in our past and present.
3. Precognitive dreams look into our future and alert us to events to come.
4. Karmic dreams inform us about our past and future lives.
5. Spiritual dreams focus around such phenomena as out-of-body experiences (OBEs), spirit guide contacts, occult, and symbolic dreams.

There may be a combination of categories, depending upon the subject matter. Some authorities would combine precognitive, karmic, and spiritual dreams as one class.

The Continuity of Consciousness

It is interesting to note that we are no more self-aware in waking reality than we are in dreaming reality. The difference appears to focus on the fact that our waking reality seems to have greater continuity. Consciousness is a funny thing. We may lose track of time while reading a book, watching a movie, or while driving on a routine trip.

These daydream states are the same alpha brain waves registered in sleep laboratories during our rapid eye movement (REM), or dream stage. Is it any wonder that we fail to recall most of the three hours of dreams that we have each night? As you progress through these chapters, it will become clear that our dream life has its own continuity. To appreciate it we must transfer our consciousness to the dimension of our dream life to be aware of its grandeur. When we do this, all capabilities of proving its existence on the physical plane disappears.

We can change our lives through our dreams because of this very aspect of dream consciousness. The consciousness we manifest in our dream universe is highly mutable. You can perceive yourself as the opposite sex, become 10 feet tall, fly, or appear as a cartoon character. Reality on this dimension is as free as our imaginative powers.

By exercising this ability to experience any form of being or perform any function, our mind can create and exhibit immortality, and we can become fully empowered. This mutability of consciousness also represents a change of consciousness location from the dream world (astral plane) to the physical realm.

What we accomplish in this dream world can become incorporated into our physical body and mind by this transfer of consciousness from the dream dimension to our physical plane. Because our dream/astral body is a reflection of our earth/physical body, any healing we initiate on our dream body can manifest in our physical body. Quantum physics supports this concept. Our thoughts can literally create or own reality.

This is why I use the expression "Dream your problems away." All therapeutic resolution will take place in your dream universe before it manifests as a cure in your waking consciousness.

This book is not a dissertation on astral travel. If that is where your interest lies, however, I have already made certain references to the astral plane, which I will deal with again in Chapter 2, as well as in Chapters 10 and 11.

One basic rule is that *all dreams represent out-of-body experiences (OBEs)*. This is what has been referred to as astral projection, or interdimensional travel. Because reports of OBEs are only anecdotal, scientists can't really prove they exist. They use the physical realm as the only standard by which to judge objective reality. We don't even know if the physical plane is real!

The Chinese philosopher Chuang Tsu contemplated a dream he had during which he was a butterfly. He wondered whether he was a man dreaming of being a butterfly, or was he a butterfly dreaming that he was a man?[3] This existential query has persisted throughout history.

These people who have experienced OBEs do not doubt their reality. From Robert Monroe to Ingo Swann to those from all over the world who have had near-death experiences, there is much agreement about the reality of the phenomenon. Reports from nearly every country in the world and throughout history have established a model of characteristics that, not surprisingly, are quite consistent.

I will detail these characteristics in Chapter 2. For our current discussion, the real question is not whether OBEs are real. The query we should be answering is: What is the nature of reality?

All dreams are OBEs, and the body we occupy on the astral plane is far less physical than its physical counterpart. This astral body is composed of a somewhat different order of energy and substance. This new body allows us to travel at the speed of light, and provides a means for our physical and astral body to recharge itself and continue with life as we know it.

Dreams play a critical role in our spiritual development. They are a sneak preview into realms far beyond the physical plane. They teach us about expanding our consciousness by reaching for the assistance of our Higher Self and Spiritual Guides.

Always bear in mind as you begin dreaming your troubles away that the ultimate purpose of a dream is to empower you. This is the identical goal of life itself. Whether it be working out, karmic lessons, problem solving, or other forms of spiritual growth, a dream is a means to our soul's evolution.

You will quickly see that life is no longer a random collection of unrelated events, but a purposeful sojourn designed by you. With this paradigm, all things are possible.

Waking Dreams

There are certain signs in our daily waking life that function in a manner similar to our nightly dreams. For example, let us assume you have a dream featuring a large letter C. This may be the size of a building in your mind.

The following day you are exposed to pictures of water (the sea) and other such representations. A school for the blind (see) may solicit you for funds. Perhaps a friend suggests you reevaluate your vitamin regimen. You now supplement your diet with vitamin C, and head off a potential cold. Note how all this stemmed from a simple dream of the letter C. Your Higher Self communicated with you through your subconscious and these waking references educated your conscious mind to take action. This is a waking dream.

Dreams can be considered as five-dimensional movies. These visual forms of communication often rely on brightly colored images, with frequent use of irrational and surreal environments. The dialogue used is far less than in our waking life, but often more meaningful. Communication may be received from third parties, and the interpretation is often clouded with abstract symbolism.

Our conscious mind functions quite differently. This waking component of our consciousness translates impulses and experiences from the five senses into words, intellectual understanding, and logic. As we may describe the dream state as a movie, the conscious mind can be thought of as a newspaper.

Guided Daydream

During breaks throughout the day, you may apply the principles of dream control to suggest a specific plot to a waking daydream. By guiding both the content and the conclusion, you are effectively reprogramming the subconscious with positive thinking and a greater likelihood of a rewarding outcome.

This technique is used to treat cancer in visual imagery exercises during which, for example, the patients are trained to see their T-lymphocytes of the immune system as sharks gobbling up meat representing the cancer cell. You can substitute positive moods, younger skin, the elimination of pain, and so on with this method.

Neurophysiological research[4] has revealed that for right-handed people, the left hemisphere of our brain deals with rational thinking and analytical processes. Creative and intuitive aspects of our thinking are performed by the right hemisphere. By practicing guided daydreaming, we are facilitating an integration of our mind by having both hemispheres work together to shape our dream life and use the results of our dream components to improve our role in the material world.

The Cultural Trance

I previously mentioned Chuang Tsu's question concerning the illusion of reality as represented by what we term the physical world. Ever since we were children growing up in Western advanced civilization, society has told us what reality is. Suppose we all dream the same dream, more or less, and that becomes society's reality.

Don't children have imaginary playmates and angels whom they can talk to? Early on in children's education, they quickly learn that this behavior is unacceptable. This results in feelings of guilt or shame from these remnants of altered states of consciousness. It may even entail punishment from their parents for not acting "normal."

All dreams represent altered states of consciousness (ASCs). In fact, they exist because of our ability to transfer our consciousness from the physical plane to the astral plane.[5] We are most familiar with ASCs in our waking state, such as moods, reverie, and daydreams. They can be induced by drugs, hypnotism, or meditation. They can be hurtful or healing. They can be subject to scientific investigation as parapsychological phenomena, or beyond all analysis, as is mysticism. They can be private variations on ordinary experience, or they can be collective experiences.

Our dream state provides us with a certain stimulation that allows us to emotionally cleanse our physical body and mind simultaneously. To understand this concept of stimulation, consider how our brain works. Something new sensed by our brain activates the reticular formation cells the brain contains. Repeated stimulation from the same source causes this mechanism to cease functioning.

Only changing concepts become a part of this data input cycle. If information is insignificant, we ignore it. Because we are in constant contact with an altering world, we respond to it in continually changing ways. We are always in an ASC. Dreaming is experienced by us day and night.

Children thrive on stimulation. IQ studies have demonstrated that as much as a 50-point spread can be observed when young children are placed in a stimulating environment.[6] They are free to play in their make-believe world with their imaginary playmates. These children describe the events of these worlds, as well as those of their dreams, without making the careful distinctions between fact and imagination that adults in our mainstream culture expect.

Evidence of the Immortality of Consciousness

When I described the four basic types of dreams earlier, I listed them as physical, mental, emotional, and spiritual. Spiritual dreams include psychic dreams and dreams of past and future lives.

For the time being I will focus on past-life dreams. A discussion of future lives is handled rather thoroughly in my book *Soul Healing.*[7] We may consider eight phenomena that point to the survival of consciousness, or soul:

1. Apparitions of the dead.
2. Spirit photographs and recording of spirit voices.
3. Near-death experiences.
4. OBEs.
5. Medium communication and channeling.
6. Possession cases.
7. Spirit Guide (angel) contacts.
8. Past-life memories.

The fact that we have past lives demonstrates the immortality of our soul and empowers us by removing the fear of death. It is fear that prevents our spiritual growth, and inhibits both our OBEs and our ability to use the dream state to solve our problems.

A rather well-documented case of mine dealing with reincarnation is presented in my book *The Search for Grace.*[8] Many of you may have seen the TV movie based on this book that first aired on CBS on May 17, 1994. Space does not allow for any more than a cursory treatment of reincarnation in this chapter. The beauty of our dream life is that it presents us with data verifying the immortality of our soul and highly suggestive evidence of reincarnation. *The Search for Grace* describes the case of a patient I call Ivy and her past life during the 1920s as Grace Doze in Buffalo, New York.

This case was independently corroborated and stands today as one of the most documented cases of reincarnation on record. Ivy received her first glimpses of this past life in her dreams, prior to my hypnotically regressing her during an office session.

Documented cases give far more credence to the reality of previous incarnations, as compared to simple anecdotal reports. The soul or subconscious lives in the dream world or on the astral plane, just as the soul survives the death of the physical body.

We can experience the nonphysical destiny of our soul every night through our dreams. This mechanism can produce a form of "Heaven on Earth." The in-between life state is the astral plane, with the same physical laws, or lack of them, that we have been discussing. Linear time and the limitations of three-dimensional space will cease to exist.

All of our past, present, and future lives will be at our disposal through our Akashic records (the detailed descriptions of all our past, present, and future lives stored on the causal plane). The exact experiences we have and characteristics we observe now are formed instantaneously from our feelings and conceptions on this astral dimension. This is exactly what we experience during our dream state.

Mystics throughout the ages have insisted that consciousness exists prior to and beyond physical reality. These same sages aver that our soul transcends both time and space. Furthermore, they declare that time and space, as well as the entire physical plane, are illusions derived from consciousness.

Because it is my premise that our life after death is identical to our current dream state, a familiarity with our experiences during this REM cycle while we are focused in physical reality will make easier the transition to the state we refer to as death.

By using our dream levels to explore past lives, we may eliminate the need to fear the death of the physical body. This practice of OBEs and past-life regression will, once and for all, allow us to continue with the process of living free of the fear of dying.

When we discuss reincarnation, we must take into consideration that this is a philosophy that has been around since humans have lived in some form of group culture. Such historical figures as General George Patton, Benjamin Franklin, Goethe, Schopenhauer, Emerson, Yeats, Thoreau, Plato, Pythagoras, and a host of others have publicly declared their belief in this doctrine of rebirth.

Past, present, and future have no meaning outside the physical plane because of the simultaneity of time I discussed earlier. This affords us the advantage of easily viewing our past lives. Many of our dreams are sneak previews of previous incarnations.

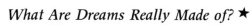

Your physical appearance will be different, and the topography and technology observed will be quite different from what you are accustomed to. The sex you perceive yourself to be, along with your race, may also be quite different from your current persona.

2
The Dream World

The world of dreams is quite different from the physical realm we label as our reality. The medieval alchemists called that dimension the astral plane, and this world is equivalent to the Christian concept of purgatory, the bardo of the Tibetans, and the Greek underworld of Hades. This astral plane is a real world, with inhabitants, houses, objects, and other structures.

This realm of illusion is partially created by our emotions and imagination. The astral plane is reportedly considerably larger than our physical world. Every object in the material world has an astral counterpart composed of astral matter.

What we have referred to as the fifth dimension is actually the dream world of the astral plane, where all past, present, and future events occur simultaneously. Time does not exist there as we have come to know it. Actions that take several hours on our world occur "in the twinkling of an eye" in the dream universe.

That is another reason why I frown upon dream interpretation. Even when one is lucky enough to recall a dream, it often represents several different dreams or dreamlets haphazardly edited together, resulting in utter confusion.

In discussing the dream world we must always keep in mind that entering this dimension frees us from the limitations of the Earth plane and the laws of space and time. This etheric or unreal environment is characterized by shadowy figures moving through a fog-like mist. This environment may take the appearance of heaven, with vivid colors and a brilliant white or gold light.

The dream body that we possess in this environment is composed of a less material substance known as astral matter. This body has been called various names throughout history. Some of these are: the double, subtle body, soul body, light body, astral body, *ka* by the Egyptians, *doppelganger* by the Germans, *vardger* in Norwegian, *taslach* in Scottish, *fetch*, *waft*, *task,* and *fye* by the English, *ruach* in Hebrew, *eidolon* in Greek, *larva* by the Romans, *bardo* body by the Tibetans, *Pranamayakosha* to the Hindus, *rupa* to the Buddhists, *thankhi* in China, *desire body* to the theosophists, *vital* body of the Rosicrucians, and the *perisprit* to the French spiritualists.

This astral body is weightless, but possesses very acute perceptive abilities, especially toward bright, vivid colors, and sound. It appears to sparkle and resembles our physical body in size and shape. It appears somewhat transparent, yet filled with many tiny white stars. Whatever we call it, this dream body is the home of the chakras or energy centers described by the yogis.

The spirit body of the shamans that travels to the Upper World and Lower World also describes the dream realm. Regardless of how we refer to it, our world of dreams allows us to interact within this dimension through the use of a nonphysical body.

From this discussion you will note that I am equating our dream world with the realm of the astral projectors, soul travelers, bardo voyagers, near-death experiencers, and the like. A thorough presentation of this topic, along with several dozen exercises to travel outside our physical body, is given in my book *Astral Voyages*.[1]

The dream body is subject to the laws of the dream environment or the astral plane. Positive dreams take place in the upper astral plane, while nightmares are remnants of trips to the lower astral plane. These two realms correspond with the Upper World and Lower World, respectively, of the shamans.

We can compare these two aspects of the astral plane as follows:

Lower Astral Plane

☆ Feelings of confusion and bewilderment.

☆ Misty or foggy environment.

☆ The presence of biazarre and evil inhabitants.

☆ No possibility of spiritual growth.

Upper Astral Plane

☆ Feeling alert, secure, peaceful, and happy.

☆ Earhtlike and beautiful environment.

☆ The presence of human inhabitants.

☆ Unlimited spiritual growth.

It is not difficult to see how the concepts of heaven and hell evolved from ancient dream voyagers to the astral plane. Since our dream body is not subject to our physical plane, we cannot be injured regardless of what takes place on the dream dimension. This nonphysical body is affected by nonphysical stimuli and interacts with nonphysical beings and objects.

You may be wondering why so many of our dreams place our dream body in peril if our physical body cannot be harmed. This is done to create an atmosphere and environment for projecting our fears and insecurities in such an adventurous manner that we can easily relate to it. It is equivalent to watching an action/adventure movie!

Always remember that recurring dreams are ways in which our subconscious is trying to tell us something we have repeatedly ignored. Observing yourself again and again fighting the same dragon or being chased by an identical saber-toothed tiger requires deep introspection and an objective evaluation about your life. You are most likely not facing some challenge if your dream consistently places you in a position of being unable to climb a mountain or reach a certain destination.

Our hopes, fears, desires, and inclinations are manifest within our dream world. Fantasy scenarios abound to satisfy our every whim. For example, dreams dealing with fame and success are common among ambitious people. If you are poor you might very well dream of being wealthy and flamboyant in your spending habits.

Social interactions in this dream world give us further understanding of this fascinating realm. We may see ourselves with people that exist in our waking lives. Of course, we created these images of them, but not all individuals we encounter are of our creation.

On various occasions we meet with the dream bodies of people who call the dream world their home. They are permanent residents of that domain. These independent entities afford us the possibility of learning from them during our dream encounters.

Another confusing aspect of the dream dimension is that our dream is only partially created by us. The astral plane has certain fixed components, and we may access a "party line" of other individuals' dreams. When some person seems to unexpectedly enter our dream scenario, the continuity may be disturbed by the dream of someone else entirely.

The dream world consists of a basic framework of permanent structures. An emotion-like substance is present on this realm that responds to every thought, desire, and emotion we have on the physical plane. All of our negative thoughts and emotions create evil and bizarre creatures and conditions on the lower astral plane.

These fixed areas of the dream world exist without our efforts, and cannot be altered by our consciousness. No form created by us may be allowed to enter these specially designated areas. Reality here is organized by a completely different set of laws.

For example, you may find yourself totally immersed in tones and hues of energy and feeling. You may be deeply moved by waves of emotions, leaving no visual impression whatsoever. Strange and alluring music of unearthly character may engulf you.

Colors may be felt and sounds could very well be seen in certain unconventional regions of the dream world. This may seem alien to you, but it is important to get what you can from this exposure. In time our subconscious may choose to inform us what this all meant in our quest for spiritual growth.

Another unusual, yet beautiful, experience in this dream realm is a merging with our Higher Self. This exposure is characterized by feelings of exaltation and bliss. You may now see the workings of reality more clearly than ever before. A feeling of greater purpose will be one result of this union.

Some have described this as a face-to-face encounter with a god-like being who radiated light and represented pure love. This is awe inspiring, and may result in a feeling of renewal and revitalization when we return to our waking life.

As we create this vast panorama, we may experience only a certain facet of it that we care to explore. This can result in our failing to perceive some things that are clearly within the range of our perceptions. Sometimes we just can't see the forest for the trees.

We may also sense the presence of departed souls, some we know, others unfamiliar to us. The astral body of people undergoing near-death experiences and simple astral projection may also be encountered in dream world.

The distance our dream body travels is at the speed of light and is directly proportional to the desire and will of the astral body. All the dream body has to do is think of a location, and it arrives there in an instant.

The Functions of Sleep

We must sleep to renew our physical and dream bodies. It is suggested by many astral voyagers that the separation of the dream from the physical body actually produces sleep. The vital force of the astral body is facilitated by its exposure to the cosmic energy at night.[2]

Another purpose of our nightly rest and dream cycle is to establish a communication with our Higher Self and Masters and Guides for the purpose of spiritual growth, or raising the frequency vibrational rate of our soul. I refer to this as *cleansing*.[3] This concept has been established by the Eastern yogis and others since ancient times, and will be discussed at length in Chapter 13.

Sleep itself is characterized by the astral body moving out of alignment with its physical counterpart. You need not be concerned about the OBEs as represented by your nightly dreams. You will always be both protected and assisted by your Higher Self. Eventually your dream body will return to your physical body, perhaps with a light jolt.

This attainment of wisdom and love (if we listen to our spiritual advisors) is made possible more easily by transcending the physical body. This way we avoid the interference of our defense mechanisms (rationalization, projection, repression, displacement, etc.), which do not function at any time during our sleep cycle.

Because it is our consciousness that creates our reality, a change in our soul's energy is needed to create a better universe. This is possible through the rigorous training we are exposed to in dream world.

Our physical plane is within our control. It has been a time-honored illusion to assume that the material plane is organized and run by factors beyond our direction and influence.

Thought-Forms

This brings us to one of the basic principles of the realm we called dream world. Thought-forms are actual objects and entities created by our subconscious and are given life in this dream world. These thought-forms have a temporary life, but so long as the thought of this object or entity is held, it exists within our dream dimension. It is immediately perceivable and tangible.

The theosophist clairvoyants Annie Bessant and C. W. Leadbeater were reportedly able to perceive these thought-forms during their waking state. Their observations were published in a classic book titled *Thought-Forms*. These researchers considered thought-forms as a form of discarded portions of our nonphysical body that exist in the super-physical realms that surround our world.

Each of our thoughts produce vibration and form. These thought impulses accumulate the vitalized nonphysical "matter" of the astral realm that is most representative of that thought. This matter then vibrates in harmony with the thought impulse itself in such a way as to result in a materialization of the idea presented by that thought.

These theosophists classified three types of thought-forms:

1. Images created by the thinker that are often mistaken for the dream body.
2. A representation of some material object that an individual is thinking about.
3. A projection that takes on a life of its own.

This type takes its shape and form by gathering the astral matter around it and creating an object or entity from its composition.

Meetings with traditional creatures of mythology could take place in our dream world. The vital spirits of stones, fire, rivers, and trees may be encountered. The consciousness of all things affords us with the opportunity to grow and learn.

Color in dream world is determined by the quality of the thought itself, while the nature of our cognitive processes affect its form. The clarity of the thought-forms outline is created from the definiteness of our thought. So in our dream world, our thoughts shape what we observe and create in its subjective region, which results in a coalesced pattern to which the dream environment somehow gives form and motion.

Our desires, attitudes, and beliefs help in the final appearance of our thoughts. For example, if we believe that all dream world entities must look human, we are less likely to encounter an alien creature or a beam of light.

Once we create a set of images, additional components are added that are compatible with that point of view. A dream enemy about to attack you is more likely to carry a weapon than a flower. You created both the adversary and his or her accessories.

Our thoughts are shaping instruments in dream world. Our wishes, desires, and beliefs give our thoughts form and motion, and the permanence of this creation is directly proportional to our intensity.

Emotions color our dream images by giving them mood and tone. The adversary example I presented before wouldn't mean much to you if it were just an entity with a weapon. He or she could be taking target lessons, or hunting for food. Your emotions, such as fear, are what make this entity an enemy versus merely a resident of dream world.

You can change the theme of an innocent scene by your emotions. Let us assume you were walking in a beautiful garden on a sunny day. In your waking life, for example, you saw a rather large spider in your home and killed it. Your guilt concerning this deed could now create a giant tarantula suddenly appearing out of nowhere in this garden and threatening you. Your emotions shaped the tone and mood of this stroll in the garden of dream world.

It is possible to recall another dream while in dream world. This dream within a dream sounds rather existential, but in reality represents a continuity of experience afforded by this realm. Certain feelings will accompany this dream within a dream. Often patients describe this phenomenon as a sense of returning to a familiar location—a *déjà vu*.

One of the advantages, as well as purposes, of dream world is to provide us with an environment in which we can shed rigid notions of self and experience our self and other selves in new and intriguing ways. This has unlimited spiritual growth potential, if only we listen to it and learn.

During our dreaming state it is not commonly observed that we remind ourselves that we are dreaming. Lucid dreamers know that their nighttime visions are dreams. How often do we remind ourselves that we exist on the physical plane in our daily lives? Most likely the answer to that is rarely to never. So we can now understand why the ordinary, versus lucid, dreamers fail to regularly acknowledge their presence in dream world during the course of their dreams. We will discuss lucid dreaming in detail in Chapter 10.

The single greatest obstacle to exploring dream world is fear. Fear originates from our insecurities and belief in our vulnerability to some form of danger. Ironically, this set belief is the only thing that can make us susceptible to dream world threats.

This is a very important principle to master in order to grow spiritually. Fear is the one emotion that will, if unchecked, absolutely stifle our spiritual growth. I do not feel there is anyone or anything out to "get us" in our waking or dream world. It is our thoughts, beliefs, and emotions that create evil and other dangers to our realm. We may have been programmed by the world to think it is negative, but we can always transcend our limitations. That's what dreams are all about.

No matter how frightening an experience is on dream world planes, no harm can possibly come to you. These scary instances are rare, but may occur. If you encounter such a situation, here is what I suggest you do:

- ☆ Remain completely passive. Any threatening person or creature will also become quite passive.
- ☆ Initiate some aggressive behavior such as punching the creature, regardless of its size. The creature will not counter with aggression, but will depart.
- ☆ Say "In the name of [whomever you pray to] go away!" This order will result in the creature disappearing immediately or becoming nonaggressive.
- ☆ Repeatedly remind yourself that nothing can harm you.

Dream World Communication

It has been known since ancient times that symbols are presented to us in our dreams. Why doesn't our subconscious simply communicate with us literally? The mechanics of multidimensionality and

distortion in translating these messages may explain some of these symbols, but that is not the main reason for this dream riddle.

If we face our insecurities directly, we undoubtedly would come to the realization that change is required. Our defense mechanisms, general laziness, and aversion to change would not find that insight compatible. Also, we may not enjoy the close self-examination. Our fears and guilt concerning being evil or sinful would create anxiety. So symbols are used to avoid the pain that might result from discovering the source of our fears. This prevents a feeling of loss of self in our psyche.

Our dream world is ideal for reflecting upon the events of the day at our leisure. Without the restraints and stress from daily life, we can replay some of these events, reshaping them into symbolic forms that incorporate our desires and hidden motives. We can rewrite the script, star in the production, and kill off the competition, all in one night.

This dream world allows us to try various options, examine possible courses of action, and assess the choices available in making a decision. We are probing probable sequences or events that are likely to result from these choices. The lesson we learn from this is that we can alter our future by what we do in the present.

What Is Reality?

In Chapter 1, I alluded to the philosophy of Chuang Tsu concerning the true nature of reality. Does not any perception of ours have the possibility of being a dream within a dream? Just because society has brainwashed us to assume our physical world manifested through our five senses is reality does not make it so.

It is merely a manner of custom, based on repeated experiences, to link the causal connections perceived by our rational mind and label that as the true nature of the universe. I do not question the fact that our material world is consistently ordered and organized by specific laws that apparently direct the minds of the inhabitants of our planet. What I do challenge is the absoluteness of these laws and propose the existence of other realms, dream world being one of them.

Can we really be certain of anything that we perceive? Our world is considered to be one of space-time. Since we are space-time observers, let us define these terms. Space functions as a type of foundation for our perception of a stable manifold of simultaneously existing objects. Time is the framework for our observations of a rather dynamic combination of forms of items existing sequentially.

These concepts of space and time must be a part of our consciousness prior to our perceptions of the various objects through which we perceive in the material world. This is necessary because the perceptions themselves are always in terms of space and time.

What I have just described helps explain why we all tend to perceive roughly some form of consistency in the physical realm. Our experiences repeatedly assure us that there are objects in a real world that can be relied on to interact with us in certain known ways. We can learn about our world. The knowledge can accumulate and form the basis of physical reality.

This may all sound existential, because it is. Truth has a strange way of becoming accepted by society. At first, a new truth is ridiculed. Some may respond to this assertion with anger and violence. Eventually, this truth is accepted, and most of us simply pretend we always shared that view. We may even wonder how we ever got along without it!

I can point to the discovery of fire, electricity, and the invention of the automobile, telephone, and computers as examples. The list is endless. Consider this paradigm before you dismiss the ideas I present concerning the dream world and our ability to use it to solve our problems. Who knows? You may dream your prejudices away.

3
How to Change Your Life Through Dreams

Ernest Rossi feels that any component of a dream that is unique, strange, or in any way out of the usual content pattern represents the beginning of a new level of awareness for the dreamer. This is one of the strongest arguments for keeping a dream journal or diary. I will discuss these diaries at length in Chapter 14.

Growth may now occur by focusing on this new level of awareness. If you integrate this new awareness with your current persona, a fresh identity is formed and this will result in behavior, emotions, and sensations not previously experienced. The cumulative effect of this mechanism is a generation of new and different dream images and other components. The cycle of understanding and growth now is perpetual, and an unlimited opportunity to learn more about ourselves is opened up.

Psychosynthesis is the term we apply to this integration of images to develop a new awareness. This paradigm of making dream images part of your conscious awareness, rather than the breaking down of these components and analyzing them, is a diametrically opposite approach to traditional psychoanalysis.

Your entire future psychological development can be enhanced by a constructive use of these unique dream images. Reflect upon these, animate them, bring them into your consciousness, compare and contrast their changes throughout your dream journal, and you will learn from your subconscious mind and Higher Self.

Rossi feels that ignoring these new dream images may actually confuse us and contribute to mental illness. Purposely rejecting these components of our REM cycle can induce them to take on frightening proportions. Never ignore what your mind is trying to tell you.[1]

A form of empowerment is felt when we are creative, heroic, and have interesting experiences in our dreams. We feel energetic, happy, and confident for several hours the following day. On the other hand, dreams of violence, abuse, frustration, and failure leave us disoriented, anxious, and uneasy.

You can follow some simple rules to begin to control your dreams and take charge of your life. Here are some of these:

☆ Attach importance to your dreams. The meaning of dreams is what we give to them. Your belief in their significance results in an increased frequency of meaningful dreams. This also applies to their quality. If you believe your dreams are creative, you remember many creative dreams. Our waking attitudes have a lot to do with the content and images we remember experiencing at night.

☆ Concentrate on what you would like to dream about prior to retiring. You may decide to solve a problem, choose a wonderful destination, or engage in a fantasy sexual encounter. Keep this preparation at a high level until just a few minutes before you go to sleep.

☆ Do not be afraid to experiment with your dreams or use them for any type of growth purpose.

☆ Draw upon your life's knowledge and experience in setting the stage for a dream you desire to have. Keep open to new and unusual ideas and mechanisms surfacing during these nightly excursions.

☆ Establish a peaceful reference point for your dreams, and make this sanctuary a regular component in their plot. Return to this place if and when the dream's scenario becomes uncomfortable in any way.

· ☆ Program yourself before going to sleep to remember while dreaming what you intended to accomplish in your dream. Set specific growth-oriented and positive parameters, and have confidence that you will be able to benefit from this exposure to your subconscious mind's nightly cycle.

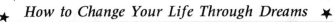

☆ Establish friendly relationships with your dream figures. If necessary, ask your Higher Self to assist you in this goal. Transform dream antagonists into allies. Always confront a dream enemy with absolute confidence. Your inability to express fear will force them to leave, or transform them into less threatening components.

☆ Prior to retiring, visualize a dream scenario you would like to have that night. Repeat this summary several times and focus on remembering this dream upon awakening. The more you contemplate and plan this dream while in full consciousness, the easier it will be to have these plots and goals appear in your dream.

☆ Custom design your dream. Anything is possible in a dream. If you want to fly, explore the ocean floor without equipment, go on a safari, and save a damsel in distress, you write the script, star in the movie, and complete the final edit. Be organized in your approach.

☆ Record your dreams immediately upon awakening. Take a few moments and visualize what occurred. Log all the details in your journal. Pay special attention to unusual dream images and recurring themes.

☆ Share your dreams with your family and friends. Discuss the characters, plots, emotions, and other sensations you experienced. Listen to the dreams of others and compare notes.

☆ Perseverance is the key to dream control and dream power. Use the techniques I present in this book and let the seven to eight sleeping hours of which you are usually unaware, work for you and facilitate your own empowerment.

☆ Refrain from using drugs to get to sleep or to deal with its effects. Alcohol, caffeine, aspirin, barbiturates, and tranquilizers decrease dream time and facilitate co-dependencies.

☆ Always reinforce the notion of developing a dream consciousness. Be all you can be and dream all you can dream under your direction and with the very best of motives. Whatever else you do, enjoy these nightly feature films.

You have within your grasp one of the most ancient and time-tested approaches to psychological stability, problem solving, and spiritual growth. The process of dreaming, properly guided, will:

☆ Build up your coping mechanisms to any form of stress.
☆ Induce pleasurable sexual adventures.
☆ Improve your memory and concentration.
☆ Enhance creativity.
☆ Increase self-understanding.
☆ Allow you to program your thoughts and feelings.
☆ Encourage empowerment in all forms.

Regardless of how many times you wake up with no knowledge of dreaming, do not think for a moment that a blank void occupied the seven or eight hours of rest you had. Dream laboratory studies reveal that we all dream for about three hours every night; that's approximately 1,100 hours each year!

My specialty is hypnotherapy. Hypnosis incorporates the art of suggestion to reprogram the subconscious to effect positive changes in a person's life. The state of mind we enter when self-hypnosis is experienced is called alpha. That is the exact same state we function in during a dream. Dream control is nothing more than practicing therapeutic hypnosis while we sleep.

Throughout this book I will be emphasizing the various principles of·hypnosis that you can apply to controlling your dreams and literally dreaming your problems away. In Chapter 7, I will present some basic principles of self-hypnosis, but for now consider the following paradigms for taking charge of your dreams:

1. Place your body in the most relaxed state you are capable of by any method that is comfortable for you.
2. In your mind, clearly formulate a specific dream that will solve a problem, resolve a health issue, or accomplish some other constructive purpose.
3. Develop a belief system that removes any doubt about your ability to induce whatever dream you desire.
4. Edit your dream theme into a clear, positive, and concise phrase. Repeat this phrase several times aloud or silently.
5. Focus intensely on this dream theme and visualize your custom-designed dream as though it were happening at

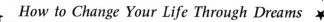

this very moment. Picture yourself in your mind and feel your body having this dream.

6. Converse with the characters that appear in your dream. Redirect their actions by simply thinking about a subplot to this scenario.

7. Take over this dream, place your persona in the roles of others in the nightly play, and act in a positive manner to make this a fulfilling experience.

8. Record your dreams in a journal immediately upon waking.

9. During your waking day, engage in activities that reflect the content of your most recent dream. Keep your mind open to any stimulus from your environment that can be used to direct a dream. For example, if you would like to have a flying dream, observe birds in flight in your local environment.

Remember, inducing specific dreams and controlling the plot is a learned skill. It will require persistence, time, and confidence. You can influence your dreams by specific actions prior to the dream and following this nightly mental activity.

Do not become frustrated if this technique requires additional practice sessions. Even highly experienced controlled dreamers do not manifest all of the desired components they intended. Sometimes additional elements surface that your subconscious (or superconscious) mind wants you to experience for the purpose of spiritual growth.

Insomnia Exercise

Note to Reader: Using self-hypnosis tapes is by far the easiest and most efficient way to practice self-hypnosis. If you are making your own tapes from these models, substitute the word "I" for "you" in this and all subsequent scripts.

For those of you suffering from insomnia, here is a simple self-hypnosis exercise that will both relax you and promote a good night's rest. While lying in bed, try this exercise:

With your eyes closed, take a deep breath and hold it to the count of six. (Pause) Let it out slowly and take a second deep breath, this time holding it to the count of eight. (Pause) Let it out slowly once again.

Let all of your muscles go loose and heavy. Just relax to the best of your ability. (Pause) Now, while the rest of your body continues to relax, I want you to create tension in your arms and fists by clenching your fists tighter and tighter. Breathing normally, just clench your fists, and straighten your arms by stretching them in front of you, tighter and tighter. (Pause) Feel the tension in your fists and arms while the rest of your body relaxes. Now let your hands and arms relax completely. Let go and appreciate the relaxation. Once again, clench your fists and straighten your arms. Notice the tension while the rest of your body relaxes. (Pause) Now let go, let your arms and hands relax, relaxing further and further on their own. Relaxing all over. (Pause) Just picture your hands and arms relaxing more and more, your whole body relaxing. Now, while the rest of your body relaxes, point your toes away from your body, thereby tensing your feet and legs. Just point your toes away from your body, increasing the tension that way. Notice the tension in your leg muscles and feet, study the tension, (pause) and now do the opposite. Relax. Let your feet and legs relax as completely as possible. Appreciate the relaxation. Note the contrast between tension and relaxation in your legs and feet. (Pause) Let the relaxation proceed on its own. Now point your feet toward your face, creating tension that way. Once again notice the tension and study it. (Pause) Relax your feet and legs now. Just continue relaxing your legs further and further, the deeper relaxation spreading throughout your body.

Now let us concentrate our attention on the neck, head, and facial areas. While the rest of your body continues to relax on its own, press your head against the back of the bed. Notice the tension in your neck and the back of your head (pause), and now relax your head and neck. Let go of the tension and relax. Note the relaxation in your neck and back of your head, your whole body relaxing more and more.

As you count backwards now from seven to one, each muscle in your body will become completely relaxed. Seven...deeper, deeper, six...deeper, deeper, five...deeply relaxed, four...three...two...so deeply relaxed, one.

Now you are in a deep level of hypnosis and are going deeper into this naturally relaxed state with each breath you exhale.

As you exhale each breath, you are going to program your subconscious mind to have the most comfortable and restful night's sleep you have ever experienced.

Your sleep will be undisturbed throughout the night unless there is a true emergency, when you will awaken immediately. In the absence of an emergency you will awaken at the appropriate time you desire and this new sleep routine will be a part of your new reality. Now, sleep...sleep...sleep.

The only real obstacles we have to our growth are our defense mechanisms. These components of our consciousness function to prevent change. They like business as usual. To grow we must change. To change we must overcome our defense mechanisms.

Here are some of the defense mechanisms that we will be overcoming as we progress through this book:

Rationalization: Finding reasons other than the real ones to make actions, thoughts, or words acceptable to the self-image. "Everybody cheats."

Displacement: Disguising a wish (fear or hate) by substituting another object to blame. The wife takes out her feelings against her husband on the child (and the child kicks the dog).

Regression: Resorting to behavior that is characteristic of an earlier age. "I'm going home to mother."

Repression: Subconscious forgetting or simply inhibiting any threatening stimuli. "I forgot my dentist appointment."

Projection: Attributing one's own faults, thoughts, or desires to others; projecting guilt on them. "My father is stingy." ("I'm afraid that I'm stingy.")

Withdrawal: Daydreaming to escape reality, pain, responsibility, or decisions; inability to get things done. "People don't care about me, so I'd rather be alone."

Identification: Establishing a oneness with a valued person, group, or thing. "I belong to group X and that makes me important."

Reaction formation: Exaggerating the opposite of true feelings. "We've got to wipe out pornography" (enjoys pornography).

Aggression: Hurting and attacking oneself or others either verbally or physically. "The best defense is a good offense."

Compensation: Substituting achievements in one area to make up for weakness in another. "I'm homely so I try to get good grades."

These defense mechanisms are not active when we sleep. Our dream world affords us the perfect opportunity for growth, and eliminates the one major obstacle (defense mechanisms) that can inhibit that growth.

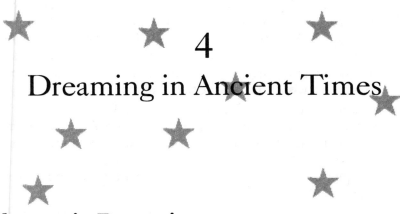

4
Dreaming in Ancient Times

Shamanic Dreaming

We can trace techniques utilized by shamans back to approximately 50,000 B.C. in Siberia. *Ecstatic journeys* is the term applied to the journeys these shamans made to the Upper World and Lower World in search of lost souls. These ecstatic journeys were often conducted in the dream state.[1]

Because all dreams represented out-of-body experiences (OBE's), the shamans were the first to document these techniques. One well-known example is a cave in France that has been dated to about 20,000 years ago. The Lascaux temple cave printing depicts a male shaman with his arms spread out like wings, and an erect penis. His bird-staff is located behind him and before him is an enormous bull.

What is most interesting about this are two details of this painting. The first is that the shaman's body is at an exact 37-degree angle. I point out in *Astral Voyages* that this precise position is ideal for OBEs and was also reported by the ancient Egyptians.[2]

Second, the fact that the shaman has an erect penis is most consistent with modern-day sleep laboratory studies on OBEs. Penile erection is often associated with REM sleep, and may very well be a similar type of energy that separates the astral body from the physical counterpart during our dreams. The yogis would refer to this harnessed sexual energy as the raising of the *kundalini* or the "serpent power."[3] This serpent power is at the heart of all real magical techniques.

The Lapp shaman, traveling to the Upper World in his dream state on a magic sleigh and drawn by his power animal, the reindeer, is a type of primal Santa Claus. Modern day shamanic journeys, such as those developed by Michael Harner at the Foundation for Shamanic Studies, emphasize a visual focus to gain entry into the Upper World and Lower World.[4]

These techniques suggest an image of a passage leading down into the earth, such as an animal's burrow or a tunnel, to enter the Lower World. The Upper World is attained by riding on a large eagle, or being shot out of a volcano. Other methods taught by modern Mystery Schools use patchworking images and guided visualizations.

The gateways to these worlds involve the use of the images of sacred sites, the construction of Inner Temples, or the application of tarot symbols. Exercises based on the connection of the Major Arcana of the tarot to the Cabalistic Tree of Life reportedly yield very powerful results.[5]

Celtic Dreams

The head Druid priest in ancient Celtic societies would be instructed in his dream state to offer himself as a sacrifice to save his people in times of great danger. It was their belief that by submission to a triple death—by strangling, cutting, and either drawing or burning—his soul's energy would be unleashed and assist with the community's protection. This was achieved by his soul working in conjunction with the gods.[6]

Ancient Egypt

The Chester Beatty papyrus is one of the earliest records we have of Egyptian man dreaming. It dates back to approximately 2,000 B.C., and was kept by the ancient Egyptian priests. They firmly believed dreams were messages from their gods. Interpretations were based on the theory of opposites; a dream of death represented an omen of long life, for example.

The men selected to interpret these dreams in ancient Egypt were called "Masters of the Secret Things," or "Scribes of the Double House." A disturbed individual slept in the temple following the administration of a potion to promote dreaming. The priest would then interpret the dream and follow the advice put forth by his interpretation of the dream for this cure. We will discuss this dream incubation technique in greater detail when I report on the ancient Greeks.

The ancient Hindu scriptures, known as the Puranas, reported that dreams were also messages from gods. The *Upanishad* (approximately 1,000 B.C.) states that dreams took place in a land between the real and the promised world. This dream world freed us from inhibitions to allow our true nature to surface. Many scholars feel that the concept of a soul and its existence after death of the physical body originates from dreams of primitive man.

Jewish Dreams

Cabalistic writings, Hasidic scriptures, the Babylonian Talmud, and the Old Testament contain many references to dreams that had divine revelation as part of their content. In the Talmud, for example, we find a rabbi interpreting a dream of a man pouring oil on a palm tree as an indication of incestuous urges for his mother. This scripture was written approximately 3,500 B.C.

Joseph interpreted the dream of a pharaoh, because of the failure of the Egyptian interpreters to satisfy their king. This dream involved the replacement of seven fat sheaves of grain by seven withered ones, then of seven thin cows consuming seven fat cows. Joseph's analysis was that there would be seven years of famine following the previous seven years of plenty. That is exactly what happened.

The ancient Jews strongly believed that God communicated with them directly or by way of angels through dreams. The word angel literally means messenger. This differed from the Greek concept of dreams originating from the realm of the dead.

If a Jew had a difficult dream, it was referred to as "wrestling with an angel." Jacob had one such dream in which people were working in the field and his sheaf of grain stood upright, while those of others bowed to his.

Jacob changed his name to Israel and eventually sired 12 sons. The 12 tribes of Israel were the descendants of these 12 sons. The dream Jacob had proved quite prophetic and changed the course of Jewish history.

One last dream that greatly affected the course of the Jewish people involved Moses. He woke up in the middle of the night after "wrestling with an angel" and cajoled his wife to circumcise their son. By this act, Moses and his son converted from being Egyptian to that of Judaism. Eventually Moses would lead his people out of Egyptian bondage during the Exodus, bring the Ten Commandments to them as law, and guide them to the Promised Land.

Dreams in Ancient Greece

The *Oneirocritica*,[7] a five-volume work of the Greek Artemidorus (second century A.D.), represented the first significant published work on dreams. Artemidorus stated that a dream was unique to the individual. This work underlined the principle of association—a dream image evokes some image or meaning in the conscious mind.

Artemidorus's work was published in English in 1644 for the first time. This book has had a tremendous influence on modern psychological schools of thought on dream meanings. He stated that dreams are infused into men for their advantage and instruction. This Greek author condemned arbitrary and overly literal interpretation of dreams, studied recurring dreams, and believed in the concept of the "great dream," which he felt was the most difficult to understand.

Hippocrates (460 B.C.–360 B.C.) felt that the stars, moon, and sun represented the organic state of the body in a dream. This Greek physician felt that if the dream stars shine brightly and follow their natural orbit, the dreamer's body is functioning normally. If dream stars become clouded or fall from their orbit or a cosmic catastrophe occurs, some disease is taking shape in the body.

Prodromic dreams are those that reflect symptoms of an illness just before they actually manifest in the body. Hippocrates deduced that certain dream images of health, such as white clothing, bright stars, radiant sunshine or mighty rivers, could be used to restore health. He based this approach on the accuracy of these Prodromic dreams. Other names for Prodromic dreams are precognitive, prophetic, prognostic, and theorematic.

Dream Incubation

The reasons the ancients spent so much time and energy devising dreaming strategies and building temples for their practice were two-fold. Initiating cures for various ailments represented one of these goals. The other had to do with obtaining answers to their questions.

A technique known as *dream incubation* was employed. This consisted of going to a sacred place to sleep for the specific reason of having a god instill a dream in you. Many scholars feel that the original purpose of dream incubation was to cure sterility.

Somewhere between 300 to 400 temples existed to honor the god Aesculapius in the ancient world from the end of the sixth century B.C. until the end of the fifth century A.D. Greek temples such as the ones at Epidaurus, Pergamon, Tyana, and Cos are well reported in the literature. Here is a sample of what a pilgrim took part in during this 1,000 years of making pilgrimages to a dream temple and its god:

- ☆ Fasting for several days was common. Wine, meat, "broad beans," and certain fish were especially forbidden.
- ☆ Abstinence from sex was required.
- ☆ Purity of the mind and body was supposedly achieved by bathing in cold water and thinking only holy thoughts.
- ☆ Activities for them to participate in during their stay included athletic events, dancing, concerts, and plays.
- ☆ Poisonous serpents were present in the sleeping dormitories or *enkoimetrion*.

The rituals, desire to please the priests, secondary gain received by having the appropriate dream, and the motivation for a cure or a question answered accounted for some of the success rates at these temples. The vivid dreams of the god Aesculapius dominated many of these pilgrims' experiences.

Since sterility was a major issue dealt with, many of the priests presumed that a type of sexual union commenced between a goddess or god and the dreamer during the night. Sacred prostitution was often employed as part of their rituals.

The setting of these temples made for an ideal retreat. In Greece, for example, their temples were large and beautifully constructed. They were placed in natural environments of splendor and isolated from the large cities. This model was also utilized by the Chinese, Assyrians, and Egyptians.

The pilgrim was also exposed to tales of miraculous cures told by the priests, inscriptions on stone slabs (*stelae*) around the temple, and fellow pilgrims at the temple. This ancient use of hypnotic suggestion is the basis of much of modern psychotherapy and Madison Avenue advertising strategies.

We have many records of Greek magical papyri from the early centuries of the Christian era documenting dream incubation techniques. These writings were prepared by gnostic and pagan practitioners, and describe various rituals designed to bring about healing or prophetic dreams.

For instance, consider the following ritual:

Take a linen strip, and on it you write with myrrh ink on the matter, and wrap an olive branch and place it beside your head, and go to sleep, pure, on a rush mat on the ground, saying the spell seven times to the lamp: "Hermes, lord of the world, who are in the heart...who send forth oracles by day or night...Reveal a sign and send me your true gift of prophecy."[8]

This spell could be strengthened by adding the blood of a crow or a dove to it. The 16th century German magician Cornelius Agrippa left us the following dream incubation following the Greek tradition:

"Let there be made an image of dreams, which being put under the head of him that dreams, makes him dream true dreams concerning anything that he hath formerly deliberated of: and let the figure be that of a man sleeping in the bosom of an angel...Thou shalt write upon the breast of the man the name of the effect desired, and in the hand of the angel the name of the intelligence of the Sun."[9]

The basic philosophy of all dream incubation approaches is to offer the dreamers guidance while they slept. The pilgrim had to be patient, as it might take several days to a few weeks to receive the appropriate dream.

The recipients had to do three things to ensure success. First, they were required to make a clear and formal request for assistance, and to have either a healing or prophetic dream to bring that aid. Second, the mind and body had to be receptive to this information. That meant diet control, abstinence from drugs, and the achievement of a peaceful and tranquil state of mind.

Last, the pilgrim had to agree to accept and work with the dreams they received. The factor of faith was all-important in this system. As soon as the confidence in these methods faded, the success rate of these incubation temples dropped dramatically.

Alexander the Great was known as a man who could dream his problems away. This Greek general studied with Aristotle, and used his dreams to conquer the Phoenicians en route to establishing one of the greatest empires of antiquity. Zeus came to Alexander in a dream and instructed the general to build a bridge from land to the base of the Phoenician island. This worked quite well.

Dreams were used by the priests at these healing temples to expand their growing knowledge of medicine. For cures, they would carefully record the instructions from these dreams, and would interpret them if they appeared symbolic.

The fact that religious rites and ceremonies of all types took place day and night added to the mindset of the pilgrims. The Greeks slept on animal hides in these dormitories. This was significant, as it represented a carryover from shamanistic eras.

Normally, pallets of straw, or a frame with ropes strung across it forming a net covered by a mattress, was used by the Greeks for their nightly rest. These hides added to the suggestion of dreams originating from this close contact to a former living animal. It is also interesting to note that the god Aesculapius communicated with the sleeper in the hypnagogic state (between wakefulness and sleep) to impart cures or advice.

Many of the dreams experienced at these temples instilled miraculous cures immediately following a therapeutic dream. For instance, one pilgrim was instructed to take ashes from the altar, mix them with wine, and apply this combination to the side of his body affected by pleurisy. This individual was quickly healed.

Some of these cures occurred simultaneously with the incubated dream. In another reported case, a pilgrim infested with lice dreamt that the god undressed him and swept him with a broom. The next morning this pilgrim's body was free of all insects. I discuss the power of faith and suggestion in my book *Soul Healing*.[10]

Roman Dreams

In Rome, the Temples of Serapis functioned in a similar fashion to those of Aesculapius. Dreams were taken quite seriously by the Romans, and they literally helped shape history.

Julius Caesar had a dream during which he had intercourse with his mother. This occurred on his way back from Gaul. This general's interpretation of this dream was that he was destined to conquer the "motherland." Caesar did take over as the emperor of Rome shortly after this. Fortunately for him, Freud wasn't around to discuss this dream.

Caesar's ego helped to shorten his reign as Rome's emperor. In another dream, Caesar saw himself ascend above the clouds and shake the god Jupiter's hand. This was accompanied by his wife's equally precognitive dream of him in her arms stabbed as he lay in a gable ornament shaped like a temple. All of these signs including the famous "beware the Ides of March" were ignored by Caesar, and his assassination from the stabbing by several senators took place on the Ides of March in 44 B.C.

The philosopher and Roman senator Cicero also helped shape the history of Western civilization by his acting on one of his dreams. Following Caesar's death, Rome engaged in many civil wars. Cicero's dream involved the selection of the new emperor by Jupiter in the Senate.

In this famous dream, the sons of various senators were seated in the temple to Jupiter Optimus Maximus (the Senate building). Jupiter, represented as a statue in this building, rejected one by one each of the senator's sons. Finally, Caesar's son Octavian walked by and Jupiter reportedly held out his hand and inferred that civil wars would end when Octavian was made ruler.

Cicero was unaware that Octavian (later known as Augustus) was Caesar's nephew. After the philosopher and senator became aware of this connection, he supported Octavian's selection as ruler. This support proved to be necessary for Octavian's success, and greatly affected the history of the Roman Empire.

Islamic Dreams

We have seen how the dreams in the ancient temples were readily shared. Mohammed asked his disciples to describe their dreams. In addition to sharing his dreams with his followers, he elaborated on interpretations of them.

According to Islamic tradition, the Prophet Mohammed considered dreams a conversation between man and his God. Their attitude was quite discriminatory, as unimportant people did not need to dream. Thus, a slave's dream was really meant for his master, the child for its parent, and that of the wife must be for her husband.

A prayer ritual was known in Islamic societies and referred to as *istipâra*. This special prayer was recited just before sleep in order to elicit an answer to a difficult problem. Drugs were sometimes used to induce dreams by the Dervishes (a Muslim ascetic order) and the people of Kurdistan (a mountainous and plateau region in Iraq).

Chinese Dreams

The Chinese authorities felt that dreams occurred when the soul (called the *hun*) temporarily left the physical body. This hun could converse with souls of the dead, the gods, or other spirits. As late as the 14th century A.D., all visitors to an important city spent the night in an incubation temple so they could receive messages from the gods.

Dreams and Christianity

The Roman Catholic Church adopted a narrow-minded view toward dreams in ancient times. Their war against the pagans included all aspects of life. Apuleius's work *The Golden Ass* describes a nobleman's dream that reversed a magical spell. This nobleman had been turned into a donkey and in his dream the goddess Isis showed him how to restore his human form by consuming roses carried by one of her priests. This priest also received this dream, and the nobleman was saved from this spell.

St. Augustine, a contemporary of Apuleius, saw to it that dreams were condemned. The Third Council of Nicea in 787 A.D. and the Council of Constantinople in 869 A.D. made this form of repression official. Dreams not sanctioned by ecclesiastical authorities were assumed to originate from the devil. The Roman Catholic and Orthodox Churches still maintain this position.

Dreams During the Middle Ages

The Middle Ages saw a continuation of the association of the Devil with dreams. This was especially pronounced with sexual dreams. The confessions elicited through torture during the Inquisition were well represented with dreams containing sexual escapades.

Demons were alleged to have had sex with mortals, as these negative entities took the form of Incubi and Succubi. This belief persisted in Europe until the Age of Enlightenment. During this time of scientific materialism, secular scholars increasingly replaced the Church monks as authorities on the significance of dreams.

Even Christians today declare the presence of saints in dreams that cure their ills. Yakushi (the master of healing) is seen by modern-day Japanese as a monk in their soul-healing dreams.

There are only two real possibilities functioning here. First, the dream image is the result of some outside source. Second, the dream results from the expectation of the dreamer, which is formulated and shaped prior to the actual dream. ·

It is a known fact that the mind can create its own suggestions and manifest them into reality with incredible efficiency when properly motivated. This is the basis of modern-day psychosomatic medicine and visual imagery techniques used in hypnotherapy and other alpha approaches.

All true knowledge is *anamnesis*: the act of remembering what the soul already knows. We recall who we are and what we may become in our dreams. It is only through active dreaming that we return to our true source, and remember why we chose this physical plane sojourn. Through properly directed dreaming, we can heal and empower ourselves and others, and dream our problems away.

5

A Culture That Takes Its Dreams Seriously

The Senoi of Malaysia have been studied since the 1930s through the work of Kilton Stewart and Pat Noone. This primitive tribe lives in mountainous jungles and is divided into two groups: the Semai and the Temiar. The term Senoi is applied to both groups, although the Temiar culture is a more dream directed culture.

These Senoi represent one of three large groupings of aborigines who live on the peninsula. They are more civilized than the Negrito group, but more primitive than the Proto-Malays group. All three groups are isolated from and more primitive than the modern Chinese and Malaysian people, who also reside on this peninsula.

What one dreamt about the previous night is a critical component of the Senoi culture. We will discuss the Senoi because their system of dreaming will assist you in eliminating nightmares and formulating creative solutions to everyday problems.

Dreams are the most central aspect of Senoi life. Each morning at breakfast, all family members are questioned about their dreams. Each one remembers these dreams. In fact, all activities from birth through and including death are the result of individual dreams.

Children are praised for reporting their dreams. Each dream is thoroughly discussed and evaluated. They ask the children about their behavior in the dreams; they tell the children what they did wrong in it, according to their system; they congratulate them on their correct behavior; they question on past events relevant to the dream; they give suggestions on how to change their behavior and attitude in future dreams; and finally, they recommend social action based on events in the dream.

After breakfast, the family members go to the village council, where their dreams are shared with the other members of the community. The significance of each dream situation and symbol is discussed. An opinion on the meaning of these dream elements is expressed by each council member. Group projects are created by those who agree with the interpretation of the dream.

More activities of the Senoi life arise from interpretations of their dreams. Moving to a different location, the forming of friendships and the construction of mechanical objects or art derived from a dream are but some effects of Senoi nightly sleep activities.

Dances are performed, costumes are created, songs are sung, and virtually their entire day's activities are determined through the dream state. When they go to sleep at night another day's agenda is being set by their subsequent dreams.

Food is not a problem for these Senoi. They fish by crushing a fruit on a rock by a stream so its juice flows into the water. This drugs the fish so it floats to the surface and is easily caught. The richness of the soil there makes it easy to grow yams, bananas, rice, tapioca, and pumpkin.

The dream-conscious Senoi are an interesting people. We would classify them as primitive, but on many levels they are far more advanced than we are. For example, violence of any sort is practically unknown to them. Although there are warlike tribes near them, the Senoi maintain their peaceful culture. The other tribes fear the "magic power" of the Senoi.

Another trait of the Senoi is the level of cooperativeness. The expression, "cooperate with your fellows—if you must oppose their wishes, oppose them with goodwill"[1] represents their cultural viewpoint. Everything is shared. This includes land, food, dreams, and life itself.

Senoi tribal members develop their own unique personalities and solutions to domestic and social problems. Neuroses and psychoses are reportedly nonexistent among the Senoi. They exhibit a high level of maturity, and make efficient use of their time so they can enjoy the relaxing aspects of life. It only requires about one week for them to construct a house that lasts five to six years.

Because only a few hours of each day is utilized for food gathering and council meetings, most of their day can be devoted to dream projects. We can't state with absolute certainty that this degree of psychological stability and health is a direct result of their unique use of dream material, but the evidence most certainly points in that direction. For instance, young children report the same type of nightmares with monsters that Westerners have. These are eliminated by the time these children reach adolescence. During this phase a consistency of benefits and creative stimulation is exhibited by the Senoi youth.

There are some general principles the Senoi teach their children in dealing with dream content. These may be summarized as follows:

1. *Confront and conquer any dangerous situation.* The Senoi advise their people to always attack a dream element that attacks you. Never run from such an enemy, or let it attack you. Always confront the danger with confidence.

2. *Always advance toward pleasure in a dream.* When children have a flying dream, they are instructed to relax and fully enjoy the experience. The same applies to sexual encounters, regardless of their age.

3. *Always establish a positive outcome despite the negativity or danger in a dream.* For example, let's say you were falling to your death in a dream. The Senoi advice would be to let yourself fall, relax, and enjoy the scenery. Then begin to fly. In other words, a child is taught to convert a fear of falling into an enjoyable activity such as flying.

The key recommendation to this rule is for the dreamer to somehow extract a gift from one of the dream images. This should be a useful or beautiful gift, which is to be brought back and shared with the dreamer's family and community. No dream should end until a positive action is completed. This could take the form of an orgasm for a sexual dream, a fight to the death in a battle, arrival at a destination in a flying dream, and so on.

The death of a dream enemy takes on a unique meaning to the Senoi. It is a good thing because the enemy's spirit now must serve the dreamer. This conversion of the enemy into a helpful and positive dream friend is a form of psychic empowerment.

We can learn a great deal about these recommendations. They facilitate a level of cooperativeness and tranquillity that is completely unknown in modern society. A diluted form of this approach could be incorporated into Western society. I don't think you would be ostracized if you shared such a dream as I previously described with a family member, friend, or coworker.

A new openness in communication has unlimited potential. Joseph T. Hart[2] reported an application of the Senoi dream approach with a small group of college students during a two-week camping trip in the Santa Cruz mountains. The results were most impressive. In addition to better levels of cooperation in their working relationships, one student experienced a lucid dream, while another had an accurate precognitive dream.

The Senoi suggest a dreamer remain asleep while falling, relax, and allow oneself to land during this initial falling dream. In future dreams, dreamers are instructed to master the art of flying when they sense themselves falling. For dreams during which flying is already established, the Senoi advise maximizing this technique with an intensification of the pleasurable experiences.

Friendly dream images are an important component of the Senoi system. The dreamer should always accept the assistance of this dream helper, express appreciation to this ally, request a gift, and share this gift with others.

An exceptionally friendly dream image is to be approached with the goal of having it become a guide for the dreamer. This is quite a contrast to the techniques of the Native Americans. In the latter's paradigm, the Indian children must endure fasting and exposure to the elements (with its isolation and inherent dangers) in order to produce pity so that a guide will assist them.

The Senoi children are empowered to conquer their dream enemies and convert a very friendly dream image into a guide. The obvious difference in the dreamer's ability to cope, the degree of independence, and self-image in comparing these two techniques is quite extreme. The Senoi system works far better. There are no negative side effects (as is occasionally reported by Native American

researchers) with the Senoi system, and the psychological health of the Senoi is far superior to that of modern Native Americans.

We must also consider the fact that the Senoi are masters of their own fate living in their homeland. Native Americans often live on reservations, and rate among the highest in unemployment and alcoholism of any American. A better evaluation of the Native American system would have to have been done before white settlers conquered them and nationalized their land.

Shaping dreams is a most interesting aspect of the Senoi system. This type of dream control results in an integration of the dreamer's personality. By neutralizing unpleasant experiences and then revising them, the fear of these negative images are effectively eliminated. This results in a disappearance of nightmares in Senoi youth and an increase in creative thinking.

Western psychologists have long recognized the power of attention in shaping behavior. By giving in to negative behavior, we encourage future incidents. However, the act of praising and recognizing a child for a dream will likely encourage him or her to dream more and to recall these dreams.

The psychological principle of reinforcement states that giving a reward for a current activity strengthens the probability of this activity occurring in the future. Applying this concept to children remembering a dream, if the children remember and tell their dream and their parents praise them for this behavior (and they like that praise), they will probably recall and tell their dreams more often in the future.

We Westerners are led to believe that dreams are mere fantasies, psychologically revealing through symbolic representation, or simply entertaining escapades. Our society does not imply that dreams can be actively utilized for growth. The possibility of using our dreams to help ourselves is virtually nonexistent. Most of us look upon our dreams with fear, titillation, or apathy.

Senoi adolescents are not granted the status of an adult until their dream characters cooperate with them and assist the dreamer in a manner that is socially acceptable. Their system obviously works, and we Westerners should look carefully at this system and learn from this most successful paradigm.

In order to effectively control dreams, the results should manifest as a positive change in the dreamers' concepts about themselves and the world in which they live. A positive growth cycle can be initiated, I feel, by applying the Senoi system. By shaping your dreams so that a change in dream behavior occurs, followed by a carryover in your waking life, you are more likely to alter the behavior and attitudes of your waking life in a positive and empowering manner. This new behavior fosters further changes in dream plots, and this cycle continues to the benefit of both the dreamer and society as a whole.

Most forms of Western psychotherapy merely try to understand and interpret dreams. This is not going to change behavior in our waking life. All it will do is create "educated neurotics." This is why I abhor standardized systems of dream interpretation. There are simply too many of them. Someone is obviously wrong, and you, the dreamer, are the loser for this lack of a universal answer key.

My advice is for you to interpret your own dreams. You, and only you, know your life best. No therapist, religious advisor, or well-meaning friend or family member can possibly understand your psyche as well as you can. There is considerable evidence to support the concept that altering and shaping our dream behavior will result in a comparable change in waking functions. Just look to the Senoi as a model of this.

Think of all of the time and money you could save while in therapy, just by shaping your dreams and applying those changes to your waking life. Among these obvious benefits is the ability to confront many of your issues at their point of origin and learn how to resolve them, as well as foster an integration of your own personality and psyche.

The Senoi's system is one of gradual change in the dreamer's life from fear to creativity and empowerment. Children are immediately encouraged to report their dreams, and slowly trained to shape them. After several years of using this method, adolescents have established a control over their dreams.

The Senoi philosophy concerning experiencing sexual pleasure in dreams appears controversial to the Western mind. By advocating that one cannot have too many dream lovers, and "advance toward pleasure in dreams," interesting results have been reported to me by my patients.

Most of my female patients reported either infrequent or no orgasms in their dreams. After adopting some form of the Senoi system, an increase was noted in both the quantity of orgasms and level of sexuality. This feeling of heightened passion and sexuality continued in their waking lives. I must also point out that their sexual activity increased beyond their previous established patterns, so their dream responses were not due to sexual deprivation.

This observation parallels that of the results of aggressive dream behavior toward dream antagonists. Patients who followed the Senoi techniques reported to me increasing levels of confidence and self-esteem.

My patients who have applied this system to their own life report less anxiety, higher self-images, and better levels of communication within their social network. Only people who are ready for this approach (internally motivated) should try this system. You have nothing to lose by attempting this technique. The worst that can occur is that you simply reject these approaches, and continue your present pattern of dreaming.

The Senoi system may actually present a paradigm of eliminating the true source of the dreamer's fears, and encouraging a special form of psychic empowerment by instilling the dreamers' ability to design their dreams and take charge of their destiny. This is truly a form of dreaming your problems away.

6

Improve Your Dreams Through Meditation

Historically, we find evidence of meditation in nearly all spiritual practices and contemplative religions. Its goal within these disciplines has been liberation from the confines of the egoic self, developing a sense of harmony with the universe, and the ability to increase one's compassion, sensitivity, and service to others. Meditation has been used as a clinical intervention for self-regulation, self-exploration, and self-liberation.[1]

When we consider meditation a means of relaxing the mind and enhancing physical health, our focus will be on its self-regulation mechanism. This is quite different in strategy as compared to other methods, such as hypnosis, guided imagery, biofeedback, and autogenic training.

With meditative techniques, the individual is trained to relax and to be able to face potential sources of stress with equanimity. It teaches the students to learn more about their thoughts, behaviors, and selves. The resulting sense of inner peacefulness and perspective can now be applied in everyday situations. Successful meditators recognize how much their dysfunctional behavior is controlled by their thoughts, and obtain a greater understanding of their own opinions, values, emotions, and self-image.

It is most unusual to find a spiritual accentuation as a result of regular use of meditation. For example, one of my patients informed me that his initial reasons for learning meditation were "stress management for better public speaking and in sexual situations." His reported effects from meditation were both self-regulation and a desire to help contribute something of service to the world. In other words, the self-regulation/stress management effect from meditation was not an end in itself, but a step toward developing greater compassion.

In the West, we define meditation as an act of pondering, reflecting, planning, and thinking. The Eastern approach is one of enlightenment and of spiritual growth encompassing intellectual, philosophical, and existential components.

Since the 1960s, meditative practices have become popular in the United States as a result of the work by Maharishi Mahesh Yogi. This Westernized style has been termed transcendental meditation (TM) and is the most popular form of meditation in America.

Meditative Techniques

There are many ways to describe meditation approaches. One classification divides this discipline into two sub-types: concentration meditation (CM) and mindfulness meditation (MM). A meditator may combine these two types, either in a single meditation session, or during the course of his or her meditation practice.

The mind's attention is directed to a single focal point in CM. Examples of this one focal point include one's breath, a pleasant scene, a candle flame, and so on. It is critical for the meditator to counter the natural tendency of the mind to wander by redirecting attention back to the focal point.

It is not uncommon for deeply repressed memories to surface during this process. Sometimes past life memories arise and these can be most therapeutic.

When any passing mind-objective dominates our consciousness by our direction, MM is applied. Contrary to CM, MM is more explanatory and involves a constant shifting of the mind-object paradigm. The purpose of MM is to deepen one's understanding of the nature of the mind with the ultimate goal being to attain true wisdom.

The initial stages of MM involve CM in order to discipline the mind with reference to developing a focused attention. Then MM goes well beyond CM in allowing a free exploration process during which the meditator directs his or her attention on whatever mind-object is most prominent.

The present moment as it is dominates this mind-object focus. To master this discipline, meditators must free themselves from distracting thoughts as the mindfulness state deepens. We now classify four types of meditation based on the particular focal device used. Visual concentration is the first category and this group involves focusing on an image visually. Concentrating on a flower, a peaceful environment, or mandala (a geometric design that features a square within a circle, representing the union of man with universe) are examples of this group.

Focusing one's awareness on some physical act or simple physical repetition represents a second category of focal device. Ancient yogic breath control called *pranayama* is an example of this physical repetition focal device. Jogging is another example.

A third focal device group involves problem contemplation with paradoxical components. The Zen *koan* provides an excellent example of this category. "What is the sound of one hand clapping?" is one of the most commonly known koans.

Dwelling on some mental event in the form of mental repetition is the fourth type of focal device. When one uses a *mantra* (a word or phrase that is repeated over and over to oneself silently) this category is being used. Chanting out loud is still another example of mental repetition.

The precise mechanism for meditation is simply the quieting of our rational and analytical left brain (defense mechanisms) and permitting our subconscious (right brain) to surface and dominate. This leads to an altered state of consciousness (alpha brain waves on the electroencephalograph), which eventually results in a state of extraordinary awareness. Easterners have described this state as *nirvana* or *satori*, while Westerners refer to this state as *cosmic consciousness*. The term *enlightenment* is the most universal description of this state.

Meditation does not suggest an escape from reality or a loss of consciousness. One important aspect of this approach is to have a room that is quiet and conducive to relaxation. This sanctuary is where this daily regimen can be performed in peace and quiet.

Many people practice meditation while lying in bed. The danger with this approach is that you are likely to fall asleep. However, because we will be using this method to guide our dreams, this is highly recommended. I suggest you use a recliner or other comfortable chair if you do not want to lose consciousness at the end of this procedure.

After you have assumed a comfortable position, simply relax the entire body. Rhythmic breathing, a gentle humming, and a slight swaying of the body while seated has proven very effective in creating such a relaxed state. A method that has been increasingly popular in the West is one of going over the parts of the body from the feet; first the toes, then knees, stomach, neck, hand, shoulders, face, jaw, forehead, eyes, the back of the head, the scalp; ensuring that each part in turn is free from strain. With the body relaxed, it becomes easier to achieve tranquillity. Finally, one is instructed to empty the mind of every distracting thought, as it intrudes and misdirects our awareness.

Try this single meditation exercise to get a feel for this technique:

Focus all of your attention on your breath.

Concentrate on the mechanics of breathing, not the thought of the breath. Note how it comes and goes. As the breath enters and leaves the nostrils, feel the expansion and contraction of the lungs.

Focus on the awareness of breathing. Remove all other thoughts and feelings from your awareness.

Observe this natural life process. Do not try to change it. Merely be one with it.

Let yourself receive the changing sensations that accompany this process.

As you inhale and exhale, one breath at a time, let it happen by itself. If it is deep, let it be deep. If it is slow, let it be slow. If it is shallow, let it be shallow.

If you sense the mind is interfering with this process, just focus on the inhalation and exhalation. Be one with your breath. Nothing else matters.

Observe the uniqueness of each breath. Don't analyze. Note the changing sensations. Be one with your breath.

Ignore all other functions of the body. Remove all thoughts from your mind. You are the breath. Be one with your breath.

You are now floating with the universe. As the wind carries a feather, you are being carried by your breath.

Notice how the distracting thoughts fade. How they become meaningless. All that matters is that you breathe. You are your breath. Be one with your breath.

Let go of the body. Feel as if you have no body. You are weightless, as is your breath.

You are floating in the universe. You are at peace with the universe. You are one with the universe.

Notice how relaxed you are, now that you are free of the confines of the body. You are totally one with the universe.

There is nowhere to go. Nobody is expecting you. You have no schedule or deadline. You are free. Enjoy this moment, for you are one with the universe.

Be quiet. Do not cough or make any movement or sound. Just be still and merge with the universe. You are consciousness. You are one with the universe.

Let each moment occur by itself. Observe it and enjoy these intervals of time. Do not resist this merging with your consciousness.

You are now nothing but consciousness. You are the universe.

Play New Age music for 15 minutes.

Now it is time to return to your body. Again, concentrate on your breath. Now note the other functions of your body. Slowly open up your eyes and do what you feel is important at this time (this is deleted if you are practicing meditation just prior to bedtime).

Hindu writings present the most precise meditative techniques. In yoga, for example, the goal is union with the Absolute, and this is accomplished by progression through eight stages of development. The first two levels deal with internal and external ethics. These stress the elimination of negative emotions such as greed, lust, and anger, and the attainment of peace of mind. Principles dealing with not harming other living things are also emphasized.

The third stage concerns itself with body postures. Following this comes breath control and the mastery of the *prana* or life force in the fourth stage. Our breath contains this prana. This life force is a component of the air we breathe. The yogi extracts the prana from the air and conducts it through his dream body.

Control of the senses constitutes the fifth stage. By this stage the body should be properly conditioned, the mind directed to a single goal and the emotions under control. It is now easier to withdraw all attention from external distractions and concentrates on the focal device we have chosen.

The sixth stage is one of concentration or *dharana*. Focusing one's full attention on a spot on a blank surface such as a wall, a point of light, the flame of a candle, a flower, the picture of a deity such as Krishna or Shiva, or a letter of the alphabet are examples of this stage.

Yogis sometimes begin their meditation by concentrating with closed eyes on some part of their body; the top of the head, the space between the eyebrows (the third eye), and the tip of the nose are commonly used.

We must differentiate concentration from meditation. The former implies an exercise of the will: The mind centers its powers on an object or idea until it yields its essence. Concentration brings mental energy to bear on a certain point so that with its conquest, further doors are opened to the mind. Meditation, on the other hand, does not require any forcible harnessing of the will. It is something that emerges from the cessation of thought.

Dhyana or contemplation is the seventh stage of this process. By contemplation, we refer to a turning within of the consciousness, and a focusing of the mental faculties inwards. The last stage is called *samadhi*. This is a state of superconsciousness or Higher Self contact. Samadhi is the ultimate goal of yogic meditation. Its characteristics can be listed as follows:

- ☆ A positive mood (tranquillity, peace of mind).
- ☆ An experience of unity or oneness with the environment; what the ancients called the joining of microcosm (man) with macrocosm (universe).
- ☆ A sense of inability to describe the experience with words.
- ☆ An altercation in time/space relationships.
- ☆ An enhanced sense of reality and meaning.
- ☆ Paradoxicality, or, acceptance of things that seem paradoxical in ordinary consciousness.

A Mantra Exercise

The mantra is simply a vehicle to assist in preventing our mind from wandering during meditation. Often, a word or phrase is utilized to achieve this purpose.

The word *om* is an example of a mantra. By concentrating on a word without emotion or significance, your mind's order of processing begins to change. The mind begins to wander, with a quieter, more subtle state of consciousness.

1. Each time you breathe out say the word om. Om. Om. Om. Breathe softly and normally, but now do not concentrate on your breathing.

2. Now repeat your mantra (or om) in your mind. Just think of saying it. Do not actually move your lips. Just think of it. Do not concentrate on your breathing. Let the mantra repeat itself in your mind. Do not force it. Just let it flow. Gradually the mantra will fade. The mind will be quiet.

3. Occasionally, the quiet will be broken by sporadic thoughts. Let them come. Experience them, then let them leave your mind as quickly as they entered, by simply going stronger to your mantra.

4. Keep your movements to a minimum, but if you are uncomfortable, move. Discomfort or anxiety will prevent full attainment of the relaxed state.

5. Now practice this method as reflected in steps two through four for five minutes.

Here is a simple meditation technique that combines a mantra with visualizations:

1. Visualize your inner black screen prior to going to sleep, and place one blue speck of light on it. Your eyes are now closed.

2. Say out loud, "OM," or any mantra you have used in the past. Repeat this mantra several times.

3. Imagine yourself watching a sunset with someone you care about, walking in a park, or perceive yourself in a weightless body inside your physical body.

4. Keep this awareness as you drift off to sleep or keep a constant but vague awareness of your own identity. Then shift your focus from your body into blackness.

This meditation exercise is designed to train you to experience the depths of your inner being. To do this, you must detach yourself from your normal attachments to thoughts. These thoughts come from your conscious mind (willpower) or enter your conscious awareness from outside.

Every time such a thought enters your awareness while doing this meditation, simply say the word "stop." You may say it aloud. This functions to dissipate the thought without diverting your attention and creating an emotional response.

The following exercise will help you to attain this goal:

1. Sit comfortably with your back straight and apply protection (visualize a white light aura surrounding you, shielding you from any negative forces in the universe). Breathe deeply for one minute. Say to yourself, "I am totally relaxed," and let your mind create an ideal place of relaxation (a sanctuary).

2. This sanctuary you created in step one can be on any plane other than the Earth plane. There are no responsibilities, tedious chores, or distractions in your sanctuary. Remain in this place for a minimum of five minutes.

3. Mentally return to the room where you are meditating and take a deep breath to go even deeper into this relaxed state. Any extraneous thoughts that may be encountered are to be immediately neutralized by saying "stop." Say this word in a relaxed manner, without any special emphasis.

4. Continue your breathing and return to your sanctuary. Stay with this process for 15 minutes, saying "stop" every time a distracting thought enters your mind.

The TM approaches practiced in the United States and other Western countries forgo the ascetic doctrines and other disciplines professed by the Easterners. We in the West seem to demand a fast-food approach to our spiritual growth, and TM provides a certain degree of the instant results required by Westerners.

We can learn quite a lot from meditation approaches. In addition to relaxation and focused concentration, the detachment from negativity and acceptance of the love, warmth, and joy that life has to offer is well worth the time and effort required of these techniques. All this leads to spiritual growth, and this can be accomplished in just 15 to 20 minutes a day of a simple exercise.

7

Improve Your Dreams Through Hypnosis

The word hypnosis is derived from the Greek *hypnos*, which means sleep. Unfortunately named, this state of mind is a waking state that is characterized by physical relaxation and an openness to accept suggestions. The only stage of our sleep cycle that entails hypnosis is our REM (rapid eye movement) or dream cycle. This stage is a waking, rather than unconscious, level of mind.

We enter into this hypnotic state naturally for four hours during our waking day, and three hours manifested by our dreaming. Because hypnosis is natural, we can induce it by detaching ourselves from our external environment and entering an altered state of consciousness (ASC).

One of the forms of evidence we have that hypnosis actually exists rests in its ability to relieve pain. When I practiced dentistry, I would use hypnosis as the only method of pain control on about 25 percent of my patients.

This type of hypnoanalgesia (pain relief) was not due to the production of endorphins. Endorphins are a morphine-like neurotransmitter produced by the body in response to pain. It does explain pain relief derived from acupuncture, but not that derived from hypnosis. We still do not know the physiological or biochemical explanation of how hypnosis functions in reducing stress and pain control.[1]

Everyone can experience hypnosis. We all enter this state for seven hours every day. This state is perfectly natural and safe. If not for natural self-hypnosis, we would die of a heart attack or a cerebral vascular accident.[2]

Those most difficult to hypnotize are the highly intellectual who constantly analyze and find it difficult to accept suggestions, and the unintelligent who have little control over their conscious mind. The best subjects are those with average intelligence and a good imagination, and who find it easy to express their feelings.

There is no real neurological difference between meditation and hypnosis. They are merely used differently, meditation being passive while hypnosis is a more active approach. I refer you to my book *Soul Healing* for a comprehensive discussion of this principle.

Whatever the mind can conceive, it can achieve. That is empowerment, and the basic premise behind my use of hypnosis. Later in this chapter, I will describe how we can use hypnosis to direct our dreams for therapeutic purposes. For our current discussion, consider that following relaxation with self-hypnosis, you can now suggest any goal to your subconscious mind. If a suggestion is to be accomplished after the trance has ended, we refer to it as a posthypnotic suggestion. This also includes ending the trance by your falling asleep.

Here are just some of the goals you can accomplish through the use of self-hypnosis:

☆ Elimination of all types of headaches, including migraine.
☆ Elimination of allergies and skin disorders.
☆ Strengthening one's immune system to resist any disease.
☆ Elimination of habits, phobias, and other "self-defeating sequences."
☆ Improving decisiveness.
☆ Overcoming insomnia.
☆ Improving the quality of people and circumstances in general that you attract in your life.
☆ Increasing your ability to earn and hold onto money.
☆ Overcoming obsessive-compulsive behavior.
☆ Improving the overall quality of your life.
☆ Improving psychic awareness.

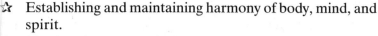

☆ Establishing and maintaining harmony of body, mind, and spirit.

☆ Slowing down the aging process.

All our decision making takes place in what I refer to as our conscious mind proper. This beta brain wave as measured by the electroencephalogram (EEG) is most often called "the self." The data collected by our five senses are received, evaluated, and acted upon. This decision-making process of the conscious mind proper is continuous throughout our waking life.

Our conscious mind proper comprises our free will and defense mechanisms. From here on I will refer to it simply as the conscious mind. The main purpose of our defense mechanisms is to keep our behavior constant, and change is the enemy, as I have discussed previously.

Any form of therapy and growth requires change. The conscious mind is the one element of our consciousness that we must battle daily. Whenever you want to lose weight, stop smoking, overcome procrastination, end a relationship with Mr. or Ms. Wrong, you are going to run into the obstacle known as the conscious mind.

The other component of our waking mind is the subconscious mind, or alpha brain level, as measured on the EEG. We can compare the function of our subconscious to that of a computer, because it stores every piece of data that is collected by your five senses. Your conscious mind both programs the subconscious and accesses its files when it makes a decision, or simply reacts to a stimulus. This overlap of functions of our two waking minds somewhat muddles the picture of how our mind works. Your actions and reactions to life's circumstances are based upon the sum total of our previous experience. This involves emotions, prejudices, response to media ads, and a host of several other factors.

The conscious mind's territory also includes regulating the functions of the body's organs. In reality, these life preservation duties are under the competent guidance and control of the subconscious. If for any reason the conscious mind is unable to monitor these vital functions, the subconscious immediately takes over and facilitates the preservation of life.

The unconscious levels of our mind function during five of the eight hours we sleep. These states are referred to as light sleep (theta brain wave) and deep sleep (delta brain wave), respectively. We will discuss these four brain waves at greater depth in Chapter 8. Here is a figure that illustrates the two main divisions of our consciousness.

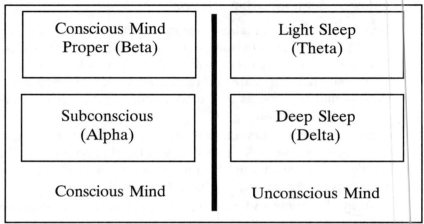

Conscious Mind Proper (Beta)	Light Sleep (Theta)
Subconscious (Alpha)	Deep Sleep (Delta)
Conscious Mind	Unconscious Mind

figure 1. Consciousness

To further illustrate these four brain wave levels, think of our cycle of waking and sleep. When we get up in the morning we have just gone from natural hypnosis (alpha) to full conscious (beta). The process of falling asleep at night is progressing from beta to alpha (REM cycle or dreaming) to theta (light sleep) to delta (deep sleep) to theta (light sleep) to alpha, and the cycle repeats itself.

Examples of hypnosis are daydreaming, reading, watching television, observing white lines on a highway, crossing over into sleep, and waking up from your nightly rest and dreams during our REM cycle.

The subconscious mind learns from experience and operates without reporting to the conscious mind when an emergency arises. This super-computer known as the subconscious has the capability of storing trillions of pieces of data without losing so much as one fact. Our conscious mind's memory bank is about 10 percent efficient, and has nowhere near the success rate of its subconscious colleague.

Thinking by itself is not within the prerogative of the subconscious. This alpha brain wave stores information relating to motivations, basic instincts, and memories. It reviews information and attitudes, and, where necessary, reacts according to its predetermined programs. But it does not *reason*. If the subconscious mind is programmed to react in a certain way to a given set of circumstances, it will continue to react blindly in this way, even if the individual no longer wants this reaction to continue.

A suggestion is an idea implanted in the mind from an exterior source and subsequently incorporated within the recipient's thinking and/or reactions. The ability to accept suggestion is not a weakness, but a sign of intelligence. Most data collected from our environment by our five senses contain an element of suggestion.

You cannot make people do anything in the trance state that they would not do in the waking state, and the same truth applies equally to self-hypnosis. Response to suggestion can vary from one person to another and, within the individual, many variable factors can cause a wide range of reactions to suggestion on different occasions.

Our consciousness has a component known as a *critical censor*. Without this element, your subconscious mind (which possesses no sense of judgment), would simply react to *every* suggestion that came along, with possibly quite disastrous consequences. Without the censor, each suggestion, would have the power of a command that could not be refused and even the most ridiculous suggestions would compel you to react in a manner that would wreck your life. The censor nullifies over 90 percent of the suggestions it receives daily. In most cases, the critical censor is much more efficient in fending off direct suggestion than indirect suggestion and, the more closely the suggestion matches the requirements or fears of the individual, the more likely it is to be accepted.

One common enemy we all face is negative thinking. Society, mostly through the media, continually brainwashes us with cynicism, doomsday mentalities, and other forms of negativity. Because of the power of suggestion, this negative programming can have quite destructive effects upon your psyche. By counteracting this negativity with positive self-hypnotic suggestions, you will begin to feel more fit, healthier, happier, and much more dynamic within yourself because now you will begin to take charge of your life and exhibit a special form of empowerment. At all times, strive to maintain a totally positive attitude of mind and, in doing so, you will ensure ultimately to succeed in all your efforts.

The great majority of people experiencing self-hypnosis merely feel completely relaxed mentally and physically, yet still retain awareness of their surroundings. There is no sharply defined borderline between the waking and the trance state, just a gradually increasing sense of mental and physical relaxation. In self-hypnosis in particular, you very rarely go beyond the light-trance state because you need to retain sufficient control of your consciousness in order to be able to make the requisite hypnotic suggestions to yourself. This is one reason why I always recommend using self-hypnosis tapes.[3] These tapes remove that obstacle, and equally eliminate memorizing scripts or worrying about what to say or phrasing suggestions incorrectly.

In the world of the mind, nothing can be said to be absolutely impossible. With a correct attitude of mind, coupled with patience and perseverance, many so-called impossible changes in your life can be ameliorated. Self-hypnosis used correctly and with total positive objectivity, in truth is the means by which all things become possible. In the final analysis it comes down to this: If in doubt, you don't; if you believe, you succeed.

The hypnotic trance state will have certain basic characteristics. These are:

1. A generalized feeling of relaxation.
2. A sense of time moving quickly. You will actually have no idea how much real time elapsed.
3. Focused concentration.
4. A lack of movement in your body.
5. Your eyes may move back and forth (rapid eye movement, or REM).

In deeper levels of hypnosis (as well as in all dream states), it is possible to experience an OBE. When you have an OBE, you are in a truly altered state of consciousness. In this state of deeper trance, you may observe the following features:

☆ Alterations in thinking. Subjective interruptions in memory, judgment, attention, and concentration characterize this feature.

☆ Sense of the ineffable. People who experience an ASC (altered state of consciousness) appear unable to communicate the essence of their experience to someone who has not had one. Amnesia is also noted.

☆ Disturbed time sense. Common to this are subjective feelings of time coming to a standstill, feelings of timelessness, and the slowing or acceleration of time.

☆ Feelings of rejuvenation. A new sense of hope, joy, and purpose is exhibited by the experiencer.

☆ Change in meaning or significance. Feelings of profound insight, illumination, and truth are frequently observed in ASC.

☆ Changes in emotional expression. Displays of more intense and primitive emotional expressions that are sudden and unexpected. Emotional detachment may also be exhibited at this time.

☆ Body image change. A sense of depersonalization, derealization, and a loss of boundaries between self and others or the universe are observed. These encounters can be called "expansion of consciousness," or feelings of "oneness" in a mystical or religious setting. Not only may various parts of the body appear or feel shrunken, enlarged, distorted, heavy, weightless, disconnected, strange or funny, but spontaneous experiences of dizziness, blurring of vision, weakness, numbness, tingling, and analgesia are likewise encountered.

In reference to using self-hypnosis for your positive programming, there are certain principles you should understand to relieve any fears about this technique:

1. The best hypnotic subjects are people who are imaginative and intelligent. The more determined you are to attain a goal, the greater your chances of success.

2. You cannot be forced to do anything as a result of hypnosis that you would not normally do.

3. Hypnotic programming works by repeated exposure. Eventually when you raise the quality of your soul's energy, you will establish a new spiritual as well as emotional foundation, and your programming becomes a permanent part of your awareness.

4. You will remember everything that you experience during a trance, unless you are a very deep-level subject.

5. After a self-hypnotic experience, you will awaken feeling more at peace, relaxed, and cleansed (both emotionally and spiritually) than you felt prior to this experience. If you practice this technique at bedtime, you will probably fall asleep and guide your dream level based on the suggestions you gave yourself.

To get a feel for self-hypnosis, try this simple exercise. First, assume a comfortable position and prepare your room so that you will not be disturbed for about 10 minutes. You may find it more convenient to make a tape of this script and play it on your cassette player while listening to it through headphones. Remember to substitute the word "I" for "you" in these scripts.

Take a deep breath and let it out slowly.

Close your eyes.

Lie back comfortably in the chair.

Let yourself go...loose, limp, and slack.

Let all the muscles of your body relax completely.

Breathe in and out...nice and slow.

Concentrate on your feet and ankles and let them relax.

Let them relax...let them go...loose, limp, and slack.

Soon you will begin to have a feeling of heaviness in your feet.

Your feet are beginning to feel as heavy as lead.

Your feet are getting heavier and heavier.

Let yourself go completely.

Now let all of the muscles of your calves and thighs go loose, limp, and slack.

Let all of these muscles in your legs relax completely.

Your legs are beginning to feel heavier and heavier.

Let yourself go completely.

Give yourself up totally to this very pleasant...relaxed...comfortable feeling.

Let your whole body go loose, limp, and slack.

Your whole body is becoming as heavy as lead.

Let the muscles of your stomach completely relax.

Let them become loose, limp, and slack.

Next the muscles of your chest and your back.

Let them go completely loose, limp, and slack, and as you feel heaviness in your body, you are relaxing more deeply.

Your whole body is becoming as heavy as lead.

Let yourself sink down deeper in the chair.

Let yourself relax totally and completely.

Let all of the muscles in your neck and shoulders relax.

Let all of these muscles go loose, limp, and slack.

Now the muscles in your arms are becoming loose, limp, slack, and heavy.

As they relax, they are getting heavier and heavier.

As though your arms are as heavy as lead.

Let your arms go.

Let your whole body relax completely.

Your whole body is deeply and completely relaxed.

Now a feeling of complete relaxation is gradually moving over your whole body.

All of the muscles in your feet and ankles are completely relaxed.

Your calf and thigh muscles are completely relaxed.

All of the muscles in your legs are loose, limp, and slack.

And as you relax...your sleep is becoming deeper and more relaxing.

The feeling of relaxation is spreading through all of your body.

All of the muscles of your body are becoming loose, limp, and slack.

Totally relaxed.

Your body is getting heavier and heavier.

You are going deeper and deeper into relaxation.

Play New Age music for four minutes.

Whenever you desire to reenter into this wonderfully relaxing state of self-hypnosis, all you have to do is say the number twenty three times and you feel yourself sinking down into a deep relaxation. Slowly count from one to five and when you say the number five to yourself, your eyes will open and you will be wide awake. (This is eliminated if you are practicing this method just prior to falling asleep.)

Try this hypnotic exercise to relax, establish a sanctuary for your spiritual growth, and guide your dreams to make this a reality. Practice this script, or play a tape of this, just before falling asleep:

Lie down comfortably, close your eyes, and begin to relax. Allow yourself to become more and more relaxed. Breathe very deeply and send a warm feeling into your toes and feet. Let this feeling break up any strain or tension and as you exhale, let the tension drain away. Breathe deeply and send this warm feeling into your ankles. It will break up any strain or tension and as you exhale, let the tension drain away. Breathe deeply and send this feeling into your knees, let it break up any strain or tension there, and as you exhale, let the tension drain away. Send this warm sensation into your thighs so any strain or tension is draining away. Breathe deeply and send this warm feeling into your genitals and drain away any tension.

Send this warm feeling into your abdomen now; all your internal organs are soothed and relaxed and any strain or tension is draining away. Let this energy flow into your chest and breast; let it soothe you, and as you exhale, any tension is draining away. Send this energy into your back now. This feeling is breaking up any strain or tension and as you exhale, the tension is draining away. The deep relaxing energy is flowing through your back, into each vertebra as each vertebra assumes its proper alignment. The healing energy is flowing into all your muscles and tendons and you are relaxed, very fully relaxed. Send this energy into your shoulders and neck; this energy is breaking up any strain or tension and as you exhale, the tension is draining away. Your shoulders and neck are fully relaxed. And the deep relaxing energy is flowing into your arms; your upper arms, your elbows, your forearms, your wrists, your hands, your fingers are fully relaxed.

Let this relaxing energy wash up over your throat, and your lips, your jaw, your cheeks are fully relaxed. Send this energy into your face, the muscles around your eyes, your forehead, your scalp are relaxed. Any strain or tension is draining away. You are relaxed, most completely relaxed.

And now float to your space, leave your physical body and move between dimensions and travel to your space, a meadow, a mountain, a forest, the seashore, wherever your mind is safe and free. Go to that space now. And you are in your space, the space you have created, a space sacred and apart. Here in this space you are free from all tension and in touch with the calm, expansive power within you. Here in this space you have access to spiritual information and energy. Here is the space where you can communicate with your spirit guides. Your flow is in harmony with the flow of the universe. Because you are a part of the whole creation, you have access to the power of the whole of creation. Here you are pure and free.

Past-Life Regression

In Chapter 1, I briefly discussed the concept of reincarnation. These people who are close to you now may have been involved with you in that previous existence. Experience is the best teacher. Try this exercise before going to sleep to experience one or more of your past lives:

Imagine a bright white light coming down from above and entering the top of your head, filling your entire body. See it, feel it, and it becomes reality. Now imagine an aura of pure white light emanating from your heart region. Again, surrounding your entire body, protecting you. See it, feel it, and it becomes reality. Now only your Masters, Guides, and highly evolved loving entities who mean you well will be able to influence you during this or any other hypnotic session. You are totally protected by this aura of pure white light. Now listen very carefully. In a few minutes, I'm going to be counting backwards from twenty to one. As I count backward from twenty to one, you are going to perceive yourself moving through a very deep and dark tunnel. The tunnel will get lighter and lighter and at the very end of this tunnel, there will be a door with a bright white light above it. When you walk through this door, you will be in a past-life scene. You're going to reexperience one of your past lives at the age of about 15. You'll be moving to an event that will be significant and explain who you are, where you are, and why you are there. I want you to realize that if you feel uncomfortable either physically, mentally, or emotionally at any time, you can awaken yourself from this hypnotic trance by simply counting forward from one to five. You will always associate my voice as a friendly voice in trance. You will be able to let your mind review back into its memory banks and follow the instructions of perceiving the scenes of your own past lives and following along as I instruct. You'll find yourself being able to get deeper and quicker into hypnotic trances each time as you practice with this tape or other methods of self-hypnosis. When you hear me say the words "sleep now and rest," I want you to immediately detach yourself from any scene you are experiencing. You will be able to wait for further instructions.

You absolutely have the power and ability to go back into a past life as your subconscious mind's memory banks remember everything you've ever experienced in all your past lives as well as your present life. I want you to relive these past life events only as a neutral observer without feeling or emotion, just as if you were watching a television show. I want you to choose a past life now in which you've lived to at least the age of 30. I want you to pick a positive, neutral, or happy past-life experience. I'm going to count backwards now from twenty to one. As I do so I want you to feel yourself moving into the past. You'll find yourself moving through a pitch-black tunnel that will get lighter and lighter as I count backwards. When I reach the count of one, you will have opened up a door with a bright white light above it and walked into a past-life scene. You will once again become yourself at about the age of 15 in a previous lifetime. Now listen carefully. Number twenty you're moving into a very deep dark tunnel surrounded by grass and trees and your favorite flowers and very very inviting, as you feel very calm and comfortable about moving into the tunnel. Nineteen, eighteen, you're moving backwards in time back, back, seventeen, sixteen, fifteen, the tunnel is becoming lighter now. You can make out your arms and legs and you realize that you are walking through this tunnel and you're moving backwards in time. Fourteen, thirteen, twelve, moving so far back, back, back, eleven, ten, nine you're now so far back— you're over halfway there, the tunnel is much lighter. You can see around you and you can now make out the door in front of you with the bright white light above it. Eight, seven, six, standing in front of the door now feeling comfortable and feeling positive and confident about your ability to move into this past-life scene. Five, four, now walk up to the door, put your hand on the doorknob, the bright white light is so bright it's hard to look at. Three, open the door two, step through the door one, move into the past-life scene. Focus carefully on what you perceive before you. Take a few minutes now and I want you to let everything become crystal clear. The information flowing into your awareness, the scene becoming visual and visible. Just let yourself become oriented to your new environment. Focus on it. Take a few moments and listen to my instructions. Let the impression form. First, what do you see and what are you doing? Are you male or female? Look at your feet first—what type of footwear or shoes are you wearing? Now move up the body and see exactly how you are clothed. How are you dressed? How old are you? What are you doing right now? What is happening around you? Be able to describe the situation you find yourself in. Are you outdoors or indoors? Is it day or night? Is it hot or cold? What country or land do you live in or are you from? Now focus on this one carefully—what do people call you? What is the year? Take a few moments. Numbers may appear right in front of your awareness. You will be informed exactly what year this is. Take a few more moments and let any additional information crystallize and become clear in your awareness about yourself and the environment that you find yourself in. Take a few moments. Let any additional information be made clear to you.

Play New Age music for three minutes.

Very good now. Listen very carefully to my voice now. Sleep now and rest. Detach yourself from this scene just for a moment. I'm going to be counting forward from one to five. When I reach the count of five you're going to be moving forward now to a significant event that's going to occur in this lifetime which will affect you personally. It will also most probably affect those close to you—it may involve your parents, friends, people who are close to you in this lifetime. I want you to move forward to a significant event but it's also going to be a positive event. Focus carefully now. Sleep now and rest and listen now as I count forward from one to five. On the count of five you will be moving forward in time to a significant positive event that is going to occur to you. One moving forward, slowly, carefully, comfortably, two feeling good as you move forward in time, three halfway there, four almost there, five. Now again focus on yourself and the environment you find yourself in. What are you doing now and why are you in this environment? Has anything changed since I last spoke with you? What is happening around you? Are there any other people around you who are important to you? If there are, are they male or female? Are they friends or relatives? How do they relate to you? Why are they important to you? Focus on your clothes now starting with your feet first. How are you dressed? Are you dressed any differently from when I last spoke with you? Move all the way up your body and perceive how you are dressed. Then look at the people next to you—are they dressed any differently? About how old are you now? Focus on that for a moment—a number will appear to you—about how old are you right now? Where exactly are you? Are you outdoors or indoors? Is it day or night? What season is this? What is your occupation? What do you do to pass the time? What do you do with your day? Focus on how you spend your time. Now I want you to focus on an event taking place right now in which you are involved. I want you to take this event right through to completion. I want you to spend a few moments and whatever this event is I want you to carry it through to completion. This will be a positive or happy event only. Take a few moments and carry this event through to completion.

Play New Age music for three minutes.

All right now. Sleep now and rest. Detach yourself from this scene that you are experiencing and listen to my voice again. You're going to be moving forward now by a period of a minimum of three years. It can be as long as necessary, but a minimum of three years. You will not have died or undergone any traumatic episode. It will be at least three years further in time. Now I want you to move forward to a significant event that is going to affect not only the kind of work you do but also yourself personally. Affect the way you relate to certain people—people who are close to you perhaps, certain goals that you have. I want you to move forward to this very significant time that is going to be positive, neutral, or happy and it will be at least three years from now. On the count of five move forward very carefully and comfortably. One moving forward, two moving further forward, three halfway there, four almost there five. Now perceive what you observe around you. What has transpired since I last saw you? Focus on yourself first. Perceive where you are, how you are dressed, what environment, you are in, where you are located if it was a different physical environment and who you are with. Take a few moments and let this information crystallize and become clear into your awareness.

Play New Age Music for three minutes.

All right now. Sleep and rest. Detach yourself from this scene. We're going to be moving forward again on the count of five. This time you're going to be moving forward to a scene that is going to signify or illustrate the maximum achievements that you accomplished in this lifetime. This scene will illustrate the maximum accomplishments personally or professionally. You'll be surrounded by the people that affect you the most in this lifetime. You will be achieving the maximum amount of success or goals or whatever else you wanted to accomplish in this lifetime. Move forward to this maximum accomplishment in this lifetime, on the count of five. One moving forward slowly, carefully, comfortably, two moving further forward, three halfway there, four almost there five. Now take a few moments and see where you find yourself. What is your environment? What has happened and why is this time of your life so important to you? Focus on it and see what you've accomplished and let all the information be made clear to you.

Play New Age music for three minutes.

Now that you've been able to perceive this particular period of your life, I want you to be able to evaluate your life. I want you to find out what goals you were supposed to accomplish and what you actually did accomplish. What do you feel that you learned from this lifetime? What do you feel that you have gained from this lifetime—in your own personal goals, family life, relationships? Let the information flow— what did you gain? Now let's focus on what you weren't able to achieve. Focus on what you felt you would have liked more time for. What do you feel you were unable to accomplish and why? Focus on that. Let the information flow. Now remember in this particular lifetime you are still alive now. I want you now to focus upon the activities in which you're involved in this particular scene to evaluate why this lifetime was important to you. What necessary or needed experience did you gain from this lifetime? Focus on this now. Let the information flow into your awareness.

As you drift off to sleep, your subconscious is now programmed to access its memory banks, known as the Akashic Records, and review one or more of your past lives to assist you in finding out your karmic purpose or other avenues of spiritual growth.

The best way to practice this exercise, or any other self-hypnosis script, is to make a tape of this technique. I discuss this simple procedure in detail in my book *New Age Hypnosis*.[4] Tapes I have recorded are also available through my office.

Hypnosis is a more directed type of concentration than is meditation. In hypnosis, a rigorous attempt is made to hold specific ideas or visual images in the mind while the body is equally relaxed. I personally and professionally feel self-hypnosis is the easiest method to use for guiding dreams and facilitating spiritual growth.

8

What Do Sleep Labs Tell Us About Our Dreams?

Laboratories use the EEG to measure changes in the electrical activity of the brain in the direction of lower frequencies of brain waves and higher voltage patterns.

Our sleep cycle presents itself as four distinct stages, and are referred to as Stage I, II, III, and IV. The brain wave rhythm is rather slow in Stage IV, but the voltage waves are high. Most of what occurs in this last stage are the thoughts of waking life, with occasional reports of dreams.

Once Stage IV is attained, there is a reverse process back through Stage III, II, and finally to Stage I. This Stage I is now called an *Emergent Stage I*, and most dreams take place here. This cycle takes from 90 to 120 minutes to complete.

We will experience Emergent Stage I between four to seven times each night, depending on how long our sleep cycle is. Each succeeding dream cycle lasts longer than the preceding one. The last one may go on from 40 minutes to an hour. Our total amount of time spent in our nightly dream cycle is about three hours.

REM Sleep

The dream period is characterized by sudden episodes of rapid movements of the eyes, both vertically and horizontally. These quick eye movements have led to the term rapid eye movements or REMs being applied to the dream state.

REM sleep was discovered by physiologists Nathaniel Kleitman and Eugene Aserinsky at the University of Chicago in 1953. The four distinct sleep stages were first proposed by physiologist Frederick Snyder in the 1960s.

The REM State is a distinct and separate phase of the sleep cycle, differing physiologically from the other or non-REM phases. This was discovered by Richard Jones. Eye movements in peaceful dreams tend to be small and sparse, whereas larger and more continuous movement are prevalent in more active dreams. We see REMs in newborn babies and congenitally blind individuals. Premature babies in the womb exhibit far greater than normal quantities of REM sleep before the expected time of birth.

Dreaming begins and ends for most of us when the REM cycle begins and ends. Although external stimuli, such as loud noises or smells may become part of a dream, they do not create our dream content.

Dream recall is richest and most detailed immediately after a REM period ends. When awakened in sleep laboratories, these subjects reported varying degrees of memories of their dreams as follows:[1]

☆ When awakened during their REM cycle, sleepers reported an ongoing dream story.

☆ Upon being aroused during a body movement immediately following REM, these subjects described complete, vivid, specific dream scenarios.

☆ Sleepers awakened five minutes after their REM cycle ended reported vague memories of dream plots.

☆ Subjects aroused 10 minutes following REM had no dream recall, merely a blurry impression of having dreamt.

We can see from this that a dream tends to break up into fragments after only five minutes of its completion, and by 10 minutes it is gone. If you want to recall a dream, you must record it immediately upon its termination.

REM sleep is important for brain growth in children and emotional renewal or cleansing in all of us. One piece of evidence from dream laboratory studies further suggests this stage is essential for the development of learning, memory, and thinking. People who are mentally challenged have little REM sleep. Drugs, such as alcohol and barbiturates (sleeping pills), tend to suppress normal REM sleep.[2]

When we are dreaming, our subconscious is still receptive to data from our five senses. The sensations may be distorted and affect our dreams. Sleep laboratory subjects may be stimulated to dream of treading in a puddle if their feet are moistened, or picture themselves being attacked if tapped on the head. Although these stimuli may affect the content of a dream, they cannot by themselves start a dream.

Because the stimulus is intruding on a relatively calm sensory field, it doesn't have to compete with other sensory stimuli, and can exert a greater influence on the dream content. Eating something that doesn't agree with us doesn't *cause* our dreams, though it may *affect* them. We may also remember our dreams better at this time, because our sleep is lighter and more restless.

Commonly, a single theme dominates the dream content, although the imagery may depict it in ways that, at first glance, show no relation. The content of our shorter initial dreams tend to be more present-oriented, less emotional, and less disordered in terms of time and space than our later dreams. We usually remember our last dream because the early morning REM is the longest in duration and our general arousal level is higher.

During a REM dream, there is an increase in oxygen consumption in the brain, increased adrenaline in the blood, and erections observed in men, which may last for the entire duration of the dream. These erections do not appear to be of a sexual nature. Anxiety dreams will not result in an erection.

Our brain is aroused during REM and the EEG shows that our dreams are biologically very similar to the waking state. For example, our breathing becomes more regular, while our pulse rate increases. Concurrently, there is a lessening of muscle tone.

This REM stage of sleep is sometimes referred to as *paradoxical* sleep, because even though the state of mind is rather active, the muscles of the body are in an extremely relaxed state. Although this part of our sleep cycle resists most arousal stimuli, such as touch or noise, its EEG pattern suggests light sleep. Scientists feel that it is the preoccupation with the dream itself that accounts for the high resistance to waking characterized by REM sleep.

The average amount of time spent in REM changes as we age. Sixty to 70 percent of a newborn's sleep is REM sleep, while about 35 percent of adult sleep is spent dreaming. In old age, this percent is reduced to about 20 to 25 percent.

The Biological Purpose of Dreams

Dreams seem to serve the purpose of maintaining our mental and emotional balance. REM sleep allows us to remove memories of the previous day's events we no longer need and to store those of value. This form of computerized emotional cleansing is necessary for the preservation of life.

The innate ability we possess to access this computer accounts for many inspirations. A novelist finds a natural expression for characters that would never occur to him or her consciously, a poet is given a verse or entire poem, and so on. This vocabulary is individual and based on our unique subjective experiences.

Most animals have REM cycle. Perhaps from an evolutionary point of view, an animal when asleep was more vulnerable to danger than when awake, so a biological arrangement ensured fixed REM periods when the animal could be more easily aroused when confronted by a predator. Our sleep cycle is far more complex than that of lower animals. We are focused more on changes in our immediate social environment than to predators threatening our physical existence. We use the dreaming phase of the sleep cycle to explore the potential impact of such changes upon our lives.

A sleeper uses the REM cycle to deal with residue emotions. Often we are faced with a challenge that is too ambiguous to act on without further information. We require the truth to act responsibly. The truthful reflections of our feelings are critical to our subconscious.

In a dream, our mind attempts to present ourselves as we truly are. This is often contaminated by our ego and its insecurities, superimposed upon the programming it initiates by its dysfunctional thoughts just prior to our falling asleep.

For example, let us assume that a recent event results in a tension that continues to trouble us. The feelings connected with it surface during dreaming sleep and are represented as the initial images of a

dream. Our subconscious now has the opportunity to present information to us without the interference of our defense mechanisms or ego in a state of mind that is quite conscious, namely our dream level. The first question deals with whether or not we should remain asleep.

Faced with the decision of whether or not it is safe to remain asleep, we have to check out the intruding stimulus by exploring what light our past can shed on it. By accessing into our perfect computer memory bank, our subconscious retrieves images from our past experiences. These images sometimes go back to early childhood, or even past lives. All are in some way related emotionally to the current issue.

After compiling this data, we need to assess our current circumstance and devise a solution. Through the use of imagery, we explore possible solutions. We will awaken if the feelings connected with the imagery are too intense to be compatible with the continuation of sleep. From this paradigm we can see that dreaming is a complex and remarkable way of getting the data we need to arrive at this decision.

Hypnagogic Dreams

This type of dream takes place at the borderline between waking and sleep. Components of this dream may appear as strange conversations, disembodied faces, unusual body sensations, and other types of hallucinations. There are no REMs at this time, and these dreams are less dramatic and much shorter in duration.

What we would call a hallucination during our waking state is referred to as a dream during our sleep consciousness. These images are perceived as being real in both instances. Hypnagogic images are visual representations of the last thoughts that occupy our mind prior to our drifting off to sleep.

These hypnagogic images are more static, less vivid, chaotic, and complex than true dreams. We are quite unaware of them unless awakened as they occur.

NREM Sleep

The NREM sleep is sometimes called *orthodox* sleep. The dreams found in this stage tend to be less vivid, less visual, and shorter as compared to REM sleep. NREM stage subjects describe their dream experiences as one of thinking rather than dreaming.

The production of our growth hormone increases dramatically during this stage. This hormone increases the synthesis of proteins and facilitates the repair, maintenance, and growth of the body.

When we compare the infrequent dreams of NREM sleep to that of REM sleep we find that NREM dreams are:

☆ Less emotional.

☆ Less active.

☆ Less vivid.

☆ Less dramatic.

☆ Less detailed.

☆ Less visual.

☆ Shorter.

☆ More thought-like.

☆ More focused on current problems.

☆ More realistic.

The occasional sleepwalking episodes reported occurred during the REM period of Stage II sleep. Whereas REM sleep plays a role in thinking, learning, and remembering, NREM sleep appears to be concerned with keeping the whole body in good repair. After prolonged physical exercise, athletes exhibit greater proportions of Stage III and Stage IV sleep. These deeper levels of sleep are correlated with increased production of growth hormone, which is required for maintenance and repair, in addition to growth.

Children and adolescents spend more time in NREM sleep, as compared to adults. Subjects in sleep laboratories show a worse effect when deprived of NREM sleep, as compared to REM sleep deprivation.

Sleep Clinics

Sleep clinics are often associated with sleep laboratories and can be quite helpful for individuals suffering from severe forms of insomnia. I highly recommend relaxation exercises, such as the insomnia self-hypnosis script I presented in Chapter 7. When nothing works and your physician *and* therapist have told you there is nothing they can do for you, it's time to consider a sleep clinic.

When you arrive at the clinic, any physical causes of your insomnia will first be ruled out. The proper medical referrals will be made if the cause is organic. A battery of psychological tests will be administered, followed by a clinical interview.

You will be asked to spend the night in the sleep laboratory and hooked up to electrodes throughout the night. The following morning many clinics ask you to rate your sleep by a one to seven system similar to the following:

1. Feeling active.
2. Functioning at a high level, but not at a peak.
3. Relaxed and awake, but not fully alert.
4. A little foggy.
5. Foggy and somewhat slowed down.
6. Sleepy and woozy.
7. Cannot stay awake, almost in reveries.

Next, a conference of experts convenes and a diagnosis and treatment plan are formulated. Specific recommendations are made, depending on whether your insomnia is due to medical, psychological, or behavioral causes.

What actually occurs in a sleep clinic or laboratory is quite interesting. Usually nine electrodes are attached to your body: two on either side of your head, one on the top, two more at the base of your ears, two near the outside corner of each eye (to monitor REMs), and two on your chin (for recording muscle tension).

The electrodes are dabbed with sodium chloride jelly to improve the electrical contact with your skin. Layers of white gauze are wrapped around your head to hold the electrodes and wires in place. Additional electrodes may be attached to your legs to monitor leg twitches while a single electrode in the middle of your back records your heart rate.

This entire electrical setup is similar to a polygraph machine. An intercom is located next to the bed, in case you need assistance at any time during the night. Interestingly enough, few people find the electrodes and wires cause difficulty in getting to sleep. Many insomniacs have a first-night effect, during which they obtain one of the best night's sleep ever during their initial night in the sleep clinic.

A *polysomnogram* is the technical name for the recording of your sleep. By reading this record, scientists can determine how much sleep you received, how many REM cycles you experienced, how restless your sleep was, the degree of tenseness before and during sleep, and how deep it was. The clinician can also determine such problems as leg twitches, a body rhythm out of phase with the day, and sleep apnea (breath stopping) from this data.

More than one-third of insomnia cases have some form of psychological cause. About one-sixth originate from medical causes, and one-half seem to come from vague, often unknown reasons.[3]

As I mentioned before, sleeping pills, alcohol, and many other depressant drugs result in no REM sleep. One of the first things the sleep clinic doctors do is wean you off these drugs.

Depression is also common with insomniacs. In studies where normal sleepers are purposely deprived of sleep, researchers have found one of the side effects of this induced insomnia is a depressed mood.

Dreams and ESP

The first studies of dreams and ESP using a single subject was completed in 1964 by Ullman and Krippner.[4] A New York psychologist successfully received information telepathically that was sent by an agent or sender.

Seven postcard-sized prints of well-known paintings were placed in a room unknown to the subject. For seven nights, the sender attempted to transmit the art scene to this subject by telepathy while the latter dreamt.

These target portraits were randomly selected from the target pool each of the seven nights. The agent was situated in a room 40 feet from the subject, and the subject was awakened each time he exhibited REMs. The results of this study demonstrated that telepathy was indeed exhibited during these trials.

Two years later, this study was repeated using the same subject. Again, the telepathy hypothesis was confirmed. To further ensure no sensory clues could be given to the subject, the following precautions were taken:

1. The two rooms were 96 feet apart and at opposite ends of the building. These rooms were separated by three doors.

2. Both the agent and subject remained in their rooms for the entire night.

3. Neither party knew what the target materials were beforehand. The staff that prepared these materials were never present during any of the trials.

A third study revealed eight hits and no misses. The overall accuracy rate for these experiments was 83.5 percent, and the odds of this occurring by chance calculated at more than 250,000 to one. These three studies illustrate the fact that ESP effects, namely telepathy, occur more commonly during our dream state as compared to our waking state. We can also explain this psychic ability by recalling that all dreams are OBEs. When we have an OBE, we enter the astral plane, which is the home of all ESP talents.[5]

Other studies have shown that general extrasensory perception, or GESP, is more likely to occur at night and at least one-half of these reported cases are associated with dreams.[6] Telepathy and clairvoyance are manifestations of psychic phenomena that involve minimal temporal displacement between the event and the experience. These phenomena occur more frequently and with greater intensity during the dream state.

Precognitive dreams were first scientifically investigated by Ullman and Krippner at the Maimonides Dream Laboratory in New York in 1971. They worked with the English sensitive Malcolm Bessant with remarkable success.

Ullman also reported a case of a man who dreamt the winners and runners-up of horse races on three successive nights.[7]

Dreaming is a unique display, usually visual, that occurs during the night in order to assess the impact of recent events on our lives. A dream is a remembered residue in the form of creatively assembled visual metaphors. Dreams originate from the depths of our psyche. They come to us uninvited because we somehow require, if not ask for, this communication. We will do well to listen to them, as they represent our talking to ourselves.

I mentioned in Chapter 7 that dreams provide an emotional cleansing that is necessary for maintaining life. The energy cleansing, by way of the superconscious mind tap, is one way we can utilize our night REM cycle to dream our problems away. We will discuss this technique in Chapter 13.

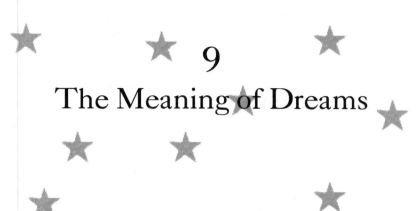

9
The Meaning of Dreams

We are far more introspective in our dreams. Our personalities are more openly and objectively dissected. All of our desires, fears, and other faults are pried open for us to view. It is during this dream state that we acknowledge things to ourselves that would normally be repressed or ignored during our waking state.

Our karma can be resolved during these nightly excursions. By listening to and following the recommendations of our perfect spirit teachers, spiritual lessons can be learned, and a resulting increase in the frequency vibrational rate of our soul is felt. This eliminates the need for this lesson to surface again while we are awake. Once a spiritual lesson (karmic debt) is learned, it is resolved for eternity.

My main objection to interpreting dream symbols is based on the fact that each and every one of us is unique. We are all different, genetically, emotionally, mentally, and spiritually, therefore our dream symbols are equally unique. There is no universal answer key for a specific dream component. A survey of the thousands of books on the market with their different interpretations of dream themes will no doubt frustrate and confuse you, if it hasn't already.

You wouldn't want to wear someone else's dentures (as a retired dentist I am permitted such metaphors), so why sacrifice your empowerment and give in to a system that has absolutely no scientific basis, and may be harmful?

Approximately 25 percent of my patients in my Los Angeles office are therapists. The majority of them use dream interpretation in their practices. Some of these colleagues are downright offended by my position concerning the efficacy of dream symbolism and their meaning.

Here is an example of dangers of dream interpretation. Several years ago, an elderly woman came to my office on an emergency call. Her son made the appointment and informed me that his mother suddenly became very depressed.

His mother, Margaret, had been seeing a Freudian psychiatrist for six years, undergoing intensive psychoanalysis. Margaret was a devout Catholic, and her hobby was playing the piano. Ever since the age of 6, she seriously practiced classical music on her baby grand piano.

One night Margaret had a most unusual dream. She was playing her piano in a concert hall in Europe during the 1700s. This was a most pleasurable dream, as this hobby today represented a high point in Margaret's life. She had lost her husband to a heart attack several years before, and although her son was close to her, he didn't see her that often.

Margaret's psychiatrist had a proverbial field day with her dream. He informed her that this dream represented a form of mental masturbation. You can imagine the shock and resulting effect this had on a devout Catholic. Margaret immediately went into a major depressive episode.

It was most fortunate that her son brought her to me, rather than a hospital. He had read my first book, *Past Lives-Future Lives*, and correctly deduced that his mother's dream was a possible previous incarnation. A past-life regression was conducted during her first session, and this 18th century life as a pianist surfaced.

Needless to say, it did not take long for Margaret to regain her emotional foundation of health and well-being. She discontinued therapy with her psychiatrist, and after a few months of follow-up hypnotherapy, her therapeutic goals were fulfilled.

In benefiting from a dream, recognize the fact that the characters and plot are not always meaningful by themselves. Although the actors in this nightly drama most likely represent you, a nightmare may bear a spiritually significant message for your karmic growth, as easily as a pleasant dream. This is why developing lucid dreaming (being aware that you are dreaming during a dream) skills are so important.

Dreams may be viewed upon in three different ways. They can be used to reflect our prejudices and attitudes. Secondly, these nocturnal manifestations point out aspects of our lives that we have ignored, or simply failed to observe in waking life. Thirdly, we can look inward through the vehicle of our dreams to discover what may be the hidden cause of our difficulties. These existential messages often reflect repressed memories and feelings that have compromised our growth. Much of our self-defeating behavior is caused by self-ignorance and self-concealment.

Dreams can tell you quite a bit about your sense of self, your self-esteem, and the value you have set on your place in the universe. Images portrayed in dream world can reflect upon your past, present, and future.

Conflicts and emotional, as well as spiritual, issues can be manifested in your dreams. We have already seen how physical problems and their solutions can be portrayed. Desires, needs, and frustrations always eventually surface in our dreams.

The relationships we have with other people often become a main feature of our dreams. Your general view of men, women, children, friends, relatives, animals, and objects are often played out in dream world. Last, the overall picture of yourself often emerges from your dreams. The ways you cope, your main concerns, and your level of functioning are commonly depicted in dreams.

Why Dreams Are So Hard to Interpret

It is not necessary to explore the symbolic nature of the events and things we encounter and perceive in our daily lives, so we usually don't. When our species lived in caves, we made better use of our senses to survive. The advent of civilization, with its farming and other technological advancements, made this less critical. We became lazy in a sensory way, and our senses reflected this vestige effect.

During our dream life, communication is often presented as symbols. By becoming more attuned to our dream consciousness, we can learn to recognize the meaning of what we perceive there. In the early stages of our astral education, we must engage in interpretation.

The images and symbols within our dreams serve as direct representations of our feelings, thoughts, and states of consciousness. They function as forms of self-expression. This creation is an outward projection in the dream dimension of what we have formulated within ourselves. Symbols can now give substance, form, and motion to our inner concepts of ourselves and the depths of our psyche.

Thoughts and feelings have an inherent reality of their own during our dreams. The patterns of our inner states of mind are naturally and automatically translated into full realization there. We can only observe this manifestation by traveling to the dream realm during our REM cycle, or purposeful OBE techniques.

Another function of these symbols is a means of communication. These representations of our mind and psyche serve as reflections of who we are. The symbols that we perceive act as forms of communication from one aspect of our own consciousness to another. This now becomes an interdimensional tool for facilitating data and messages from our dreaming consciousness to our waking consciousness. This communication is also a two-way process.

Much can be lost and mistranslated along the way. There are many different focuses of consciousness on the dream dimension. These different levels of awareness require translations within the dream realm so that our physical brain will be able to comprehend it.

Once this has been accomplished, the newly translated material is sent to us via our dreams. This multidimensional characteristic of both our dream world and our physical plane life complicates the relaying of this message. Whenever any portion of our overall consciousness experiences something, all other components experience it on their own level of awareness. Our whole being is affected by anything that occurs on any level, and each aspect of the soul's experience of the event is translated in a manner suited to its level. This is what I mean by multidimensionality.

We perceive dreams as a series of episodes that restate the same theme in different ways. The recall of a single multidimensional dream involves the perception of events enacted at various levels of our consciousness. Different symbols on each level will express the same message on different levels of this multidimensionality.

The problem with making sense out of this is that it is distorted by the time it reaches our waking consciousness that it is nearly impossible to decipher its original meaning. Our waking consciousness has its limitations that cause the true message from the dream to be lost. The exercises presented in this book will train your subconscious to better interpret this data. Tapes I have recorded are also available to assist you in this endeavor.

There are conscious methods to facilitate this interpretation mechanism. Every time you attempt to decipher a dream, you send a signal to your dreaming consciousness that you wish to understand its communication. You are also preparing your conscious awareness to be more receptive to such communications. This results in a stimulation to the flow of information at both ends of the consciousness spectrum.

You can further improve this ability to properly comprehend your dreams by recording as many of them as possible. By documenting the context in which the dream was presented, valuable clues will be provided to the actual meaning of these dreams. This will make your role as a dream detective far easier and more fulfilling.

Our waking minds are programmed to organize data according to linear concepts. Herein lies the problem, as this mechanism often distorts the true context and significance of the dream itself. The fact that dreams may be produced simultaneously with others, their multidimensionality, and the invasion of our dream plots by other dreamers (as well as our becoming part of their dreams) contribute to the difficulty we have in recalling and making sense out of them.

Sequential order is not the rule in the dream realm. The dreaming consciousness can maintain the primary plot while it simultaneously explores other scenarios. The result is a spreading of subplots like the branches of a tree. This may divert our attention and cause our dreaming level of awareness to wander. Now our perception is totally confused, as we receive dreamlets from several different sources and have lost our place, so to speak.

It is folly to assume that you can look up an image in some dream dictionary and say it means this or that. Only through personal introspect and training your subconscious and conscious minds to both receive and decipher this multidimensional message, can you hope to accurately unravel the mysteries of your dreams. That is why nobody can successfully interpret your dream messages for you. You must do it yourself.

Your intuition is always with you throughout your dream interpretation efforts. Learn to develop your psychic ability and trust this psychic component of your consciousness. Accelerating your spiritual growth is the quickest road to this end. Practicing the superconscious mind tap technique presented in this book will assist you with this goal. You might find my tape of this technique easier to use in the beginning.

We must also acknowledge the fact that not all dreams are symbolic. There are those that relate closely to events in our daily lives. For example, a manipulative and over-demanding boss you have been too timid to confront could be played out in a dream. You might very well have a series of dreams ranging from continued abuse by this boss to successfully asserting yourself.

These computer simulations are not mere trial-and-error approaches. You can actually create your own reality and empower yourself through this method. Your dream themes are quite literal in this example. Your intuition will assist you in determining whether the content of your dream is literal or symbolic.

Because everything in a dream can be associated with many other things, any component of this dream can be taken as a symbolic representation. This message may represent one thing when applied to your daily life and another when considered in light of your karmic purpose and spiritual growth. These levels of meaning can go on indefinitely.

You need not explore the potential hidden meaning behind every object, person, or event you recall from a dream. The primary significance is what counts. Any other approach would require spending your entire waking life exploring the possible interpretations of a single dream.

Pay more attention to your interrelationship with the characters in your dreams, rather than their appearance. These players may indeed represent archetypal energies or human qualities. They may even symbolize people in your everyday life, specifically the manipulative people in your dreams, as a warning that you are not dealing with this genre effectively in your waking life.

The possibilities are endless on the dream dimension. You may find yourself in a pleasant and fulfilling relationship with someone with whom you have an antagonistic association in your waking life. You might encounter a spiritual teacher, participate in someone else's dream, or experience a myriad of other possibilities in this wonderland of imagination becoming reality by mere thought and will.

The Meaning of Dreams

As I have emphasized throughout this book, your dreams are completely individual to you. Although there is a plethora of books on the market with standard interpretations for dream images and symbols, I strongly urge you not to follow any one system. No book, or well-meaning therapist, is going to be able to accurately decipher your dreams.

My colleagues will no doubt become quite defensive at my position. I am not as concerned about their fragile egos as I am for your own empowerment and spiritual growth. If you are going to engage in dream interpretation, make it a do-it-yourself exercise.

This chapter will present the major categories of dreams, and guides for your own self-interpretation. The characters, objects, environments, plot, mood, and other components present ample messages for your own growth. It is not as difficult to understand your dreams as you may have been led to believe.

Use your instincts and intuition as you ponder a dream plot. If one element appears meaningless, alter your viewpoint, and shift your perspective to another component. Always try to relate an aspect of your dream to your waking life. Look at your dream from many different angles. "Walk around your dream" and become a dream detective, following up on every clue.

The themes I will discuss shortly are presented because they occur commonly. Each component of a dream is important in its own way. The landscape, colors, climate, inanimate objects, and so on are just as significant as the characters and the plot. My goal is simply to suggest methods of considering the overall theme, along with its individual components, so that you can place it properly within the context of your everyday waking life and recognize its significance.

Sex

I have described a quite different use of sexual dreams in Chapter 11 when I discuss dream lovers. It is relatively rare to see yourself making love in a dream. Flirting and desire seem to abound more than the physical intimacies themselves. Do not be shocked by the contents of this type of dream, but instead use it to improve your sex life for both you and your partner.

Many nonsexual components and themes that surface in our dreams may actually relate to your attitudes toward sex. For example, consider the following themes:

★ Violent behavior emphasizing domination of others and aggression. This may point to a lack of consideration for our lovers.

★ Danger, excitement, and passion plots could be a sign that your current attitude toward sex requires modification.

★ Feelings of insecurity or being scolded in a dream can direct us to inhibitions we may not be aware of consciously.

★ Themes focusing on abandonment may also suggest an unfulfilled sex life.

★ Dreaming of ice or coldness in other ways or restrictions of movement has often been associated with frigidity in women.

Sexual overtones can be implied by the beauty of flowers, plants growing, the tactile shape of an object, the texture of silk, and so on. Dreams of trains entering tunnels, climbing stairs, flying, and others of this genre are more blatantly sexual in their meaning.

Sexual themes in dreams can have more spiritual connotations, referring to creation and healing, as well as fertility. Very significant dreams that have recurred over several years, but don't appear to be related to any waking theme in your life, should always be evaluated for sexual allusions. Remember the ancients' incubated dream temples were originally established to treat fertility issues.

Landscape

The landscape component of a dream can lead to tremendous insights as to the overview of global assessment of your waking life. Busy landscapes, such as a city street crowded with traffic and people moving around, could be an indication of a stressful conscious life with too little time to accomplish goals.

There is quite a difference in such a busy city scene as I just described if the people were moving briskly and freely toward their destinations versus being caught up in a traffic jam or other encumbrance. The former theme may signify efficiency and purpose, whereas the latter seems to indicate stagnation and frustration.

Sometimes we have a peaceful and happy rural landscape only to be disrupted by some rude intrusion. This often indicates an issue that requires attention. The intruder may signify a disruptive person or circumstance in your conscious life. Landscapes that appear to recede before you may be a sign that you are allowing desires or ambitions to slip away from you. Detachment in the form of a vantage point of a high window or isolated location can also be a reference to unfulfilled wishes and self-created barriers in your life.

Confidence and purpose may be represented by gliding or moving unobstructed across the landscape. The opposite can be implied if you find yourself struggling through a dense jungle, or moving with hesitation. An arrogant or superior attitude is often reflected by looking down a landscape from a height.

If you are moving too quickly through a landscape to appreciate it, is life passing you by? Rocky and arid landscapes are quite different in their meanings as compared to lush and smooth topographies. Can you find a parallel in your life here? This could refer to a need to improve your appearance, lose weight, develop more interests, and so on.

Landscape elements can also suggest the need to get away from it all and take a vacation. This change of scenery is a direct message from your subconscious. Lakes, oceans, mountains, weather, and other such aspects of your dream have a way of referring to your expression of emotions.

Water

Water aspects of a dream can literally be instructing us to "dive" to the bottom of our problems. Our deepest instincts, emotions, and intuitions can be at the root of this symbolism. Birth is typically represented by dreams of the sea. Our independence of thought can appear in our dreams as stagnant pools, deep lakes, fountains, and waterfalls.

We should be on guard against repressed emotions whenever we see confined or compressed water in our dreams. Too hot or cold water can also reflect upon the status of our emotional life. Inner stress may appear as storms and lack of water often points to a spiritual drought or "dry" emotional life.

Expanding our imagination, creativity, psychic ability, and esoteric interests are more commonly represented by water. A feeling of enjoyment with the water element can mean we are happy and confident. Fear and hatred of this component have the opposite connotation.

Water aspects usually signify a mirror image of us. It often reflects a soul that is placid, calm, or tempestuous and disturbed by the manner in which it appears. Dreams of birth for a woman do not necessarily mean a desire to have children. The breaking of water in the birth dream could also refer to the bringing of an idea to reality.

Trying to purify yourself, or rid yourself of an unpleasant person or situation, could be implied by the image of water. You could be preparing to move on in some new and positive direction by a scene involving a beautiful running stream of fresh water at a comfortable temperature.

Pursuit

There are many types of dreams during which pursuit is depicted. Consider the following possibilities:

☆ You are being pursued and you outrun the aggressor.

☆ Instead of running away, you turn and confront the enemy.

☆ In recurrent dreams of this chase, the distance between you and the pursuer increases or decreases.

This last category is especially significant. An increase in the distance may mean you are dealing with an issue properly. A closing of this gap often signifies you are allowing a problem to creep up on you. Feelings of life closing in on you and running out of room to maneuver is another interpretation of this shrinking gap between you and the aggressor.

The source of the thing chasing you may be a problem, person, or even an element of your own psyche from which you are attempting to escape. If this enemy is an animal, see what this image means to you. Are you normally afraid of it, or does it bring other emotions to

the surface? Perhaps the characteristics of this animal relate to someone you know. Your own hostile instincts have classically been represented by pursuit by unfriendly animals.

This theme could very well indicate a personal inadequacy or some inferiority complex if you were chasing another person. It may allude to an ambition or a means to becoming more empowered. Failure to catch up to this individual has been associated with "missing the boat" in some aspect of your life. One solution would be to work harder and act in a more goal-oriented manner with your career or other facet of your being.

Positive symbolism, such as outdistancing your pursuer or catching up to another person, is a compliment to your current actions. This often boosts our self-confidence. Turning around and successfully confronting the adversary is another healthy indication that whatever you are doing, it's the right thing.

Disasters

These themes are usually nightmares, and can result in our waking up in a cold sweat feeling very anxious. We must first consider our physical state. Dreaming of a flood could reflect on our need to urinate. The onset of a menstrual cycle in a woman may result in dreams of blood. Adolescents who are particularly concerned about acne have been known to dream repeatedly of volcanic eruptions.

The breaking into our consciousness of some repressed emotion is another possibility for these nightmares. It is your state of mind during this dream, superimposed on recent events in your life that gives us the key to this theme's meaning. You may find this disaster frightening, spectacular, or even humorous.

A dream of a car crash, assuming neither you nor loved ones had one recently, may be a way in which your subconscious is telling you to attend to some maintenance of your vehicle. Many possible problems have been avoided by these prophetic dreams.

Our deep-seated anxieties may be reflected by these themes. For example, a collapse of our goals or ambitions could be manifested as a building crumbling. Is some other aspect of your life falling apart?

Being buried in a dream could refer to being inundated by commitments. Dreams of earthquakes can suggest an overall insecurity in your life. They usually focus on one specific problem that is critical to your life.

Never take a dream at its face value. A scene of well-constructed buildings or other structures falling apart without harming anyone could simply allude to an architect or engineer friend's misfortunes. Battles at sea could indicate arguments about which cruise to take or fights with business colleagues or competitors.

One must always consider the possible precognitive nature of a disaster dream. The dreams reported by President Lincoln of attending his own funeral a few days before he was shot, or that of Archduke Franz Ferdinand's former tutor, Bishop Lanyi, are well known and will be discussed in the next chapter.

Flying

Flying dreams have been dealt with in detail in my chapters on the Senoi of Malaysia (Chapter 5) and Lucid Dreaming (Chapter 10). For our current purpose, we will deal with more conventional associations of these types of dreams.

The classic psychoanalytic interpretation of flying dreams revolves around sex. However, do not limit yourself in this rather narrow paradigm. If you have been "flying high" in some aspect of your life, a dream of flight would not be out of the question. Being on top of a situation is another possibility.

Sometimes we invent flying scenarios, especially from the perspective of great heights, to symbolize our attempts at escaping from a circumstance or person. Perhaps you have to make an important choice, and want to see the whole picture.

There is quite a difference between dreaming of just clearing an obstacle versus soaring above the Earth and floating on a cloud. A fear of heights could be reflected by this type of dream, especially if falling was involved.

Were you a bird, an angel, in a craft, or some other scenario? These have very different meanings. Always look deeply in your own life for its significance. Dreams of flight are far more common among the elderly. This may indicate a need for freedom and relief from everyday stress. Sometimes a flying dream points, a lack of being "down to earth." The association of flying dreams with OBEs is clearly stated in my book *Astral Voyages*.

Colors

Most of our dreams are in color. Colors may represent a person, often relating to their clothes. The reason many of us don't recall these color dreams is that unless there is some significant reason for recalling them, they quickly fade from memory.

Some authorities state that dreams dominated by flamboyant colors suggest extroversion, while black and white depictions allude to introversion. Colored dreams may be evidence of great animation of our subconscious and demonstrate special vitality in the dreamer. It is not uncommon for artists and professional athletes to have such dreams.

We can recall blue skies, a deep black void, forest green landscapes, bright red objects, and so on. The key is to properly determine the meaning of this hue to you. Consider some of these associations with the more frequent colors that appear in our dreams:

Green: Nature, especially plants, is often quite apparent in our dreams. This color may symbolize gladness and hope, abundance, paradise, innocence, folly, immortality, jealousy, and other connotations. The ancient Chinese associated green with "the beginning of great work." It was a good sign when contemplating starting a new project.

Red: Along with green, red is the most common color noted in a dream. It is considered a positive hue, and represents passion and sexual excitement, joy, festivity, and activity in general. In a negative content, it can mean vengeance, lust, cruelty, martyrdom, and anger. For the Mayas, red indicated success and victory; for the Chinese, happiness, warmth, and joy; for the Christians, power, love, faith, and Christ on the Cross; and for the Hindus, creativity, expansion, and the basic life force or prana. More modern interpretations suggest vivacity, gaiety, or a warning to stop.

Black and White: White is almost universally associated with a positive force, while black denotes a negative one. Black may represent a void, death and the underworld, or protest. White has been identified with establishing a truce and surrender, purification of the soul, spiritual authority, simplicity, and chastity. A distancing of yourself from problems may also be suggested by the predominance of white in your dream.

Blue: Christians have used blue to represent the Virgin Mary, faith, fidelity, and eternity. It is also associated with justice, truth, spirituality, intellect, piety, magnanimity, and peace. Often in dreams, it is a way of telling us to slow down, be more contemplative, and relax more.

Yellow: In its bright form, yellow has been identified with pure goodness, intuition, and faith. It is considered the light of life and immortality by Hindus and Native Americans. Faithlessness, betrayal, avarice, treachery, and secrecy are meanings given to dark, muddy yellow. Buddhists consider saffron yellow to indicate lack of desire, renunciation, and humility. One of the most accepted interpretations of yellow is that of representing health in some form.

Clothes and Nudity

We all have had dreams at some time of being naked, usually with others around us being fully dressed. The classical association of sexual inadequacy is not necessarily its true meaning. It may refer to a desire to break away from conformity or boredom.

The reactions of others to your nakedness is important. Complete acceptance often indicates that you have nothing to worry about, sexually or in any other way. Expressions of disgust or shock could suggest a more self-critical attitude toward sex, or an unsympathetic partner. Only recurring themes of this nature imply real trouble.

Being nude could also indicate a certain vulnerability, lack of preparedness, or disorganization in your life. It could point out the fact that you are seeking undue attention, or perhaps just the "bare facts" (undisguised truth) concerning something.

Meanings of nudity are quite different if you are enjoying this state, such as sunbathing, swimming, or playing the role of a stripper. Is this latter example a plea for attention, or an attempt to shock someone in your life? Only your own honest evaluation of your life can answer this question.

The opposite situation also can manifest. In certain dreams, we may be dressed in clothes totally foreign to us. Are you having an identity crisis, and trying to act like someone else? Perhaps your subconscious is suggesting a new image and accompanying wardrobe.

If you have been chastised recently by a mate or employer, outlandish attire could indicate a rebellious attitude or an acceptance of this label as "unsuitable." Self-confidence and the correctness of certain actions may be implied by your new outfit, looking good, and feeling right.

Always consider belts, handbags, sunglasses, hats, shoes, and other accessories as extensions of your image and personality in a dream. Evaluate them in this context to gain additional insight to the full meaning of your wardrobe.

Food and Drink

If you are dieting, don't be surprised if dreams of food dominate in your dreams. The appearance of food in our dreams can also refer to a lack of self-discipline. Nibbling instead of eating properly could imply holding back emotionally in your waking life. Are you "nit-picking" about something, or afraid of a commitment?

Sitting down at a feast or banquet quite often is associated with sensual pleasure. It may also mean a deep desire or lust to accomplish something. A hunger for security or affect can be alluded to by gorging on food. This may refer to another type of personal nourishment.

Preparing food in a dream is often a reference to the way you express love to others. Compare the richness of the food, the generosity of the servings, the stinginess or excessive quantity of ingredients, and other factors from this perspective. Any lack of quantity or quality could be a warning of being drained emotionally or unrequited love.

Other sexual connotations with food dreams revolve around greed for the food, and its shape. Tomatoes, salami, and bananas are commonly used in this manner. Money is often associated with food. Did you have to buy the food? Are you trying to buy the friendship or love of someone in your life?

Crowds

Dreams of crowds may have a claustrophobic meaning. If not literally, it may denote a stifled lifestyle, in which you can't get to where you are going. Housewives commonly have this theme and relate to me how unfulfilled they feel, and express a desire for greater freedom of expression in their lives.

Men who want to grow more professionally or intellectually can have this same type of dream. Boredom, depression, and cumbersome obstacles are common associations with crowd dreams. We see this form of dream reported in middle-age dreamers who are not happy with their lot in life.

Dreaming of being one member of a crowd could also be a message that you need to conform to some societal convention. These themes may also suggest the manner in which we attempt to deal with everyday problems. If our problems are getting the best of us, the dream state may represent this as our being trampled, or failing to stick up for ourselves.

If you are a "team player," your dream may depict you as a part of an orderly crowd. You may perceive yourself as disrupting this precision, which could indicate a desire to break out on your own, or a failure to keep up with others.

An unexpressed desire to have influence or control over others could be illustrated by a dream that you are giving a political speech or preaching. A favorable response by the crowd suggests that you are in a strong position to affect others. You should consider acting upon this urge if this dream is repeated several times.

Passive and unresponsive crowds to your oratory have the opposite meaning. It could also be conveying to you that your actions lately may be pompous and manipulative. This may also indicate a need to give others more breathing room.

Travel

The old term of *déjà vu* ("I have been here before") is commonly applied to the dreams we have of travel. These can very well be precognitive dreams that give us advance notice of places we are about to see.

When we are about to begin a new venture, make some significant change, or establish a new relationship, dreams of strange places and travel in general often surface. Problems with your trip, a car breakdown, or long lines at the airport, symbolize obstacles in your plans now.

Another reason we have exotic dreams of travel is a hint to break our current routine and take a vacation. It could also be an indication to change jobs, move to a new city, or end a relationship.

The quality of the weather and landscape reflect your mood and emotional state. A dream of travel can indicate an escapism desire on your part. Do you really want to run away from it all?

Cars in a man's dream often have strong sexual connotations. This also applies to motorcycles and even bicycles. An attack by someone could be represented in a dream involving a car accident. This may suggest a narcissistic aspect of your personality. You may very well

have spent too much time on superficial pursuits and interests. The general expression of affection or love is often the symbolism for a woman having this dream.

If you are feeling inadequate, you might see yourself not having enough money for a ticket, or losing the ticket just as the trip is about to begin. Self-satisfaction could be the meaning of an arrival at your travel destination. This feeling of accomplishment is usually accompanied by the appropriate emotional response associated with goal attainment.

Weather

When we have stomach problems, dreams of thunder and wind are occasionally reported. Reassurance can be suggested by dreams of happiness, warmth, and the shining sun. A sense of inner contentment and confidence that our recent actions and decisions are correct often accompany the warmth and brightness of a sunny day in our dreams.

Concerns about purity and your attitude about virginity may be reflected in snowy landscapes. A hot, scorched desert scene could be a warning that feelings of unfulfilled passion and frustration are being ignored. Inhibited suggestions can be suggested by icebergs and frozen lakes or streams. These are more significant if they appear in recurrent dreams, as with all other themes.

If you observe changes in the weather of your dream, consider an evaluation of your present attitude as expression of feelings. A storm may mean act more assertive. Considerable anxiety to this storm could imply a fear to speak your mind. Decision-making interpretations are also assigned to weather changes.

Birth and Death Change

Do not be overly concerned that a dream of the death of yourself or a loved one means something that is ominous. This more commonly symbolizes a change, and often a deep-rooted psychological or spiritual one at that.

This death dream should always be viewed as referring to physical health first. If that is not accurate, then consider why you have been given this information. Perhaps you are the only one who can assist your friend or family member in some crisis.

Your own death can mean a major change in your life is in order. Is it the time for ending a relationship, discarding an outdated concept, or other modification in your present lifestyle? You may find yourself acting as the Phoenix of ancient times and rise from your own ashes.

Birth dreams more commonly represent the initiation of new projects or ideas. They can refer to new relationships, and can have a literal meaning for women. As with all potential forms of symbolism, never discard the possibility of its literal meaning.

Environment

It is easy to see how a very modern building could represent a manner in which we are in fashion and current in our behavior and thinking. The desire to present a flamboyant image to others may be depicted as an ornate and very decorated structure. Ambitious aspirations can be represented by mansions, castles, and cathedrals.

Your tendency to be pompous and arrogant has a way of surfacing as palatial settings with marble "halls." Having an ivory tower in this setting also suggests this type of remoteness. Many authorities have related the appearance of a house in a dream as symbolizing our body. The windows may represent our orifices, and climbing the stairs a desire for sex.

The desire for new challenges should not be ignored when considering the empty rooms of a house. Empty cupboards and unused space may also suggest untapped potential and opportunities. Be wary of doors that are locked and windows that can't be opened as signs of blocks and obstacles in your life.

Different areas of your life and other facets of your personality can be represented by the different rooms of the house. A hospital room scene implies a need to concern yourself with your health. Preparing food in the kitchen could indicate you are planning something. Scenes of confinement in a prison cell often point to guilt and the subconscious desire to be punished.

When you are attempting to interpret your dreams, consider these helpful hints:

1. Dreams offer us the opportunity to connect to a greater level of awareness.
2. Consider all elements of your dreams important, and record everything you recall in a journal.

3. One of the best times to remember dreams is the state of consciousness between wakefulness and sleep.

4. Dreams afford us the possibility of accessing a source of knowledge and wisdom not usually available to us in our waking, daily life.

5. The content of a dream may not be symbolic, but most commonly is.

6. Our subconscious communicates with us through our dreams.

7. Dream symbols are often quite personal in nature. Only you are in a position to properly decipher them.

8. Recurrent dreams are always more significant, and indicate we are not following through on some communication from our subconscious.

9. You are responsible for dream content and frequency.

10. The information and significance of dreams can be determined by comparing the differences and similarities between how you feel when awake and your reactions during your dream itself.

11. Properly encoding the initial component of your dream will make it easier to understand the rest of it.

12. Consider several different levels when attempting to understand a dream. These are multidimensional messages and often require time to search out the deeper meanings.

13. Dreams never lie or misrepresent the truth.

14. To obtain the most benefits from a dream, approach it with complete honesty and openness.

15. Real-life characters in your dream symbolize past and present associations, in addition to other aspects of your psyche.

Experience in applying the techniques presented in this chapter will train you to approach your dreams in ways that result in the most efficient stimulation of your spiritual growth. Do not be concerned if you lack psychotherapy training. Your dreams are unique and personal.

You will succeed in empowering yourself through a conscientious effort of the methods I presented here. This will result in accessing a far greater level of consciousness than you are using at this moment. Dream interpretation is an art that requires practice over time to perfect. It may appear overwhelming at first, but don't be discouraged. A 1,000 mile journey begins with but a single step.

To obtain the greatest benefits from the material I discussed in this chapter, consider these principles:

1. An honest and deep understanding of yourself will result as you apply these methods.
2. Your own intuition, subconscious, Higher Self, and Masters and Guides will assist you in this endeavor.
3. Maximum benefits from your dreams will *not* be the result of simply looking up a list of symbols and their possible meanings, or by use of your conscious mind alone.
4. A deep desire for understanding yourself and others, coupled with a willingness to be guided by inspirational forces within your psyche, will lead to the quickest road to self-realization and spiritual empowerment.

Conscious Daydreaming

To explore one of your dreams further, simply practice relaxation with one of the meditation or self-hypnosis exercises given in this book and follow these steps:

1. Give yourself permission to explore and understand one or more of your dreams.
2. Ask your Higher Self to assist you with this exercise.
3. Keeping your eyes closed, replay a dream that you would like to interpret and explore in greater depth.
4. Relive this dream emotionally, mentally, and spiritually. Your mind should ask yourself how it felt, what sounds you heard, what you saw, and so on. It may be easier to imagine a large movie screen with this dream projected on it.
5. Simply relax and enjoy this movie without analyzing or judging it. Gently instruct your Higher Self to complete this dream if you woke up prior to its natural ending. Allow your Higher Self to do your interpreting for you.

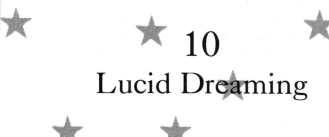

10
Lucid Dreaming

When you are aware that you are dreaming during a dream, this is referred to as a lucid dream. This cognitive awareness can range from a thought, "This must be a dream," to a comprehensive freedom of consciousness and of all restrictions of time and space.

One of the great advantages of lucid dreaming is that anything is possible. You can design any scenario you please. Imagine the pleasure and enjoyment potential of the following possibilities:

☆ Make love with any celebrity or other desirable person anywhere in the world or from history.

☆ Communicate with departed loved ones.

☆ Solve any current or future problem.

☆ Brainstorm creative ideas.

☆ Fly anywhere in the universe.

☆ Experience any type of positive emotion or existential paradigm.

To become a lucid dreamer, you must learn the technique of becoming conscious during your dreams. This is not commonly encountered by most of us. When our dreams are routine and dull, we ignore them. Dreams that become too bizarre or fearful overwhelm us and make it impossible to assimilate the dream figure.

The ideal is to establish a healthy balance in your dreams in which you both interact with your dream players in exciting scenarios and still retain your awareness that it is still a dream.

By not preprogramming the entire plot, the lucid dream retains its characteristic of a "stimulating adventure," so the element of surprise is still a component of the dream. You are aware that you can change, stop, and shape negative events to convert them into positive resolutions.

Celina Green, director of the Institute of Psychophysical Research in Oxford, England, quotes a lucid dreamer as follows:

...in conscious dreams, the awareness of the fact that I am dreaming, is the only point of contact with reality. Everything else belongs to the dream which, although more or less directed by my will in certain respects, still contains a very considerable degree of scope for the operation of the unforeseen, independently of my will and controlled by factors outside of my consciousness. Everything appears vividly objective and as convincing as the events of real life, in a way which is quite different from the feeble impressions of daydreams.[1]

Lucid dreaming instills a competence concerning your ability to achieve desired goals. This newly acquired competence will improve your waking life by carrying over that confidence and knowledge imparted during the dream.

The goal of a lucid dreamer is to attain consciousness during the dream state. This dream method is considerably more difficult than those we have already discussed. The exercises I present at the end of this chapter are easy to master, and will facilitate your introduction to the fascinating world of lucid dreaming.

According to Green, most people surveyed report only one or two lucid dreams in their lifetime. Whether it is the lack of knowledge of this marvelous technique, or their general disbelief in the concept, advanced societies report far less incidences of lucid dreaming than more primitive cultures.

The Senoi method involves only a semiconscious awareness. When Senoi dreamers fight a dream attacker, they are only vaguely aware that they are dreaming. Senoi techniques concentrate on the action required, not awareness. Lucid dreaming, as with the Yogis, makes awareness a central focus. Action is secondary and may take any one of several forms.

Lucid dreaming requires a constant state of awareness. This is not so easy, as your mind will oscillate in and out of awareness. One simple method to assure lucidity is to repeatedly say to yourself, "I'm dreaming, and anything is possible." Failing to do this results in a conversion of a lucid dream into an ordinary dream. This is uncontrolled, and none of the empowerment we will discuss with lucid dreaming approaches is now possible.

The other extreme may also nullify your lucid dream. If you become too aware during the dream state, you will awaken. As with many therapeutic techniques, a delicate balance must be established. The significance here is that you are responsible for this balance, not a therapist. This further fosters independence and empowerment.

To develop the ability to experience lucid dreaming, the initial step is to recognize when you are in a *prelucid state*. A prelucid dream is characterized by your suspecting that you are dreaming. You are not fully aware that you are dreaming at this time. An expression common to this phase is, "Am I dreaming?" or, "Is this real?"

Reality testing is the mechanism used to determine both prelucid states and lucid dreaming. It is imperative that you test the reality of your experience during the actual dream. Becoming more aware of these prelucid states makes it easier to transform the dream into a true lucid one.

False awakenings are common during lucid dreams. If you feel you have awakened during your dream, but soon realize that this is still a dream (due to the results of your reality testing), you are experiencing a false awakening. These phenomena are known to occur in prelucid dreams also.

It is possible to induce a lucid dream from events that occur in ordinary dreams. For instance, nightmares that scare you so much become lucid dreams when you realize that this impossible scenario *has* to be a dream. Most people simply wake up very anxious. If you say to yourself calmly, "I know this is only a dream. I can wake up at any time, but I decide to convert this nightmare into a pleasant dream...." This lucidity can be used to awaken from that dream in a calm manner also.

Mary Arnold-Foster devised a formula for her lucid dreaming: "Remember this is a dream. You are to dream no longer," or "You know this is a dream; you shall dream no longer—you are to wake."[2]

She would repeat this to herself throughout the day and right before falling asleep.

Becoming lucid during a nightmare is an excellent way for the novice to establish a lucid dream. The trick is to keep from waking up. We saw this approach to a degree with the Senoi concept of *confront and conquer*.

Another method to convert an ordinary dream into a lucid one is to focus on the strange dream-like quality of the images. You now begin to recognize that you are dreaming, and this is the first step toward lucidity. This technique is far less stressful than converting a nightmare into a lucid dream. In addition, it is far more common for the average person to recall unusual components in a dream and realize they are dreaming. If only they understood lucid dreaming advantages and weren't culturally conditioned to ignore these dreams, lucid dreaming would be as natural and common to us as it is to more primitive societies.

Analyzing your thought processes in a dream is another system to induce lucid dreaming. Whenever you initiate critical thinking during a dream, you are laying the foundation for transforming this dream into a lucid dream.

Later in this chapter, I will focus on the fact that all lucid dreams represent out-of-body experiences (OBEs). The first person to fully document his astral projection excursions was a lucid dreamer named Hugh Callaway. Callaway wrote under the pen name of Oliver Fox and described four levels of critical attitudes during many lucid dreams:

1. *The dreamer recognizes an incongruity in his dream only after he is awake. For example, in one of the above dreams I might have puzzled about the image of my daughter turning into a ball of snakes after I woke.*

2. *The dreamer notices an incongruity during his dream, is somewhat curious about it, but accepts it—for example, I might have observed the image of my daughter with some mild curiosity during the dream.*

3. *The dreamer notices an incongruity in his dream and is surprised by it at that time. For example, I might have seen the image of my daughter and said, 'That's peculiar,' in the dream.*

4. *The dreamer notices an incongruity in his dream, says in effect, 'But that's impossible; I must be dreaming,' and thus*

becomes lucid. This is essentially what I did when con-
fronted with the image of my daughter turning into a ball of
snakes.[3]

Entering a lucid dream from a waking state is also possible. These dreamers observe their own thought processes as they drift off to sleep. This method requires a deliberate attempt to turn this into a lucid dream. Yogis have mastered this approach. So did the Russian philosopher Ouspensky.

Ouspensky created what he termed "a particular half-dream state." Because he found it difficult to go back to sleep once he induced a lucid dream, this philosopher limited his lucid dreaming to early in the morning, when he already was awake but still in bed.

He held a definite image in his mind, and induced the lucid dream based on that topic. It is important to note that all lucid dreams are easier to induce after several hours of sleep. Statistically, the hours of 5 a.m. to 8 a.m. are ideal for lucid dreaming.

Comparing Lucid Dreams to Ordinary Dreams

Lucid dreams differ from ordinary dreams in several ways. In addition to being aware you are dreaming, lucid dreams are typically far more realistic than ordinary dreams. Your body rarely changes form, and other dream characters act in a normal manner. The exceptions to this characteristic are dreams of falling, flying, moving through a tunnel, and manipulating the environment.

Lucid dream perceptions are vivid—the tastes, odors, temperatures, sounds, noises, and kinesthetic sensations all appear real. Although behavior of the dream images and the physical seem real and the dreamer's perceptions appear normal, thought processes are less realistic than in waking consciousness. Your memory regarding immediate and specific details of your current life may appear distorted.

The Dutch psychotherapist Frederick van Eeden journaled over 352 lucid dreams. One of his lucid dreams was reported as follows:

On September 9, 1904, I dreamt that I stood at a table before a
window. On the table were different objects. I was perfectly well
aware that I was dreaming and I considered what sorts of ex-
periments I could make. I began by trying to break glass, by

beating it with a stone. I put a small tablet of glass on two stones and struck it with another stone. Yet it would not break. Then I took a fine claret-glass from the table and struck it with my fist, with all my might, at the same time reflecting how dangerous it would be to do this in waking life; yet the glass remained whole. But lo! When I looked at it again after some time, it was broken.

It broke all right, but a little too late, like an actor who misses his cue. This gave me a very curious impression of being in a fake-world, cleverly imitated, but with small failures.

I took the broken glass and threw it out of the window, in order to observe whether I could hear the tinkling. I heard the noise all right and I even saw two dogs run away from it quite naturally. I thought what a good imitation this comedy-world was. Then I saw a decanter with claret and tasted it, and noted with perfect clearness of mind: "Well, we can also have voluntary impressions of taste in this dream-world; this has quite the taste of wine."[4]

Waking memory about a lucid dream is usually rather clear. Because it tends to generate excitement, lucid dreams are often more easily remembered than ordinary events in our waking life. You most certainly know when you have had a lucid dream.

In order to keep a lucid dream from ending, a form of emotional detachment must be maintained. Emotions may very well run high at this time and such conflicts tend to terminate lucidity. Engaging in an act that is physically dangerous or too anxiety ridden will cause you to wake up. The key to this delicate balance is to enjoy the dream without allowing your emotions to get out of hand.

Two dream events that abruptly end a lucid dream are flying dreams and false awakenings. We have briefly discussed false awakenings and described this state as looking back on the dream and realizing it was a dream that you just awoke from, but discovering (through reality testing) that you are still dreaming.

A series of false awakenings may be experienced, establishing a cycle of three or four dreams within a dream before the realization that a false awakening was manifested. Now you can see why I place such an emphasis on reality testing.

Celia Green describes two types of false awakenings. In the first type, the dreamer appears to be thinking about or discussing a prior dream. Occasionally this happens during reality testing.

A strange atmosphere appears to be present in the second and rare type of false awakening. Apprehension, suspense, or excitement are felt by the dreamer, who appears to awake in a realistic manner in his or her own bed. This type *always* begins with the dreamer in bed. The first type sometimes places the person dreaming in bed.

We can use a false awakening to induce a lucid dream. You should always attempt to determine whether your awakening from a dream is real. If your reality testing demonstrates that this is a false awakening, use this state to precipitate a lucid dream.

Flying Dreams

Flying dreams are reported in every culture. They have been noted throughout history. Later on in this chapter I will discuss OBEs and demonstrate how all dreams, especially lucid dreams, represent a separation of our astral body from our physical one. Before we engage in parapsychology, a survey of how conventional science responds to flying dreams is in order.

Lucid dreamers report more flying dreams than ordinary dreamers. These flying excursions commonly precede lucid dreams. Studies show nearly half of the general population report flying dreams. Interestingly, psychiatric patients show a smaller percentage of flying dreams.

Many well-known lucid dreamers speak of attaining lucidity while flying or floating during their dream state. You can even learn to fly in your dreams. We have previously discussed the Senoi method of transforming falling dreams into flying scenarios.

If you want to have a flying dream, there are several simple ways to do so. One way is simply to think and intensely concentrate on flying right as you drop off to sleep. Make a specific effort to concentrate intensely on having a flying dream for two or three days. Discuss this idea with friends.

Another way to achieve flying dreams is to observe birds. Mary Arnold-Forster described her method as follows:

> *It was a long time before I could fly higher than five or six feet from the ground, and it was only after watching and thinking about the flight of birds, the soaring of the larks above the Wiltshire Downs, the hovering of a kestrel, the action of the rooks' strong wings, and the glancing flights of swallows, that I began to achieve in my dreams some of the same bird-like flights.*[5]

In other words, concentrate on the subjects you desire to produce in your dreams during your waking state to assure success in your lucid dreams. You could observe planes or helicopters instead of birds to induce these flying dreams.

It doesn't really matter why you fly in a dream. This activity may appear suddenly and is unrelated to the plot of a dream. Often you fly to escape a danger, to observe something, as an efficient means of pleasurable travel, and so on. Flying dreams are also easier to induce between 5 a.m. and 8 a.m.

Flying is different from falling in a dream. Almost all flying dreams are pleasurable. There is not the fear of being killed as a result of this activity, as is common with falling dreams. Because lucid dreaming allows us to exert a great deal of control over our dreams, we can perform any flight maneuver we choose and fly to any desired location.

Using Lucid Dreams for ESP Enhancement

When you engage in lucid dreaming, anything is possible. You can select your goal when you establish lucidity, or delay this choice until the dream is in progress. One experiment you can attempt while lucid dreaming is a form of "traveling clairvoyance."

This technique involves an attempt to gather information or current knowledge about a person or place that you have no contact with at present. Today, scientists refer to this as remote viewing.

Oliver Fox described a conversation he had with two friends, Elkington and Slade, concerning dreams. A meeting on Southampton Common in their respective dreams was scheduled. That night both Fox and Elkington had lucid dreams and met at Southampton Common. They remarked that Slade was not there.

The following day Fox and Elkington discussed their mutual lucid dreams, and the absence of Slade. Slade arrived and criticized the experiment as a failure, because he hadn't dreamt at all. This astounding example of preprogrammed lucid dreams worked in two out of three cases. The absence of Slade confirmed the accuracy of these dreams.

The vivid details and complete memories of these dreams are ideal for this form of psychic expansion. You can ask your Higher Self for answers to questions concerning yourself or others, including your own future. Using lucid dreams to stimulate precognitive dreams allows your mind to function as your own personal ESP laboratory.

Therapeutic Applications of Lucid Dreaming

In addition to problem solving, consider using lucid dreams to eliminate a phobia. In psychology we use the term systematic desensitization, in which the subject is presented a hierarchy of feared objects consisting of graduated levels of anxiety, coupled with a relaxation feeling to neutralize this anxiety.

By systematically showing resistance to these fearful stimuli, from lower levels of anxiety to higher levels, the phobia can be removed. The lucid dreamer knows this is just a dream, so harm is not a possibility.

Variations of this approach can be applied to recovering alcoholics and former drug users. In their lucid dreams, situations could be created during which fears of relapsing would be dispelled, and more acceptable behaviors substituted. They could see themselves as drug-free and completely empowered.

The lucid dream state could also be used to learn or perfect motor skills. Such tasks as typing, basketball, golf, tennis, and many others have been improved through the establishment of a two-way communication between the conscious mind and subconscious. Recall the improvement Jack Nicklaus made in his golf swing from a single lucid dream! Even ordinary dreamers have been trained to perform simple motor responses during sleep.

One research project conducted by the University of Chicago tested college students on their ability to shoot basketballs. Group one was instructed not to engage in basketball for one month. One hour a day of practice in shooting baskets was assigned to Group two. Group three was told to spend one hour each day imagining that they were successfully shooting baskets.

When these groups were initially tested, before this month of trial, their results were recorded. After this month they were tested again. The results were as follows:

☆ Group one tested the same.

☆ Group two improved their basket shooting abilities by 24 percent.

☆ Group three improved by an amazing 23 percent. This was only 1 percent less than the Group (two) who practiced one hour daily.

Always bear in mind that travel is instantaneous during a lucid dream, if you desire it. Anything is possible. The possibilities are endless. With the background I have presented concerning lucid dreaming as a foundation, let us practice this fascinating technique.

Shamanic Method for Lucid Dreaming

Carlos Castaneda, anthropologist and author, discussed shamanic techniques to experience lucid dreaming. He was instructed by his Yaqui shaman guide Don Juan to control his dreams by visualizing his own hands prior to falling asleep.

When his hands appeared in his dream, Castaneda would realize that he was dreaming. This technique can also be fostered by vividly recreating a specific dream world with our imagination while we are completely conscious. This method makes it progressively easier to reenter the conscious state while we are dreaming at night. Another variation of this approach is to seek a particular melody, object, or person just prior to falling asleep and thereby exert a form of conscious control over our dreaming.

Several other possibilities of this technique can be utilized such as:

☆ Imagine yourself dreaming of common actions like driving down a certain street, patronizing a certain store, or visiting a friend. Frequent repetition of these imageries throughout the day will increase their likelihood of appearing in your dream. When they do occur, you realize you are dreaming.

☆ Repetition of a specific suggestion just prior to falling asleep that conscious awareness will be exhibited during your dream allows your subconscious to institute the mechanism of lucid dreaming.

☆ While awake, imagine yourself having a specific dream. Focus on each detail of this "virtual" waking dream and constantly remind yourself that these illusions are created by your mind and are completely under your control. You are now devising a single level of awareness that encompasses both the waking and dream world. This bridge between waking and dream consciousness will train your mind to be a competent lucid dreamer.

Here is another simple technique to induce a lucid dream:

1. At some time in the early morning when you have awakened spontaneously from a dream, quickly go over every detail of the dream in your mind and repeat the process several times until you have completely memorized the dream.

2. While you are still lying in bed, repeat to yourself several times, "Next time I'm dreaming, I want to remember to recognize that I'm dreaming."

3. After repeating this phrase, picture yourself back in the dream you just finished dreaming, only imagining that this time you realize that you are dreaming.

4. Keep the visualization in your mind until it is clearly fixed or you fall back to sleep.

Additional methods to create lucid dreams or transform an ordinary dream into a lucid one are presented by these simple approaches:

☆ Recognize the discrepancies in your dreams. Prepare yourself by giving your subconscious directions to critically analyze the data it receives during this imagery. Identify any irregularity and immediately focus on the unreality of this dream.

☆ Suggest you have a nightmare and program yourself to awaken from it during a specific incident. By awaken I mean a false awakening so that your dream environment will become peaceful and you will continue in this dream, now fully aware that you are dreaming.

☆ Program yourself to have a flying dream. Flying dreams are far more characteristic of lucid dreams than they are of regular dreams. This type of suggestion works rather quickly and well.

To summarize how we can use lucid dreaming to dream our problems away, consider the following:

☆ Lucid dreaming is maintaining a conscious awareness that you are dreaming during a dream. It is more difficult than ordinary dreaming, but anyone can master this technique.

☆ Practicing skills in lucid dreams improves your performance of them in your waking state.

★ Maintaining lucidity requires a delicate balance between keeping awareness, but not becoming so aware or emotional that you wake up.

★ Use reality testing to check on prelucid states, and convert these to true lucid dreams.

★ Repeat to yourself, "This is only a dream and I can't be harmed," to establish and maintain lucidity.

★ Lucid dreams may be induced by:
a) Becoming so scared that you realize you are dreaming.
b) Recognizing dreamlike qualities, unusual occurrences, and incongruities in your dream.
c) Developing a critical approach during your dream.

★ The hours of 5 a.m. to 8 a.m. are the easiest to induce lucid dreams for most people.

★ Lucid dreams are usually realistic, except for flying. Specific recent details may be distorted.

★ Use reality testing to ascertain false awakenings.

★ Anything is possible in a lucid dream.

★ All lucid dreams are OBEs.

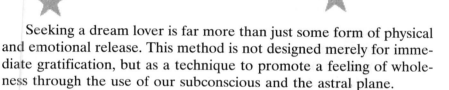

11

Dream Lovers

Seeking a dream lover is far more than just some form of physical and emotional release. This method is not designed merely for immediate gratification, but as a technique to promote a feeling of wholeness through the use of our subconscious and the astral plane.

Men have reported to me a sense of harmony and peace as a result of using these methods. Not only do they experience an increase in the qualities of the women they meet now, they also appreciate these qualities more. I will describe a case history at the end of this chapter in which a male patient resolved a long-standing sexual dysfunction problem and met his current wife through the liaison efforts of his dream lover.

Women feel far more confident and balanced in their dealings with men when they establish a relationship with a dream lover. They seem to shed their "baggage," experience better orgasms with their physical plane partners, and improve creative energies and talents.

You can gain insight and improve your current relationships through experiences with your dream lover. Another fringe benefit of these astral excursions is a tapping into a source of inner wisdom that is not found in your waking life. Couples also benefit from these techniques, as I will present later in this chapter.

There are many reasons we desire sex. A dream lover can fulfill many of these, and prepare you for a function and blissful relationship with another human being. Here are some of the reasons my patients have for a sexual experience:

☆ It reinforces the fact that they are attractive.

☆ They desire a reward for the work they do.

☆ The closeness and sharing are unmatchable by other activities.

☆ Sex helps to distract them from feelings of depression, separation, and loneliness.

☆ It keeps them healthy and makes them feel young again.

☆ Sex may be the only way they feel their lover can show that they still love them.

☆ They enjoy the erotic fantasies and other visualizations that accompany their orgasms.

☆ The emotional release and dissipation of physical tension are a welcome result of sex.

☆ This is how they can communicate feelings of love and affection to their partner.

☆ Sex makes them feel someone else cares for them.

How do dream lovers appear to us? This question is often asked of me by my patients. The answer is quite simple: in any manner we desire. Here are some examples of how your dream lover may manifest to you:

☆ A wise sage.

☆ A beautiful maiden or handsome male youth.

☆ A doctor.

☆ An artist.

☆ An executive.

☆ A saint.

☆ A high priest or priestess.

☆ Someone you know now.

☆ A Spirit Guide or angel.

☆ A healer.

Always bear in mind that your dream lover is a reflection of yourself. By accessing the energy of this astral entity, you will gain an understanding of your deeper psyche that is almost impossible to duplicate on the physical plane.

You will also improve your relationships on the physical plane as you integrate your own consciousness and empower yourself. A thorough understanding of your own inner complexities is only a dream away. A dream lover is always there for you, to support, encourage, stimulate, educate, and love you. Its therapy is free and the experience of this astral companion needs to be felt personally to comprehend its beauty.

Your experiences in dream world will be characterized by the presence of many kinds of entities, as I have previously discussed. Some of these astral bodies are available for engaging in sex.

Having sex with an astral being while in your dream body offers advantages far beyond physical and emotional release. You can significantly add to your spiritual growth by this type of encounter.

We must also consider the fact that astral sex with a dream lover is perfectly safe. There is no possibility of disease, yet this experience provides us with the possibility of support, warmth, tenderness, satisfaction, and communication that we seek in our physical plane relationships.

During our REM cycle, our dream body is quite active. We are functioning on a rather emotional dimension, during which our every thought and feeling manifests as a reality. It is critical that you maintain a high level of integrity and ethics when you engage in a relationship with a dream lover.

These entities are real, and most definitely have feelings. Karmic laws apply and purposely hurting or using a dream lover will not add to your spiritual growth. You naturally want to attract a high-level dream lover into your awareness. This means keeping your OBEs limited to the upper astral plane.

Here are some characteristics of high-level dream lovers:

☆ They do not want you to be alone on the physical plane.

☆ Their advice is always for your best interests. They can alert you of future problems and facilitate healing when you are ill.

☆ Your ability to have OBEs will be improved under their guidance.

☆ A dream lover can help you to improve the quality of your current relationship.

☆ They will not be jealous of your present lover.

☆ They only want you to be happy, and will assist you in any way possible to help your spiritual growth, health, and other aspects of your physical plane sojourn.

One question my patients pose to me concerning their dream lover is: "should I tell my significant other about this relationship?" This is a personal decision, but I strongly advise against this disclosure. Your current lover will most likely act in a jealous manner or simply ridicule you.

Another problem with informing your mate about this companionship is that he or she will be insulted. Women especially will feel quite intimidated by your having to seek spiritual (they may also assume emotional or physical) needs from someone else.

This type of rival is impossible for an insecure physical plane lover to deal with. The image of a "ghost" rival will not improve your communication with your physical plane lover. He or she may very well question your psychological stability. You most certainly would not be able to relate this situation at the office, either.

You need not be concerned with your dream lover interfering in any way with your Earth life. This dream world entity is far more tolerant of your physical plane experiences than anyone you know.

The Advantages of Having a Dream Lover

It is not difficult to see the many benefits of attracting a dream lover into your life. Among these advantages are:

☆ A dream lover can keep you fulfilled during occasions when your Earth mate is out of town, ill, or otherwise unavailable. This astral entity can teach you how to unite with your physical lover during this absence, too. Your physical lover must agree to this to keep within the bounds of spiritual ethics.

☆ The sharing of limitless travels, deep insights, and spiritual bliss enhances life as nothing else on the physical plane can.

☆ This contact will assist you in improving your life on several levels, including physically, emotionally, and spiritually.

☆ Sex with a dream lover provides you with a healthy outlet and helps reduce the anxieties, obligations, and pressures incurred from our Earth plane sojourn.

☆ Another benefit is from the lack of physical exertion required to engage in astral sex. This is attractive to the elderly and those recovering from life-threatening illness, such as heart attacks.

☆ You will be shown your Akashic Records and can use this information to facilitate your own karmic cycle and spiritual growth.

☆ The resulting empowerment is very difficult to duplicate through conventional means on the physical plane.

☆ Your astral lover can assist you in finding a high quality mate in your Earth life.

☆ Your ability to end a current dysfunctional relationship without the usual procrastination and guilt aspects will be facilitated.

☆ Because anything is possible on the astral plane, it is easy to use this experience to remove doubts and inhibitions, and build your self-image.

Meeting a Dream Lover

Before attracting a dream lover into your life, a certain amount of growth should be undertaken by you to avoid meeting a low-level astral being. I highly recommend you remove as much fear, tension, and negativity from your awareness as possible prior to practicing the exercises in this chapter.

Every thought and feeling you have manifests itself in dream world. It behooves you to get your act together to obtain the maximum benefits from this process.

Balancing your seven major chakras is a good start in the right direction. Try this *higher chakra link* method to balance these energy centers located in your dream body (see figure 2):

1. Sit comfortably or lie down. Breathe deeply and apply protection. Focus your attention on your third eye region of your forehead. This is the sixth chakra, located between your eyes.

2. As you inhale, imagine a glowing white light being drawn into this third eye area and creating a sensation of warmth. Hold this focus for a count of eight. Now exhale and repeat this procedure two more times.

3. As you inhale again, see this glowing white light being drawn up to the crown chakra located at the top of the head. See a rainbow bridge being formed here. Hold this focus on the rainbow bridge for a count of eight at the crown chakra, exhale, and repeat this procedure two more times.

4. Visualize the rainbow bridge moving into the third eye chakra and finally into the throat (fifth) chakra. As you inhale, feel this warm sensation permeating the throat. Hold this focus of the rainbow bridge in the throat chakra for a count of eight, exhale, and repeat this procedure two more times.

5. Imagine this rainbow bridge moving from the throat chakra into the heart (fourth) chakra. This is the area in the middle of the chest at the level of the heart.

6. As you inhale, feel this warm sensation permeating the heart chakra. Hold this focus for a count of eight, exhale, and repeat this procedure two more times.

7. Finally, inhale deeply and hold your breath for a count of eight. As you hold your breath, visually link up the rainbow bridges in your heart, throat, third eye, and crown chakras with a band of glowing white light. Feel this link as a warm, tingly sensation. Exhale slowly and repeat this procedure two more times.

You have activated your highest spiritual centers to facilitate your spiritual growth. I highly recommend my superconscious mind tape and chakra healing tape to assist you in this preparation.

By properly preparing yourself in the manner I just described, you are more likely to attract a higher level astral being into your consciousness. When you leave the body to initiate this astral encounter, I strongly recommend exiting through the sixth or seventh chakra. Never leave through the first or second chakra, as this will attract lower-level entities. This advice applies to those of you who are skilled at astral projection techniques. To learn these I refer you to my book *Astral Voyages*.[1]

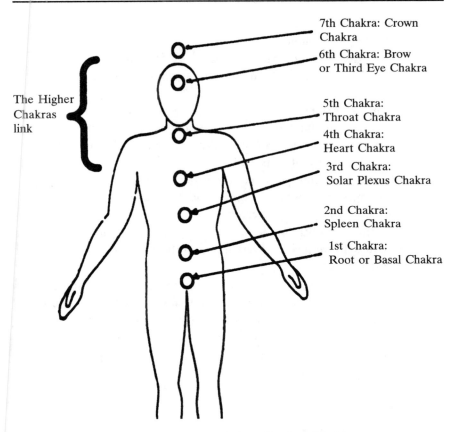

Figure 2. The Higher Chakra Link

Your First Date With a Dream Lover

To locate a dream lover, I suggest establishing a sanctuary that you can utilize for spiritual growth as well as astral plane rendezvous. Here is a simple exercise to create such a place:

1. First practice one of the self-hypnosis exercises using white light protection.

2. Create a room on the astral plane that is empty and bare. This is your sanctuary.

3. Add furniture, flowers, statues, paintings, and anything else you desire to reflect your spiritual side. There should be a pool of some sort in this large and beautiful room.

Remember, the astral pane is much more expansive than our physical plane.

4. Mentally focus on your list of physical problems. Memorize this list and state to yourself how you can resolve each issue.

5. Remove whatever clothes you are wearing and enter this pool. As you immerse yourself in the sacred and cleansing waters of this pool, you are releasing your problems to the healing energy of this water.

6. Finally leave the pool and allow the warmth of the sun to dry you and revitalize your body. This will result in the physical changes you desire.

Repeat this visualization technique with the emotional, mental, and spiritual issues in your life. Every six months or so you may want to repeat this cleansing.

Other preparations for meeting your dream lover include grooming, wearing a sexy nightgown or silk pajamas when going to bed, and programming your thoughts to love, spirituality, and companionship. In addition, you should think carefully about the qualities you would like to see in your dream lover. Here is a list of some possibilities:

☆ Physical beauty.
☆ Spiritual growth.
☆ Truthfulness.
☆ Supportiveness.
☆ Integrity.
☆ Patience.
☆ Decisiveness.
☆ Lover of animals.
☆ Gentleness.
☆ High self-image.
☆ Compassion.
☆ Concern.
☆ Intelligence.

Always remember that the attributes you seek in someone else are a reflection of your own psyche. Just prior to falling asleep, recreate your sanctuary and visualize yourself meditating there. Your dream lover will arrive shortly, if he or she isn't already there to greet you.

When your dream lover finally does arrive, take a few minutes to introduce yourself and discuss your mutual goals. This entity may have shared a past life with you. If this is the case, your lover will most likely be dressed in the attire of that era and will manifest the persona of that lifetime.

Hold hands and embrace this astral being. Feel free to ask questions, such as the following:

1. What is your name?
2. Have we shared previous lifetimes together?
3. Will we be together on the physical plane in some future life?
4. Where do you come from originally?
5. What can you teach me?
6. How can I be of help to you?
7. Why am I meeting you at this time in my life?
8. Is there anyone on the physical plane you would like me to contact?
9. Can you assist me in finding a lover in my physical life?
10. Why do you want to be with me?

You should always feel comfortable in the presence of your astral companion. Refrain from sexual activity right away. Begin a courtship and make this last as long as necessary before engaging in astral sex. When you do finally share intimacies with this entity, begin with the brow chakra, but no lower. Under no circumstances initiate sex from the lower three chakras.

Your dream lover may take you to the temple to access your Akashic Records. Any lifetimes you two may have shared together will be explored at this time. You may also explore other lifetimes of yours in which this entity did not participate. You may view scenes back or forward in time, contact a departed loved one, or solve a current problem on the physical plane you may be having. This is a wonderful opportunity for spiritual understanding and growth.

One thing you do not want to do is become obsessed with your dream lover. Never forget about your physical plane life and its responsibilities. This will result in emotional, financial, and other problems. In addition, you will retard your spiritual growth and create problems in your aura by becoming too involved with these experiences.

The first impressions you receive from any being (physical or astral) are very valuable in judging the quality of an encounter. Be very wary if your companion is quick to solicit your trust. If you are asked to make dramatic changes in your life or if you catch this entity in a lie, you are dealing with a low-level entity. Simply dismiss this being if that is the case.

Sex With a Dream Lover

The actual experience of sex in dream world with your dream lover is like nothing you have experienced on the physical plane. First, your throat chakra expands and a tingly sensation is produced throughout your entire dream body.

The next phase is a face-to-face position with your dream lover, lining up both of your now expanded throat chakras. What results is an exchange of light energy that is quite difficult to describe. As a white light descends over both of you, beams of light enter your chakras one by one. Each of these energy centers open wide to receive this rushing energy. All blockages are eliminated and a complete purification of your dream body unfolds. Finally, your first chakra creates a sudden surge of Kundalini energy that rises like an oil well gushing through your crown chakra.

This results in a burst of energy encompassing the entire room. Your dream body quivers in response to this energy surge. Next, your dream lover moves closer to you until both of your bodies are touching. A whirlpool of light energy emanating from both of your crown chakras swirls around your bodies, which now function as one unit.

Slowly, your astral lover moves away from you and decreases this energy flow. Soon you again regain your previous vibratory rate. He or she will most likely gently kiss you and disappear. Your physical body is likely to respond with a sensation of feeling completely energized and very stimulated to engage in physical plane sex with your partner.

A dream lover can act as a teacher, advisor, friend, protector, and lover all rolled into one. Your association with this being can eliminate despondency, loneliness, and frustration. You can access the wisdom of ancient knowledge thanks to your companion on the other side.

Whether we want to call this dream lover experience a state of timeless bliss, an eternal now, or merely the ability to access our past and future experiences that contribute to our personal identity, it can be most beneficial to our spiritual growth.

Sex is known to produce an ASC, and dream lovers can improve our sex life and our lives in general. This can be accomplished through three steps: expectation, desire, and merging.

Expectation is easy to accomplish. Simply state to yourself a goal of meeting a quality lover. By really wanting this relationship to occur, you are fulfilling the desire component of this paradigm. Your choices of success are directly proportional to the strength of your desire.

Merging is attained through hypnosis, meditation, visualization, dancing, music, and OBEs. When you diffuse your mind into the timeless dimension of dream world and flow with the divine energy of oneness, you have successfully merged.

Shared dreaming with your lover is another way to add to the beauty of a relationship. This can be accomplished by practicing the following steps:

1. Select a specific location to dream about and meet there in your dreams. This spot should be one that is familiar to both of you, and represents a romantic rendezvous place.
2. Both of you should visualize meeting at this location. Use your expectation, desire, and merging talents to create a detailed, yet romantic atmosphere.
3. Compare notes and share the details of your dreams and OBEs. Make sure to engage in astral sex with your lover.

The combination of dream patterning and shared dreaming will result in better sex, increased closeness, and an improved relationship.

Both of you should select the specific types of dream world experiences that best fulfill each of your desires. Dream lover experiences, whether they be with a physical plane lover or an astral entity, will expand your consciousness, add new elements of passion and intimacy to your sex life, and facilitate your spiritual evolution.

Sex on the dream world with your lover can greatly enhance a relationship. This can be facilitated by engaging in a high-quality form of physical sex on the Earth plane with this individual. Proper breathing exercises will facilitate both of the physical enjoyment for both and increase your respective sexual stamina.

This deep breathing exercise will assist you in this endeavor:

Stand upright, keeping your arms relaxed at your sides and your feet apart. Breathe normally through your nose with your mouth closed. Place both of your hands, one over the other, on your abdomen just below your navel. Breathe in deeply and distend your stomach muscles by taking in air, not by muscular force.

Breathe out and press both hands gently against your abdomen until all of the air has been released. Repeat this five times to constitute one cycle. Breathe normally four breaths and repeat the entire cycle four additional times.

Repeat this procedure except now breathe mainly from the chest.

When you practice these exercises enough times, your body will become conditioned so that with one smooth in-breath, the air is directed into your fully expanded chest, leaving some room in your abdomen. As you continue breathing in, the abdomen fills up with air.

The reverse occurs upon breathing out. Most of the air in the chest is now released, and subsequently, the air from the abdomen. Next, the remaining air in your chest, and finally your abdomen, is let go.

To summarize, breathing in, or inspiration, is from: abdomen-chest-abdomen-chest. Expiration, or breathing out, is indicated by the following: chest-abdomen-chest-abdomen.

Men typically have more difficulty with breathing from their chest. They favor stomach breathing. Women, on the other hand, find abdominal breathing harder, as they tend to breathe from their chest.

Deep-breathing exercises offer many positive effects. It is a natural method and continual adherence to this regimen will result in the following benefits:

☆ Calmness.
☆ Increased confidence.
☆ Increased stamina.
☆ Increased concentration.
☆ Relaxation.
☆ Heightened vitality.

Another technique to facilitate physical sex with your partner is to refrain from orgasm as long as possible. The application of firm pressure on the base of the penis works well in this regard. Women who are capable of multiple orgasms should also delay this response. A simultaneous orgasm by both partners is the ideal situation. This mutual satisfaction will now result in a stronger climax, a more fulfilling OBE, and better dream world sex.

A Dream Lover Success Story

Roger came to my Los Angeles office in 1992 with a severe case of secondary impotency. He could not maintain an erection long enough to ejaculate during intercourse. We refer to this as secondary impotency because there was nothing medically wrong with him.

A thorough examination by a urologist confirmed that Roger had no organic cause to his sexual dysfunction. In addition, he could successfully masturbate to orgasm. It was only when he entered a woman's vagina that this problem surfaced.

Roger had neither the time, money, nor patience to go through tedious psychotherapy. A trip to Masters and Johnson's clinic in St. Louis was also out of the question.

I guided Roger through various hypnotic techniques, including superconscious mind taps and out-of-body experiences, to facilitate his developing a dream lover.

Tanya was the name of his dream lover. This proved to be a most rewarding and therapeutic relationship. In addition to providing Roger with sexual bliss during his dreams, Tanya assisted Roger in eliminating his ED (via astral sex), and reintroduced Roger to an old college girlfriend that he dated 10 years earlier.

This meeting was set up by Tanya's instructing Roger to be at a certain coffee shop one evening. Tanya had visited this woman in the latter's dream state and detected that she still cared for Roger, but didn't know how to contact him.

The night Roger entered this coffee shop, his life was changed. He met Cynthia there and recognized her immediately. She likewise acted as if this meeting was an angelic intervention. During the next 18 months they dated and became engaged.

Today Cynthia and Roger are married and have a beautiful baby daughter. Many would scoff at the concept of a dream lover, but don't expect Roger to laugh at this theory.

Cynthia does not know about Tanya. Roger was not particularly metaphysically oriented when I first worked with him. As I stated earlier, most relationships would be compromised if the truth of this approach was discussed. The bottom line is that they are all happy, and so is Tanya.

12

Improve Creativity
Through Dreams

Just like the incubated dreams of the ancients, you can learn to discover and improve upon your own natural creativity by controlling your dreams. Your dreams can actually become your source of inspiration, as you create art, write, or design your next home. They may be utilized to solve simple to complex problems.

In this chapter, we will discuss how dreams inspired creative works while the dreamer was consciously working on an idea. Sometimes this dream solution simply appears, without the dreamer attempting to find the solution to some problem or idea. This fascinating technique is virtually unknown to most of the people who at first reaped its rewards.

These classic examples of creative dreamers are presented to inspire you to learn from their success. The mechanism consists of the following:

☆ Somehow ask our subconscious to use the dream state to create a product, or find an ingenious solution to a current problem.

☆ Extract a solution from the unlimited memory bank of the subconscious.

☆ Sift out the answer and rearrange it in some original form.

☆ Present it in a dream that is easy to understand.

One of the main advantages of using dreams in this way is an integration of self. The more we can link the waking and dreaming segments of our consciousness, the greater will be our expression of our own unique personality and empowerment.

There are two possible approaches a creative dream may take. In the first type, the final form and totality of the creative product or solution is given. In the second type, the idea or mood that leads to this creative endeavor is established. These dreams can happen by "pure chance," or be brought on by premeditated actions on the part of the dreamer.

One technique that is common to proficient creative dreamers is that they immerse themselves with the subject they desire to explore in a dream right up until the last few seconds before falling asleep. I used to have to do this with organic chemistry and physics problems in my college years.

The English artist/poet/engraver William Blake (1757–1827) was known for the dreamlike quality of his art. I described his astral projection works in my book *Astral Voyages*. Blake's dream of importance to our discussion was in reference to an inexpensive method of engraving his illustrated songs.

One night Blake's dead younger brother Robert appeared in a dream and suggested a process of copper engraving. Blake immediately acted on this suggestion, and it proved both valid and practical. This example illustrates becoming totally involved with the creative goal just prior to falling asleep.

The German chemist Friedrich A. Kekulé used a dream to make one of the most profound discoveries in the history of chemistry. For several years Kekulé tried to unravel the secret of the structure of benzene. He could not come up with a configuration to account for its chemical components.

As he gazed into a fire one cold evening in 1865, he fell asleep and had the following dream:

Again the atoms were juggling before my eyes...my mind's eye, sharpened by repeated sights of a similar kind, could now distinguish larger structures of different forms and in long chains, many of them close together; everything was moving in a snake-like and twisting manner. Suddenly, what was this? One of the snakes got hold of its own tail and the whole structure as mockingly twisting in front of my eyes. As if struck by lightening, I awoke....[1]

As a result of this dream, Kekulé realized that a closed carbon ring was the structure of benzene. This led to the establishment of organic chemistry, which evolved into biochemistry. Biochemistry is critical to the pharmaceutical industry and modern medicine in general.

Kekulé was honored at a scientific convention 25 years later. The chemist was commended on his great discovery and the process by which it evolved. He stated: "Let us learn to dream, gentlemen, and then we may perhaps find the truth."[2]

We can program ourselves to dream purposely to create something or solve a vexing problem. Upon repetition and enhancement of this technique, you will acquire the ability to induce creative dreams and stimulate your reservoir of creative talents far beyond what may have previously been exhibited.

You may consider yourself an "ordinary dreamer," and not have the need or desire to create a great work of art. These simple methods can still be of use in your daily life. Daily dream practice can result in solving mathematical problems that you found impossible to do while fully conscious.

You can use these methods to deal with career changes, facilitate the development of insights to all sorts of personal and professional applications, and even improve your athletic ability. Golfer Jack Nicklaus reportedly improved his golf swing by altering it as suggested by a dream. He was in a slump at the time, and this new grip established his "swing" that vastly improved his performance on the green. He stated:

First I "see" the ball where I want it to finish, nice and white and sitting up high on the bright green grass. Then the scene quickly changes, and I "see" the ball going there: its path, trajectory, and shape, even its behavior on landing. Then there's a lot of fade-out, and the next scene shows me making the kind of swing that will turn the previous images into reality.[3]

Recording your dreams in a journal is the first step toward applying this technique. This will assist you in maximizing your innate creative abilities. You must break old habits and "see the forest through the trees" to access new and more efficient solutions to day-to-day problems and challenges.

All we need do is look around our environment for the elements of creativity. Listening to our Higher Self, filtered through our subconscious, will answer each and every one of our queries. As children we have this talent, but society mocks this and encourages "fitting in" to established modes of behavior.

Summarizing Creative Dreaming

There are many things you can do to improve your creativity through use of your dreams. Throughout your day, train yourself to note similarities between seemingly dissimilar things. Free yourself from any form of rigid thinking.

Always allot a certain amount of time for your creative goals. Give yourself both the opportunity and the environment to turn your dreams into a reality. When you receive inspirations, refrain from judging them until your creative juices stop flowing.

Here are some simple procedures, as I have presented in this chapter, to utilize your dreams for creative purposes:

1. Develop positive dream images that assist you in your endeavors. This will eliminate the nightmarish elements of your dream and transform negative components into dream helpers.

2. Expose your conscious mind to all forms of art, music, literature, and data from several different sources. Go to movies and lectures; travel, and engage in conversations and pursuits that stimulate your thoughts, feelings, and soul.

3. Become healthfully obsessed with your topic of special interest. Read everything you can on it. See what others have produced or evaluated about this subject. Develop an emotional intensity to create something new in reference to it.

4. Prepare yourself for this endeavor by building up your conscious skills in this field. Take courses, study with experts, and use your direct observation and trial-and-error to thoroughly familiarize with its basics.

5. Spend a minimum of two days focusing in your area of interest. Limit your concentration to this discipline, and keep this an intense preparation right up until the moment you fall asleep. It is highly recommended to consciously direct your dream content at this time.

6. Visualize and note all the details of the resulting creative dreams. Record it in your journal, and make it as concrete and applicable as you can while detailing it. Your "stream of consciousness" will be active at this time.

7. Pay particular attention to your recurrent dreams, and those that try to edit or correct your interpretation or actions based on previous dream content.

Other examples of dream-inspired creativity include:

☆ Edgar Allan Poe (1809–1849) drew heavily from his dreams for the theme and mood of his surreal short stories and poetry.

☆ Luong-Vichivathlen was a writer from Thailand who was stimulated and directed to write as a career when his deceased spiritual teacher appeared to him in a dream, handed him a pair of glasses, and told him to wear them as he wrote books.

☆ Voltaire (1694–1778) composed parts of his "La Henriade" from a dream. This French philosopher and essayist used his dreams to inspire some of his other writings.

☆ The ancient Greek bishop of the Greek colony Cyrene in North Africa, Synesius (373–414 A.D.) left written accounts describing his use of dreams to solve problems and inspire his writings.

☆ Elias Howe, the inventor of the sewing machine, was unable to figure out where to put the eye in the machine needle. One night he had a frightening dream in which "savages" took him captive. They danced around him with upraised spears, threatening to kill him unless he completed his invention. Terrified, Howe noticed something odd about the jabbing spears. They had eye-shaped holes near their tips. Waking, he realized he had been given the solution to his problems; he needed to place the eye of the sewing machine needle near the point. This resulted in the invention of the modern sewing machine and a major change in the direction of the industrial revolution.[4]

An Exercise in Enhancing Creativity

Try this technique of accessing your Higher Self to facilitate the development of your creative talents. Practice this script just prior to falling asleep:

Now listen very carefully. I want you to imagine a bright white light coming down from above and entering the top of your head, filling your entire body. See it, feel it, and it becomes reality. Now image an aura of pure white light emanating from your heart region, again surrounding your entire body, protecting you. See it, feel it, and it becomes reality. Now only your Higher Self, Masters and Guides, and highly evolved loving entities who mean you well will be able to influence you during this or any other hypnotic session. You are totally protected by this aura of pure white light.

In a few moments, I am going to count from one to twenty. As I do, you will feel yourself rising up to the superconscious mind level where you will be able to receive information from your Higher Self and masters and guides. Number one, rising up. Two, three, four, rising higher. Five, six, seven, letting information flow. Eight, nine, ten, you are halfway there. Eleven, twelve, thirteen, feel yourself rising even higher. Fourteen, fifteen, sixteen, almost there. Seventeen, eighteen, nineteen, number twenty. Now you are there. Take a moment and orient yourself to the superconscious mind level.

Play New Age music for one minute.

You are now in a deep hypnotic trance and from this superconscious mind level, you may request guidance to increase your creativity. You are in complete control and able to access this limitless power of your superconscious mind. I want you to be open and flow with this experience. You are always protected by the white light.

At this time, I would like you to ask your Higher Self to assist you in connecting with someone whom you consider as a creative role model in your area of special interest. This person may have appeared to you in previous dreams.

Now ask this individual for guidance on a project that you are currently working on. Focus on the image of this teacher and select a rendezvous spot (this could be the sanctuary you created previously), for a creative brainstorming session. Trust your Higher Self and your own ability to allow any thoughts, feelings, or impressions to come into your subconscious mind concerning this goal. You will remember everything you learn from this meeting upon awakening. Now let your dream world assist you in your creative development.

When you awaken the following morning, write down everything you can remember immediately. A tape player is ideal to quickly summarize ideas, sing songs, or document anything else that surfaced from your dreams. You might want to draw or sketch any visualizations you received at this time.

Another script you can use following the standard induction, white light protection, and rising up to the superconscious mind level is as follows:

You are now going to begin the process of releasing your natural creative energy. You can unleash your creative talents by tapping into your Higher Self.

You can now draw creative inspiration from the universe. You feel creative and are creative. It is easy and natural for you to generate creative ideas and solutions.

You are open to all of the joy and fulfillment life has to offer. You can even more appreciate your natural creative expression and beauty.

The wisdom of the universe is within you. Allow your natural creative talents to flow through your awareness and manifest themselves in your present being. Do this now.

Play New Age music for four minutes.

You are deeper and deeper in trance as you access your Higher Self and tap into your natural abilities for artistic work, for drawing, or painting, writing, sculpting, or any kind of creative work. You easily generate creative and marketable ideas. Program your senses to facilitate bringing your ideas to an actual material form.

Now let your Higher Self instruct you on your particular creative interest and mentally perceive yourself applying your creative talent in a highly developed, personally and professionally fulfilling manner. Focus your creative energies upon a current project, or one that you have put aside for some time. Increase your determination to its maximum level and now mentally perceive yourself carrying out this creative project successfully while enjoying this entire process. Do this now.

Play New Age music for four minutes.

Now for this last exercise I want you to see yourself receiving formal recognition for your current talents. If your goal is to develop your creative talents into a full-time professional pursuit, see yourself being both established, rewarded, and fulfilled in this endeavor. Do this now.

Play New Age music for three minutes.

End this exercise as I previously instructed.

Hypnogogic Creative Techniques

The hypnogogic state between waking and sleeping is the level during which many creative people have received their inspirations. Thomas Edison used this method to improve his creativity, and he was responsible for approximately 1,100 patents during his lifetime! Einstein also obtained some of his basic concepts of the relativity of mass, time, and distance through hypnogogic methods.

There are many ways to prevent yourself from falling asleep while practicing this approach in the way it is intended. For example, while lying in bed or on a couch, extend your hand toward the ceiling. When your arm drops, this alerts you to the fact that you are about to fall asleep, and that it is time to refocus your consciousness.

Edison used a method of placing metal pellets in his hand while lying on a couch and having a metal pan directly beneath his arm. When the metal pellets dropped into this pan, the noise prevented him from falling asleep. You can devise whatever method you find most compatible to bring about this result.

I would suggest you recreate your sanctuary for these exercises. Another possibility is to image you are viewing a large white movie screen. Now you can project onto this screen any image that you desire.

For this technique, I want you to imagine a setting you find most conducive for expressing your creativity. It may be your study, walking through a meadow, a placid mountain scene, or any other environment that will provide a creative stimulus for you.

1. Use the hypnotic induction with white light protection I previously presented. Imagine yourself in your ideal creative environment. Let yourself become oriented to the peacefulness and beauty of this place.
2. Now focus on an example of the type of work you would like to produce. For example, if you are an artist, perceive yourself in a museum portraying the type of art you do. This might be an art exhibition in a gallery. Use this

image to obtain any creative ideas that will assist you in your next project.

3. Shift this scene to one in which you have created some of your specialty area and observe your work being objectively critiqued. Do not be concerned about the quality of these reviews. The purpose of this exercise is to learn how to improve and tap into your natural creative talents. Do not allow ego or other insecurities to contaminate this experience.

4. The last step is to program your subconscious to repeat this technique during your dreams until you obtain your desired goals.

Creating a New Vehicle for Your Talents

In this visual imagery technique you are actually picturing yourself in a new body, one that is expressing creativity to its maximum development. Begin this exercise with my standard hypnotic induction and white light protection. This may be practiced during the hypnogogic state, or just prior to falling asleep.

Mentally see an image of yourself standing before you. This is your body exactly as you would like it to appear, exactly as you want that body to be, and as it has the possibility of being. Look at it more and more closely now, and it will be a realistic but ideal body image, one that you really could achieve, and one that you will achieve, and one that reflects your higher level of creativity. When you have a clear image of your body as you would like to have it, keep observing that image, and make it a part of your own reality.

Play New Age music for four minutes.

That ideal body image is becoming more and more real, you are seeing it very clearly, and seeing it in its full size and dimensions, and now you are going to step forward and into that body, you will find yourself in that body, so that you can try it out and make certain that it is just the body you do want to have, and if there is something you would like to change, then make those changes now. At all times, focus on the specific creative talents you want to perfect.

Move around in that body, feel its strength and agility, its dynamic aliveness, its surging vitality, and make really certain that its appearance and all of its attributes are what you realistically desire. And as you occupy that body, coming to know that body very well, your present physical body is going to be drawn into that new mold. You are moving already toward the realization of that ideal body image, and you will be doing whatever is needed to achieve that body you want to have.

Play New Age music for five minutes.

You may end this trance as usual if this exercise is practiced long before you retire for the evening. If you are using this to program your dream cycle, simply give your subconscious a suggestion to have this imagery manifested in your dream world.

By focusing in on our right brain through hypnosis and visualization approaches, we are able to view our creative potential in a new light. One result of this method is an expansion of our horizons and an improvement of the image we have of ourselves and our ability to be creative.

13

Heal Yourself While You Dream

From the material I have already presented, I'm sure you see how healing your dreams can be. You can dream your problems away and both empower yourself and attain spiritual growth at the same time.

Patients who ask, "How can I change?" are really telling me that they dislike who they are now, and want to become someone different as soon as possible. Fortunately, my therapy is very short in duration.

For people in need of change, stress is their constant enemy. Even highly motivated people experience stress, especially the more radical the change and the faster the breakthrough. The classic examples are get-rich-quick schemes, instant cures, infatuation relationships, and crash diets.

Patients present themselves with various attitudes when they finally seek therapy. The ones who expect a codependency relationship with its accompanying "do it for me" approach, are not treated by me. Unless a patient is willing to accept full responsibility for all success or failure of their therapy, I will not work with them.

Another type of individual who is usually doomed to fail in therapy is the immediate gratification type. These people have dozens of stories about how they instantly became a better person, usually by going to a retreat, workshop, or watching a video. They have become a "changed person," but for some reason are still calling therapists.

My purpose is not to ridicule these individuals. The sudden changes they experience are quite real, but temporary. They neither have the attention span nor time to thoroughly eliminate the cause of their issues. Their demands for once-and-for-all transformations, with little or no effort on their part, can only be met with disappointment.

When patients represent these two types, or any other category, they may find themselves at a crossroads in their lives. They can continue with their current behavior and remain miserable, or take a different path and grow. It is at this stage that dreaming their problems away is possible.

There are five major steps exhibited by such internally motivated patients. These may be described as follows:

1. **An openness to change.** The motivation to look within ourselves should be an internal, rather than external one. We must desire, from our "heart-of-hearts," to change and grow. This process is destined to fail if it is initiated to please someone else.

A crisis may be the initial trigger zone. For example, a divorce, death of a loved one, lost job, depression, or other catastrophes in our lives may motivate us to "see the light." Usually a crisis motivation is temporary. Once this difficulty passes, the individual returns to his or her previous behavior. Motivation must be internal to assume success.

2. **Increasing awareness.** When we explore our expectations, memories, thoughts and feelings concerning important issues in our lives, our awareness has expanded. To maximize your benefits, I highly recommend you suspend judgment over what you discover about yourself.

Finding out about your inner psyche can bring to the surface qualities that you may find frightening, distasteful, and frustrating. If you are working with a therapist, make sure this clinician is not dogmatic, prejudiced, or judgmental. This soul healer should be objective, properly encouraging you to explore your deep, dark, secret self as thoroughly as possible.

3. **Admitting our faults.** This is where our ego attempts to abort the therapy process. Statements such as "I had a difficult childhood," "My husband/wife/partner [and so on] messed up," and "I was just about say that" reflected

the conscious mind's natural resistance to change. Old guilt and fears initiate this defense mechanism.

Own up to your faults. Acknowledge that you need to change, and take the necessary steps to begin this change. After reaching steps one and two, this phase is easier to contend with.

The Good Girl or Good Boy role that we may have been brainwashed to play as a child doesn't help our soul's growth. This obsessive desire to please only reflects insecurities. As the Beatles stated so well, "Can't Buy Me Love."

4. **Acceptance.** Once you accept who you are now with all of your faults, you open yourself to the process of healing and spiritual growth. It all boils down to eliminating fear, raising your self-image, and becoming empowered.

One thing you will notice is the development of compassion for yourself and others. Not only will you accept the way you are, but also the right of others to be who they are. This improvement in your tolerance is a very positive step forward in your spiritual growth.

Don't confuse acceptance with rationalizing. In the latter you simply justify why you shouldn't or needn't change. With acceptance, you admit to yourself that you have problems and commit yourself to resolving them.

5. **Keeping conscious of our faults.** Our emotions have a way of removing objectivity and distorting our reactions with subjective feelings of anxiety or inadequacy. We must refrain from the natural tendency to repress our emotions and thoughts and stay aware and focused on our goals.

This repression, if untreated, can extend to our creativity, ideals, and virtues. We notice what we are doing when we maintain our awareness. This affords us the opportunity to catch ourselves before we do something foolish, or fall back into a previous dysfunctional behavior pattern.

Using the techniques presented in this book will not only assist you in keeping conscious of your problems, but they will also train you to integrate this awareness level with the dream state to dream these problems away.

Using Imagery to Create Healing Dreams

Imagery is used in many different forms of healing, such as hypnosis and meditation. We can define imagery as a flow of thoughts you can see, hear, feel, taste, and smell. This natural way of thinking draws on your inner wisdom, becoming a powerful force for healing and growth. The unskilled imagination, manifesting as worry, may have negative effects on our health by creating high levels of stress.

We can apply imagery to:

☆ Increase our self-awareness.

☆ Deeply relax mentally and physically.

☆ Promote self-healing through visualization.

☆ Focus within and draw on the wisdom of our Higher Self.

It must be remembered at all times that imagery is not just wishful thinking. This tool accesses both the subconscious and superconscious to bring about a rise in the quality of energy of our soul. This can help you "read" the body signals we call symptoms—so that you can give yourself precisely what you need in order to heal.

A Simple Exercise to Dream Your Problems Away

This method is quite simple and effective. I suggest you focus on a relatively simple problem and follow these steps:

1. Use one of the relaxation exercises I have already presented.

2. Just before falling asleep, present a problem to your Higher Self for resolution.

3. Mentally review your previous attempts to solve it and any other factors that can assist your dream consciousness in finding a solution to this difficulty. Program your subconscious to solve this problem in your dreams.

4. Relax and keep this goal in your mind until you fall asleep.

5. Record your dreams the following morning and review their content, message, and suggestions for incorporation into your behavior or actions.

6. Follow through on these recommendations, and note your progress in your dream diary.

To use our dreams to heal, it is best to simply review what part of the body or mind is troubling you while you are in bed just prior to falling asleep. Visual imagery techniques can be applied to "see" the problem disappearing. This message you are sending the subconscious will activate a rather efficient and dramatic form of soul healing that will begin during your initial REM cycle.

Here is a script you can try just prior to retiring to facilitate your healing processes:

Feel yourself becoming a loving and forgiving person. Consider love as an end in itself. Express your desire to achieve a thorough mental housecleaning....Use positive words and positive thoughts to become a loving, forgiving person.

Imagine the illness or pain bothering you. Focus your healing energies. Quickly erase this image of your illness and see yourself completely cured. Feel the freedom and happiness of being in perfect health. Hold onto this image, linger over it, enjoy it, and know that you deserve it. Know that now in this healthy state you are fully in tune with nature's intentions for you.

I have always been suspect of the obsession many therapists have with dream interpretation. The sad commentary is that this system ignores the wonderful opportunity to utilize the dream state for healing.

We have seen how the ancients and Senoi apply the dream level to healing approaches. My paradigm in using hypnotherapy is based on a similar principle.

You might be wondering how this system could be incorporated into our dream state. The answer to this involves a discussion of a mechanism that was discovered in 1977 and named the *superconscious mind tap* or *cleansing*. This technique is equivalent to the samadhi or eighth stage of yogic meditation, without all of the tedious preliminary rituals and lifestyle adjustments. Cleansing requires only about 20 minutes and most definitely fulfills the Western immediate result requirement for spiritual growth and problem resolution.

When I speak of cleansing, I am referring to the process of introducing the individual's subconscious mind to its perfect counterpart known as the superconscious mind or Higher Self. Visualization is not a part of this process.

The superconscious mind is a remnant of the perfect God energy from which the energy component of our being (soul) originated. Our subconscious mind or soul is composed of compromised or lowered energy.

When we introduce the soul to its Higher Self, the energy of our soul is raised. This increase in the frequency vibrational rate of our soul's energy is what I mean by cleansing.

It is impossible for the soul's energy to be lowered. The worst that can happen in a cleansing is no change. What most often occurs is a permanent rise in the energy of our essence.

These energy changes result in our spiritual growth. At this higher frequency vibrational rate, we are now resistant to the issues to which we previously were susceptible.

Even death can't lower our soul's energy, so these improvements are eternal. When you die, your soul reincarnates with the exact same energy you exhibited at the moment of physical death.

It is during our REM cycle when we dream that 98 percent of this cleansing occurs. The nice part about this system is that the only obstacles to raising our energy, namely the defense mechanisms, are absent during all stages of sleep, including the REM cycle. This affords us a perfect opportunity for spiritual growth and the elimination of our problems, if we only properly train our mind to initiate this mechanism.

We spend three hours every night in REM. By applying the superconscious mind tap, we can now use this time for accelerated therapeutic progress with any issue. Normally, our REM cycle is focused on emotional cleansing, which is necessary for the preservation of life. The energy cleansing initiated by superconscious mind tap does not interfere with the emotional cleansing mechanism.

This means that there is no possibility of harm by incorporating my cleansing technique into your daily regimen. The only reason we don't all naturally utilize this energy cleansing approach is because it is not required to maintain our vital functions. Spiritual growth is a luxury, not a necessity.

There are three levels to an issue. The physical level is the lowest category, and is directly related to our emotional state. This is the basis of psychosomatic medicine. The true cause of an emotional block is not a cognitive one, rather it is our compromised soul's energy. To eliminate a difficulty we must raise the frequency vibrational rate of our soul. The most efficient method I know of to accomplish this is a superconscious mind tap.

Figure three illustrates this mechanism:

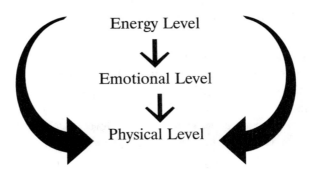

Energy Level

↓

Emotional Level

↓

Physical Level

Figure 3.Cleansing

The arrows always move from the energy level down to the physical. In the case of pain, it is often not even necessary to deal with the emotional level as an intermediary. The energy level can directly affect the physical, as noted in figure three.

The reason cognitive and analytical approaches to therapy simply do not work is because they do not treat the true origin of a problem. The whys of an issue are not going to resolve an issue. The only way patients will truly eliminate once and for all the cause of their difficulty is by raising the energy of their soul. They don't have to understand either this process or their specific issue for this method to work.

Here is a script of my superconscious mind tap for you to try to achieve your own cleansing:

Now listen very carefully. I want you to imagine a bright white light coming down from above and entering the top of your head, filling your entire body. See it, feel it, and it becomes reality. Now imagine an aura of pure white light emanating from your heart region. Again surrounding your reality. Now only your Masters and Guides and highly evolved loving entities who mean you well will be able to influence you during this or any other hypnotic session. You are totally protected by this aura of pure white light.

In a few moments, I am going to count from one to twenty. As I do so, you will feel yourself rising up to the superconscious mind level where you will be able to receive information from your masters and guides. Number one rising up. Two, three, four, rising higher. Five, six, seven, letting information flow. Eight, nine, ten, you are halfway there.

Eleven, twelve, thirteen, feel yourself rising even higher. Fourteen, fifteen, sixteen, almost there. Seventeen, eighteen, nineteen, number twenty, you are there. Take a moment and orient yourself to the superconscious mind level.

Play New Age music for one minute.

You may now ask yourself any question about any past, present, or future issue. Or you may contact any of your guides or departed loved ones from this level. You may explore your relationship with any person. Remember, your superconscious mind level is all-knowledgeable and has access to your akashic records.

Now slowly and carefully state your desire for information or an experience and let this superconscious mind level work for you.

Play New Age music for eight minutes.

You have done very well. Now I want you to further open up the channels of communication by removing any obstacles and allowing yourself to receive information and experiences that will directly apply to and help better your present lifetime. Allow yourself to receive more advanced and more specific information from your Higher Self and Masters and Guides to raise your frequency and improve your karmic subcycle. Do this now.

Play New Age music for eight minutes.

Alright now. Sleep now and rest. You did very very well. Listen very carefully. I'm going to count forward now from one to five. When I reach the count of five, you will be back in the present, you will be able to remember everything you experienced and re-experienced, you'll feel very relaxed for the rest of the day or evening. You'll feel very positive about what you've just experienced and very motivated about your confidence and ability to play this tape again to experience the superconscious mind level. Alright now. One very very deep, two you're getting a little bit lighter, three you're getting much much lighter, four very very light, five awaken. Wide awake and refreshed.

If you are using this method just prior to falling asleep, delete the wakeup section and instead add the following:

You absolutely have the ability to use your dream levels to obtain positive and practical answers to any question you have.

You will nightly use this time to access your Higher Self and find out your true purpose and the unlimited power of your superconscious mind.

Your dreams will now be quite detailed and will impart upon you solutions to problems or goals and an increase in the quality of your soul's energy.

While in hypnosis, just before going to sleep, review a problem that can be solved with information or advice. Be sure you really care about solving it. Now say to yourself, "I want to have a dream that will contain information to solve a problem, such as _____. I will have such a dream, remember it, and understand it."

Knowledge is power and you are going to train your subconscious mind to release that knowledge to you so your conscious memories will become filled with this knowledge and add to your power. Let your subconscious mind begin by giving you a sample of this knowledge now.

Using this superconscious tap, you can apply this method and your dream state to heal just about any problem. Here is a script that you can practice just as you are about to fall asleep.

Now listen very carefully. I want you to imagine a bright white light coming down from above and entering the top of your head, filling your entire body. See it, feel it, and it becomes reality. Now imagine an aura of pure white light emanating from your heart region, again surrounding your entire body, protecting you. See it, feel it, and it becomes reality. Now only your Higher Self, Masters and Guides, and highly evolved loving entities who mean you well will be able to influence you during this or any other hypnotic session. You are totally protected by this aura of pure white light.

In a few moments, I am going to count from one to twenty. As I do so, you will feel yourself rising up to the superconscious mind level where you will be able to access your Higher Self. Number one, rising up. Two, three, four, rising higher. Five, six, seven, letting information flow. Eight, nine, ten, you are halfway there. Eleven, twelve, thirteen, feel yourself rising even higher. Fourteen, fifteen, sixteen, almost there. Seventeen, eighteen, nineteen, number twenty. Now you are there. Take a moment and orient yourself to the superconscious mind level.

You are in a deep hypnotic trance and from this superconscious mind level, there exists a complete understanding and resolution of the [state your problem]. You are in complete control and able to access this limitless power of your superconscious mind. I want you to be open and flow with this experience. You are always protected by the white light.

At this time I would like you to ask your Higher Self to explore the origin of your difficulty in tonight's dream. Trust your Higher Self and your own ability to allow any thoughts, feelings, or impressions to come into your subconscious mind concerning this goal. Throughout this dream, I want you to see yourself freed of this difficulty. Open up the channels of communication by removing any obstacles and allowing yourself to receive information and experiences that will directly apply to and help better your present awareness. Allow yourself to receive more advanced and more specific information from your Higher Self to raise your soul's frequency and remove this issue once and for all from your being.

Dreams can warn us about potential health problems. When disease begins to develop, dreams often provide warnings of specific problems before physical symptoms have become manifest. Such dreams can enable you to take timely preventive measures. They can both name the problem and prescribe specific measures for our self-healing. Later in this chapter, I will describe the healing dreams of psychic Edgar Cayce.

Stanley Krippner described a woman who was afflicted with a rather severe intestinal problem. Her physician was unable to help her. A dream prescribed that she should eat papaya. Interestingly enough, the woman hated this fruit in her waking state. When she followed her dream treatment recommendation, her intestinal difficulty disappeared.[1]

In Chapter 4 we discussed dream incubation approaches used by the ancients. Modern-day approaches still incorporate hypnosis and visualizations to be applied during our dream state. Dreams afford us a tremendous opportunity for healing.

Dreams can inform us of precisely what is out of balance and can suggest solutions to our illness. They give us timely warnings of developing ailments, sometimes symbolically, but often with direct reference. Our nightly visualizations offer us opportunities to work on our healing, rather than be codependent upon authority figures.

The dream world can show us the true meaning of illness. Our dreams provide a context of meaning. They rarely treat physical symptoms in isolation. Dreams relate our diseases to the global spiritual picture of our karmic development. They illustrate how sometimes we need to rethink and redirect our lives, and illness forces us to slow down and smell the roses.

Finally, through dreams we are placed in direct contact with our inner healer, the superconscious. This provides us with a simple and effective mechanism to correct energy imbalances within our body and restore harmony in our lives.

A Bereavement Healed by a Dream

We tend to think of bereavement issues as relating to other human beings. Let us not forget our pets. Patients of mine often report a closer relationship with their pets than they have with their family members.

Fran had lost her pet dog Bonzo a year before I saw her. Bonzo was a beautiful St. Bernard, and because of several untreatable medical problems, had to be put down. This resulted in a severe bereavement period for Fran.

One evening she was watching the television debut of the feature film *Beethoven*. This movie revolved around the antics of a St. Bernard named Beethoven. At first this film brought back longings for her late pet, but superconscious mind taps took care of this issue.

What was most significant was that Fran had a dream in which Bonzo reincarnated as a German Shepherd puppy and came back to Fran as her pet. Fran informed me that she was never fond of German Shepherds, and couldn't foresee this dream as being accurate.

The following week she went to a local mall and absentmindedly left her car unlocked. When she returned to her car there was a German Shepherd puppy in the front seat. Fran had no idea how the dog got there, or who might have abandoned it.

This puppy had no collar and was not identified in any way. She took him home and kept him. To this day Fran swears that he is the reincarnation of Bonzo. In addition to several mannerisms identical to Bonzo, this new dog, now named Squire, dug up an old toy of Bonzo's on the first day Fran brought him home.

Dreams have a tremendous power of healing. Fran thinks her guardian angel brought Squire into her life. All I know is that both of them are happy and Fran was healed thanks to her REM cycle.

The Healing Dreams of Edgar Cayce

The late Edgar Cayce (1877–1945) was named the Sleeping Prophet by Jess Stearns. Cayce spent most of his life in Virginia Beach, Virginia, going into trance and using his dreams to heal others who requested his assistance.

Cayce felt that every important event in our lives is brought to our attention through our dreams. This statement referred both to precognitive and prodromal dreams. This sleeping prophet taught others how to use their dreams for healing and spiritual growth, and how to foster memories of them upon awakening.

Dr. Harmon Bro cites Cayce's philosophy concerning dreams:

It was the contention of Cayce in his hypnotic state that every normal person could and should learn to recall his dreams so that he might study them for clues for better functioning in his daily life... .Had Cayce done his work several decades later, he might well have been studied for his hypnotic interpretations of his own dreams, if not the dreams of others.[2]

It was Cayce's contention that dreams should be evaluated in series, not just individually. The dreamer was in the best position to truly comprehend this dream, he felt. Cayce divided dreams into two different types.

Problem-solving dreams were the first category, and mostly dealt with finding practical solutions to the problems of everyday life, and involved the subconscious. The second type of dream dealt with the growth of the dreamer. This class involved improving self-image, comprehending life in general, or relating better to God. They concerned themselves with the superconscious mind.

It was not impossible for dreams to combine both groups, being both transformative as well as problem solving. This mixed category could be represented in successive components of one dream, or in layers of meaning of the same dream symbols.

Cayce was quite adamant about our ability to control our own destiny. He truly felt that no event was predestined, and our free will determined the final outcome. He stated: "Destiny lies in what we do about what we know" (Edward Cayce Reading 262–78).[3]

Cayce felt dreams serve as the basis for self-analysis. He also focused on the psychic potential of this state. This sleeping prophet used his dreams to read the past lives of others, access the mystical experiences of the divine, and show others how to effect healing of their mind, body, and soul. Out of the more than 14,000 readings he gave to others, approximately 2,500 of these dream encounters dealt with the individual's past lives.

According to Cayce, dreams deal with more dimensions of human experience than any other data available to us. The dream may be of a physical, mental, or spiritual nature, and involve all manner of psychic phenomena. This includes OBEs, clairvoyance, telepathy, precognition, and communicating with discarnate entities.

Dreams can relay to us the status of our body and diagnostic treatment information for physical and mental disorders. Because all subconscious minds are in contact with one another, dreams may assist us in attuning with those in either the physical or spiritual realms.

Here is an example of a reading Cayce gave for the treatment of migraines:

Most migraine headaches begin from congestions in the colon. These poisons cause toxic conditions which make pressures on the sympathetic nerve centers and on the cerebrospinal system, and these pressures cause the violent headaches, and almost irrational activities at times.

These [migraines] should respond to colonic irrigations. But first, we would X-ray the colon, and we will find areas in the ascending colon and a portion of the transverse colon where there are fecal forces that are as cakes.

There will be required several run colonic irrigations, using salt and soda as purifiers for the colon; and we will find that these conditions will be released. The first cleansing solution should have two level teaspoons of salt and one level teaspoon of soda to the gallon of water, body temperature. Also in the rinse-water, at body temperature, have at least two tablespoonfuls of Glyco-Thymoline to the quarter and a half of water. (3400-2)

A thorough study of the dream readings of Edgar Cayce, and his overall 99 percent success rate, will impress even the most skeptical of students of his work. The Sleeping Prophet was truly able to dream away the problems of others.

A Salesman Uses His Dreams to Attain Abundance

Sam was a highly successful and aggressive salesman. He was fired from his last position and hadn't worked for nearly six months. As Sam's lifestyle was a rather extravagant one, he was in great need of money. When he finally acquired another job in Los Angeles, he decided to take advantage of his initial sales call on one of his new company's biggest customers and persuade the buyer for this company to buy additional quantities, so his commission would be large enough to cover his recent debts.

This plan backfired. The buyer was not impressed with Sam's arrogance and "take no prisoners" aggressiveness, and postponed making any purchases for three days. Sam was about to lose this job, he thought, so he called his brother for advice. Sam's brother Ernest had been a patient of mine, and he referred Sam to my office.

On the physical plane, you have only one opportunity to make a first impression. However, in dream world we are dealing with the astral plane, where all time is simultaneous. I trained Sam to revisit this buyer in his dream state and effectively negotiate their differences. I refer to this method as *astral* negotiation.[4] Sam apologized for his arrogant and overly aggressive attitude.

Back on the Earth plane three days later, Sam met with the buyer again and consummated a sizeable sale. The buyer appeared to be quite receptive, and no reference was made to the hostilities of the previous meeting. This sale was not quite as large as Sam initially desired, but it did pay most of his accumulated debts and led to additional commissions.

Sam did not initially accept the dream world concept, or metaphysics in general. He was quite desperate and highly motivated to correct this self-defeating situation he created. To this day Sam is still a type A personality, but is now far more assertive than aggressive. He has referred several of his colleagues and customers to my office as evidence of his continued success on the physical plane.

14

Dream Diaries

When you record your dreams in a journal or diary, they are preserved and foster additional memories. The mere act of summarizing these nighttime imageries acts to bring to your conscious mind more details than you may have had the moment you woke up.

The first step is to develop a positive attitude toward your dreams. Value them, and place a greater deal of importance on their meaning. Refrain from rejecting any one of them, regardless of how trivial or ridiculous its content may appear on the surface. Give all of your dreams proper respect and they will work for you in facilitating your growth and development.

Always give a dream form by writing it down. I prefer written records to tape recordings for many reasons. You may tape a summary of your dream the moment you get up from sleep for efficiency purposes, but put it in writing as soon as you can.

Simply making a tape of a dream leads to a form of laziness. It requires very little effort and critical details are often omitted. When you write it down, you encourage a "stream of consciousness" to flow, and it is easier to more thoroughly describe your dream.

Another reason relates to the practicality of review. You can scan a dream summary in a journal in a few minutes. Playing tapes can be quite time consuming. The incentive to review several hours of tapes decreases with time. Whereas, we can always find five, 10, or 15 minutes to review even several dozen pages in an organized diary to evaluate a series of dreams.

A conscientious effort to log your dreams will bear fruit quickly. Seemingly unimportant symbols will surface time and time again. Your diary affords you an excellent opportunity to trace their patterns and development over time. The result will be providing you with rather significant insights about your psyche and spiritual growth.

One of the most efficient methods to facilitate dream recall is to give yourself a suggestion immediately prior to sleep to remember your dreams. For example, you might say to yourself:

☆ "I will remember my dreams the moment I awaken."
☆ "Tonight's dreams will be clear and meaningful, and I will have total recall of them tomorrow morning."
☆ "I desire to dream about something that will assist my growth as a person. When I arise in the morning, the memories of everything I dreamt will stay with me."

It is best to awaken from your night's sleep naturally. Alarm clocks, children calling you, a telephone ringing, and other artificial and stressful wakeup calls inhibit our dream memories. When you awaken naturally it is directly from a REM cycle, during which most of our dreams occur. The last REM cycle of the night is the longest (40 minutes or more) and it is easy to recall dreams experienced during this phase of our sleep cycle.

You may find it helpful to use the weekends, vacations, and holidays to train yourself to recall dreams by awakening naturally. During these times you do not have to get up at a specific time, and it is easier and less stressful to incorporate this system. Remember, alarm clocks and other traumatic endings to your night's rest tend to block out memories of your dreams. In addition, they may wake you before your dream reached its natural conclusion, so you don't know how the "movie" ended.

When you incorporate my recommended system, consider this approach. Lie still in bed when you wake up and *don't open your eyes*. Let the dream images flow into your mind and simply let yourself receive the data. Refrain from analyzing this material, and just relax. Even the smallest fragment from your last dream can open up the floodgates of information about that one dream and its predecessors.

For example, you may wake up with an impression of some scene from your last dream. By reviewing this reference point in your mind, the scene that directly preceded it reappears, and the one before that, and so on. This effect is not like that of a film running in reverse; the entire scene and plot simply line up in reverse order and play themselves out.

Another method to facilitate dream recall is to repeat the suggestion you gave yourself the night before. This will often trigger memories. You can also review in your mind the people in your life that you feel the closest to. A dream fragment concerning one of them is likely to surface. From this fragment you can ascertain the rest of the dream by the methods I have already presented.

Another interesting technique to recall dreams deals with your body position in bed. Lie still in whatever position your body is in when you awaken, and let the dream images flow as I have already instructed. Next, roll over gently into other sleeping positions you commonly use and continue with this method. You may talk into a tape recorder with your eyes still closed to experiment with this system. The important point here is to keep your eyes closed.

Dream recall can occur spontaneously by an environmental stimulus even several days following a dream. You may see a bird flying, or respond to what someone just told you and say to yourself, "I had a dream about that a few days ago." Immediately summarize this dream and add it to your journal. In the second example, a precognitive dream was the most likely occurrence. In dreaming, as in life, timing is everything.

When formalizing your dreams it is very important to record a unique verbal expression immediately. This will facilitate its preservation in its original form. This method will allow you to keep a song, poem, invention concept, mathematical solution, or other specific idea in its complete and original form.

After you note verbal expressions and other landmarks (such as geography, buildings, emblems, etc.) unique to your dream, record the other fragments or details as they arise. Sometimes these unique elements stimulate more detailed memories of other aspects of your dreams.

A hypnagogic state, as we have been shown, precedes sleep. This is a transitional state of consciousness that represents the borderline between waking consciousness and light stages of hypnosis, which begin our sleep cycle. Dream imageries often occur during this state, and are worth noting. These are usually scenes or images, rather than dream plots. Record these images in your dream diary, and note them as such to assist you in understanding your dream content.

Directing your dreams just prior to falling sleep results in enhancement of their recall. By assigning creative problem solving or other tasks to your subconscious while in the hypnogogic state, recollections of these dreams increase markedly in quantity and quality. My patients report more detailed, more colored, more emotional, and more meaningful dreams by giving their subconscious specific predream instructions.

If you choose to record your dreams, here are some helpful hints:

1. Use unlined 5 x 8-inch note pads that are sealed with string enclosed within the plastic binding. This prevents the pages from breaking off and becoming loose. You cannot write legibly on loose, moving paper.
2. Do not use pads with thick perforated tops, as they are too bulky. Spiral bound pads are also to be avoided.
3. Write with a high-quality ballpoint pen. This pen should be attached to the pad by a string, in case it slips during your recording.
4. Always keep a second pen within easy reach to replace a pen that has run out of ink.
5. Do not use shorthand. Write slowly in your normal longhand style.

Your Actual Dream Diary

It really doesn't matter how you store your written summaries of your dreams. I always recommend you keep them neatly filed in an organized journal or diary. Many of my patients use their computers to store this data. With the marvels of technology, it is easy to access these computer files to retrieve a specific dream. Even if you do store them in your computer, keep a hard copy of your dreams as a backup.

The system I am about to recommend works quite well, and does not require much time to maintain. You are welcome to modify these suggestions to blend with your own tastes and interests. First, purchase a diary or journal that is fitting for this purpose. The more elaborate a diary you use, the higher the value you place on these dreams. I have already indicated that attitude is important, and affects recall rate of your dreams.

Take notes as you recall a dream. This may be the moment you awaken, while you have your morning coffee, or anytime throughout the day. Transfer these summaries to your journal neatly and in an organized fashion. Date your entries and emphasize any unique or unusual aspects of those dreams. Note your emotional response and any immediate benefits these dreams had to your life.

This dream diary should be kept in chronological order with monthly dividers and in a book large enough to hold several months of your dreams. However you keep your diary, make it systematic and easy for your recording style.

Another helpful hint is to assign titles to individual dreams. You can then prepare an index listing these titled dreams alphabetically for a quick reference in the future. This is routine with computers, but not always utilized by manual recordings of dreams.

These unique and idiosyncratic aspects of a dream can represent emerging components of a dreamer's personality. By giving special dreams titles, you facilitate your ability to recall it, and are more likely to recognize emerging patterns and other cues to your psyche.

To add to the value of your dream diary, I suggest you summarize the dream in the main section of the page. In the right hand column you can note associations and patterns to previous dreams. Here you can refer to other labeled dreams, or make any other notes. This translation of your dream will be of great help in the future when you want to quickly review dozens of your entries.

Always remember that no other person can interpret or translate your dream better than you. Only you know how you felt when you had the dream, what associations in it really mean, and how it has affected your life today. A well-trained and equally well-meaning therapist can only guess. As a scientist, scholar, and clinician, I discourage guesswork. Shooting from the hip may be acceptable in an old western, but it does not belong in psychotherapy.

The more you practice visual imagery, the better your dream recall rate. This book contains many exercises to assist you in developing this skill. Here is a simple visualization exercise that you can practice to enhance using your mind's eye:

1. Use a self-hypnosis or meditation exercise to relax every muscle in your body. Keep your eyes closed and breathe deeply, but slowly.

2. Imagine yourself walking through a meadow. Notice a stream in the distance...see it and hear it. Feel the sun on your skin. See yourself. (How are you dressed? How do you walk and feel?) Walk across the meadow to a grove of trees.

3. Walk into the shade of the trees and feel the difference. At the end of the grove, through to the other side, see a chapel. Walk into the chapel. In the chapel is a painting...look at all the details and colors. Down the hall is a statue...note its design, texture, shape, size. Listen to the music.

4. Before you are three doors. Select one door and open it. Notice all the details, the sounds, the temperature. When you are ready, go back out into the hall and enter a second room and experience what is there. When you are ready, go into the third room.

5. When you are through exploring, walk out of the chapel and back into the meadow. When you are ready, open your eyes and write about your experience.

Here is a sample page from a dream diary that you may want to use for yourself:

Dream Diary

Title of dream _____ Dream
Date _____

Dream:

Feelings:

Metaphors suggested by the imagery:

Precognitive or prodromal information
suggested by the dream:

Waking context:

Presleep thoughts:
(include any unusual environmental factors)

Associations:

Integrating metaphors
and waking context:

Follow up data or interpretations:

Here are some suggestions for recording your dreams in your diary that will facilitate your own spiritual growth.

1. Recall as much detail about your dream as possible without censoring or editing the data. Record this dream in your diary.

2. Request assistance from your subconscious and Higher Self in interpreting this dream. I recommend the superconscious mind tap technique to facilitate this step.

3. When reading your dream, note all thoughts and feelings that accompany the content.

4. Always write down your *first* interpretation of the dream.

5. Consider the context, mood, and other factors in your dream before you record it.

6. Encourage free association within your waking mind when recalling the dream content. Always try to record your dream while you are in an altered state of consciousness to take advantage of this "stream of consciousness."

7. Consider additional perspectives as you think about your dream.

8. Note the deeper meanings and any new ideas that surface during the recording process.

9. Review your final interpretation. If for any reason it doesn't feel right, repeat these steps and record the assessment that does feel right.

Record all dreams in the present tense, as if it were taking place as you are documenting your memories of it. This will greatly stimulate your emotional response to the dream. At this time, feel free to sketch or draw any unusual structure or symbol given to you by this dream memory.

Date each entry and review your diary on a weekly basis. Select one dream and work on it from different perspectives, revising your interpretations if necessary. Choose a regular time of the day, preferably in the morning upon arising, to write in your diary.

It is even more desirable to index your dreams by their titles and note all recurring themes and environments. Pay particular attention to correspondences between dream world action and events in your waking life.

When you are diligent about keeping a dream diary, many possible aspects of your life may surface. Your dreams represent many aspects of your life, such as:

☆ A way of looking at your fears, prejudices, and pretenses.

☆ A place to acknowledge parts of yourselves.

☆ A source of creativity, a source of discovery, a release of intuition, and insight.

☆ A way to enact solutions to unresolved problems.

☆ A way of expressing feelings you are unaware of.

☆ Compensation for what is missing in your life.

☆ A way to show you the other side of things and increase your awareness of what is around and within you.

15
See Into the Future With Your Dreams

Precognitive experiences are known to occur in altered states of consciousness, such as hypnosis, meditation and sensory deprivation experiences. The less skeptical we are about these phenomena, the more frequently they are reported. This may be the reason women more commonly describe precognitive dreams.

Montague Ullman reports a precognitive dream during which the female dreamer correctly obtained the name of winning horses prior to their races.

I would like to tell you I have dreamed who would win at the harness races and they did win. In June of this year I dreamed three nights in a row who would win the perfectas (this is the first and second horse in one race). The first night I dreamed the numbers 7-2 would win the first perfecta, the second night 5-2. It did, and the third night, 6-2. It did. The first night I ever dreamed of horses was about four or five years ago. The horse's name was circled Jimmy Cannon, as such. I had never heard of this horse. The next day it was listed, and ran, and won! I have wanted to tell someone about this. This was a racehorse. I also recently went to Latonia in Florence. I dreamed 4-7 would win the

perfecta; 7-4 won and paid $225. I bet this both ways and there-
fore won. The next night I dreamed 2-1. It won the double and I
won. I told the teller at Latonia and he was fascinated. I later
found out he was a reporter for a newspaper and he wrote an
article about me. He called me "The Dream Girl."[1]

An Old Testament Precognitive Dream

The book of Daniel was written in the second century B.C. and
contains a startling example of a prophetic dream.

I saw a tree of great height at the center of the earth; the tree grew
and became strong, reaching with its top to the sky and visible
to earth's farthest bounds. Its foliage was lovely and its fruit
abundant; and it yielded food to all...

A Watcher, a Holy One coming down from heaven...cried... "Hew
down the tree, lop off the branches, strip away the foliage, scat-
ter the fruit...but leave the stump with its roots in the ground...let
him cease to be a man's mind, and let him be given the mind of
a beast. Let seven times pass over him."[2]

Daniel's interpretation was that Nebuchadnezzar is a powerful
king, but sets himself up as god. The Jewish god Yahweh will put him
in his place and cause much discomfort for the king. Daniel warned
him that he could literally go insane unless he changed his ways.

Nebuchadnezzar ignored Daniel's advice and continued with his
megalomaniac ways. The king did go mad and "the grass like oxen...and
his nails [grew long] like eagle's talons." He did retrieve his sanity
after seven years and "blessed the Most High...praising and glorifying
the Ever-living One."[3]

The ancients most definitely felt the main purpose of a dream was
to warn us about an upcoming event. After all, they considered dreams
to be communication from the gods. The coronation of King Edward
VII in 1909 was organized by many people. One of them was William
Cavendish-Bentinok, Duke of Portland. He recorded the following
dream just prior to the coronation:

The state coach had to pass through the arch at the Horse
Guards on the way to Westminster Abbey. I dreamed that it stuck
in the arch, and that some of the Life Guards on duty were
compelled to hew off the crown upon the coach before it could

be freed. When I told the Crown Equerry, Colonel Ewart, he laughed, and said, "What do dreams matter?" "At all events," I replied, "let us have the coach and arch measured." So this was done, and, to my astonishment, we found that the arch was nearly 2 feet too low to pass through. I returned to Colonel Ewart in triumph, and said, "What do you think of dreams now?" "I think it's damned fortunate you had one," he replied. It appears that the state coach had not driven through the arch for some time, and that the level of the road had since been raised during repairs.[4]

The Duke's dream was a classic example of a precognitive dream. Another classic type of predictive dream concerned the assassination of Archduke Franz Ferdinand in 1914. His former tutor, Bishop Lanyi, had such a dream and attempted to warn the archduke, but was ignored. The result was World War I.

Abe Lincoln's Precognitive Dream

Several weeks prior to his assassination, President Lincoln described a dream to his wife and numerous friends in which he was awakened in the middle of the night by the sounds of people crying and wandered downstairs in the White House. When he arrived in the East Room in this dream, Lincoln observed a man lying in a coffin and a line of admirers bidding their farewells. As he could not make out the face of the corpse, Lincoln approached a soldier and inquired as to the identity of the dead man.

The soldier promptly informed him that it was the president and the cause of death was an assassin's bullet. Suddenly, Lincoln heard a noisy outcry of grief from those viewing the body and instantly woke up feeling much anxiety.

Lincoln was shot by John Wilkes Booth on April 14, 1865, at Ford's theater in Washington, D.C. Just three and a half hours before his death (7 p.m.), Lincoln spoke to his guard, William E. Crooke, and expressed concern about those enemies who wanted to assassinate him.[5]

Psychic Dreams

There are many types of dreams that can be labeled as psychic. Each one of these categories deals with information the dreamer cannot obtain through any of the five senses. Hans Holzer divided this genre into six subdivisions,[6] listed as follows:

1. ESP dreams. These dreams contain telepathic elements and involve the development of one or more psychic gifts (clairvoyance, precognition, etc.).
2. Warning dreams. This class involves a depiction of a future event that is changeable.
3. Prophetic dreams. This category represents the foretelling of future events that the dreamer is not able to alter.
4. Survival dreams. When communication is established with a discarnate entity, this type of dream comes into play.
5. Out-of-body experiences (OBEs). Anything from lucid dreaming to classic astral projection dreams make up this division. Remember my earlier statement that all dreams represent OBEs.
6. Reincarnation dreams. When you dream about one of your past or future incarnations, you are involved with this class of dreams. The documented past-life regression of my patient Ivy that I previously described is an example of this type.

It has been my experience, in working with over 12,000 different patients and conducting more than 35,000 past-life regressions and future-life progressions since 1974, that only dreams of tragic or very significant past lives come through our dreams to our waking mind naturally.

I cannot offer an explanation for this, other than to state that our superconscious mind wants us to learn from these past and future lives. We must separate these experiences from *déjà vu* occurrences.

Déjà vu is an outdated term and concept. This phenomenon takes place in our waking state and represents a feeling that we have been in that place before, which is not possible from our history. In reality, these are precognitive experiences that may originate from precognitive dreams, or spontaneous waking flashes of insight.

Conventional psychology is apt to classify precognitive dreams as paramnesia, which is defined as a defect of memory in which the person's sense of before and after becomes confused. This tidy little explanation fails to explain double *déjà vu*, during which two separate individuals share the same precognitive dream. Something else is going on here. The fact that all dreams are OBEs, and all time is simultaneous in dream world, is a far better overview of this phenomena.

Theories on precognition have taken one of two approaches. In one school, the future is viewed as already existing, and is as complete as our present time perspective. The other paradigm focuses on the future as a "plastic" one. This potential future is changeable based on our actions.

As I stated in *The Search for Grace*:

> *Many dreams seem to contain fragments of futuristic material, just as they contain fragments from the past. In sleep, the mind appears to wander freely back and forth over the 'equator,' an imaginary line between the present and the future. At the deepest level of consciousness, there is no sense of the flow of time, only an 'eternal now' in which all events coexist. The theory of a plastic future rejects the notion that the future already exists. It says that tomorrow is real only in potentiality. The future is capable of taking many possible final forms. Only when it congeals into the present does it really exist as an actuality.*[7]

Precognition means foretelling future events with a foreknowledge of actual data that does, in fact, take place. These may appear in dreams as visions, verbal expressions, intuitive feelings, or other types of communication. Precognitive dreams allow for a deeper and easier penetration of the conscious mind's defense mechanisms than if this data were made available during our waking state. There is, unfortunately, no possibility of changing the events received in a precognitive dream, according to this classification system.

Hans Holzer also describes the precognitive dreams of a young girl named Sandra. When she was 6, Sandra dreamt that her father was building a home on the lot between their house and that of a neighbor. Sandra observed a pile of dirt from the construction near the kitchen door. The neighbor's daughter and Sandra were both playing on this dirt mound. Suddenly the neighbor's daughter said to Sandra, "My aunt had a baby girl last night and she named her Nancy."[8]

At this time, Sandra's father had not contemplated the purchase of this lot, nor was the neighbor's aunt pregnant. Over a year elapsed before the events of this dream unfolded with pinpoint accuracy. Sandra's father did buy the lot, the mound of dirt scene also replayed as in her dream. When her playmate said, "My aunt had a baby girl last night," Sandra interrupted her and correctly stated that Nancy was the name chosen for the baby girl.

In high school, Sandra had another precognitive dream. During this time she was out sick with the flu and had no awareness of the upcoming school activities. She dreamt that there was an animal show at school that featured snakes, an armadillo, and a lion. A boy in the audience started roaring at the lion, which subsequently broke loose and chased after the boy. The auditorium was cleared to protect the students. No person was injured.

Sandra returned to school the following day. Sure enough there was an animal show featuring all of the animals Sandra perceived in her dream. The boy sitting next to her started to roar at the lion, which broke loose. The school authorities evacuated the auditorium and subdued the lion before anyone could be harmed. This was precisely what Sandra's dream revealed to her the previous night.

Warning Dreams

Warning dreams differ from precognitive types in that the dream is changeable. A potential disaster can be averted by applying the knowledge given in this dream. Betty's dream of her mother's medical problem (as I will shortly present) is a perfect example of this class. Had Sandra been able to somehow prevent her classmate from roaring at the lion, her second dream would have been typical of a warning dream, rather than the precognitive type it turned out to be.

The Prophetic Dream of J. W. Dunne

In 1902, a British Army officer and engineer, J. W. Dunne, had a dream while he was in South Africa during the Boer War. During this dream, Dunne successfully foretold the eruption of Mount Pelée in Martinique. Dunne, in his dream plot, saw himself attempting to warn the French colonial officials of the imminent catastrophe. He informed the authorities that "4,000 people will be killed."

Dunne was shocked when he read a newspaper headline from the *Daily Telegraph* that he received several days later. The headline read, "Volcano Disaster in Martinique," and the accompanying subheading stated, "Probable Loss of 40,000 Lives."[9]

This dream was both a clairvoyant and prophetic one. During the time he actually had the dream, the volcano was in the process of erupting. This is why we refer to it as a clairvoyant dream. The newspaper headline was perceived before it appeared in the newspaper, so this component of the dream was prophetic. I use the term prophetic here because there was nothing that Dunne could do to prevent this headline from appearing following his dream, because the eruption already occurred.

This event prompted Dunne to keep a dream diary for more than 30 years. He concluded that the reason his estimate of 4,000 deaths was off by a zero (it was actually 40,000 people that were killed) was that he misread the headline in his dream.

His theories, as presented in his book, *An Experiment with Time*, demonstrate that some dreams foretelling events in our future are given to us by news we receive from the electronic or print media scenario we devise in our mind as the mechanism for this data.

Dreams, according to Dunne, are able to make use of future events with the same freedom with which they select happenings from the past, wandering backward and forward through time, sometimes combining the past and future within the same dream. His book details this paradigm with intimate subtheories and illustrations. It makes for technical, but interesting, reading.

Other examples of more scientifically collected precognitive dreams include:

1. Many dreams foretelling the sinking of the Titanic were collected by Professor Ian Stevenson of the University of Virginia.
2. Professor Hans Bender of the University of Freiburg, Germany, collected a large number of verifiable precognitive dream accounts, including some from the actress Christine Mylius.
3. Duke University's Louisa and J. B. Rhine discovered many accurate dreams of the winners of horse races from among the 1,000 or more precognitive dreams sent to them between 1930 and 1955.
4. Mark Twain was also an example of a well-known person who dreamt with amazing accuracy of his brother's death prior to its actual occurrence.

The Central Premonitions Bureau in New York City headed by R. B. Nelson recorded precognitive dreams it received from all over the United States. Nelson listed 11 categories for the dreams he collected. Most of them were inaccurate, but some of these dreams hit their mark.

For example, a California woman told of a dream in which Southern California would be attacked by a foreign country. As far-fetched as that may have sounded, a few days later, a tuna boat was fired upon by a Mexican ship near San Diego.

One dreamer wrote to Nelson's organization and described a dream in which he perceived illness of the crew aboard the spacecraft *Apollo 7*, and difficulty during its landing. This was accurate in that *Apollo 7* landed upside-down in the Pacific, with the crew suffering from colds.

Not all psychotherapists reject the precognitive potential of dreams. Katherine Cover Sabin reports:

> *The psychological dream factors discovered by Freud do not rule out precognition in dreams; instead the dream psychology often forwards the parapsychological content. Dreams can be realistically true or symbolically true. Gifted psychics are more prone to receive understandable predictive material than nonpsychics who usually receive dream guidance through symbols. However, both the gifted and the ungifted should make a study of dream symbols, for parapsychological material is most often presented symbolically.*[10]

I respectfully disagree with her statement that nonpsychics usually obtain precognitive material through symbolism. Betty's case and others presented in this chapter show precise and realistic detail as to the futuristic material received. These "clear dreams" make it rather easy to verify the accuracy of these dreams. Sabin's opinion reflects her position as a professional psychic with an analytical base to her paradigm.

A Marriage Made in Dream World

Dreams have a way of foretelling our future. The ancients knew this, and used this principle in their temples. Several years ago, one of my East Coast patients reported this dream to me.

This 42-year-old man named Brent was divorced and lived alone with his dog Lancelot. He was quite lonely and one of his therapeutic goals revolved around meeting a quality woman and eventually getting married again.

One night while he was in Los Angeles during his five days of therapy with me, he had a dream in which Lancelot came home and was obviously in a fight with another dog. Lancelot was bitten, but not hurt. The next scene in this dream consisted of Brent going on a picnic with a beautiful blond woman, her dog, and Lancelot.

I completed Brent's therapy on a Friday, and he flew back to the East Coast as he planned. Six weeks later he called me to report Lancelot's run-in with another dog. It seemed that while walking him in a nearby park, a larger dog came out of nowhere and attacked Lancelot.

Brent came to Lancelot's rescue and the attacking dog's master arrived shortly. I should say mistress, because this other dog's owner, Olivia, was a 28-year-old beautiful blond woman.

Olivia and Brent began dating as a result of the most unusual meeting. Brent couldn't believe the accuracy of his dream. Olivia looked exactly like the woman he pictured with him on this dream picnic. They hadn't had this picnic date when Brent called me.

Brent and Olivia called 18 months later to let me know that they were married and totally in bliss. They did have that picnic date and their dogs get along famously. What was also noteworthy was the fact that Olivia's dog Barnaby never attacked another dog before or since that incident with Lancelot.

Was this destiny, a coincidence, or a truly prophetic dream? I vote for the latter, and list it among many thousands of other examples of the precognitive nature of dreams.

A Daughter's Dream Saves Her Mother's Life

Nearly every one has some degree of precognitive ability. Sometimes this may display itself as apprehension, sometimes as a hunch, and sometimes as joyful anticipation when you feel "something nice" is going to happen. These impressions cannot, as a rule, be predicted in advance. They come only occasionally and usually without any preliminary warning. We seldom act on them and become aware of them only in retrospect.

Certain dreams carry warnings of illness to ourselves or others close to us. The case of one of my patients, Betty, illustrates how such a warning dream saved her mother's life. Here is her description of her dream:

May 18, 1993 seemed like any other day for me, typical in every way; that is, until I was met by a guardian angel who helped me save my mother's life, and in so doing, changed my own.

It all began when I was softly awakened out of a sound sleep when the most wonderful feeling of love entered my being. I experienced an intense flow of supreme divine energy blending with mine; I felt one with it and instantly I felt a connection to the universe. Basking in the light of this true joy, I wanted to be a part of it forever.

This supreme energy showed me the importance and uniqueness of my spirit...of everyone's spirit. Each person's existence played an integral part of the workings of the universe. I had a special role, a unique role that only I could fill. I was bathed in feelings of worth, value, and complete love. Instinctively, I knew that I had just been cradled in the arms of the divine.

Something very important happened to me that day; a messenger of the divine spirit—an angel of God—expressed its love to me. I had experienced the highest level of connectedness with God and his world.

To my surprise, that feeling made way for an immediate fear of impending doom. My intuition told me that I was being given a message of utmost importance. Very vividly, I saw shining white clouds sparkling magnificently against a brilliant blue sky. Emblazoned in a golden aura on the clouds, and flashing on and off like a neon sign, was the date, December 19, 1993 (my mother's birthday).

This scene had an indescribable heavenly nature to it. Everything was glittering and shimmering and had a strange surreal 3-D presence. This vision was further enhanced with an audio and sensory dimension.

To my right, I heard voices strongly affirming the word 'maternal.' In my left visual field, my mother's face, surrounded in black, flashed before me. Death, darkness, and impending doom tore through my soul like a lightning bolt. I was struck with the eeriest uneasiness and despair. I had an inner knowing that she was going to die!

Betty was very disturbed by this dream. She came to my office and underwent superconscious mind taps. Her Higher Self confirmed the seriousness of her mother, Linda's, medical condition. This led to Betty's convincing Linda to return to her physician for the additional tests.

An undiagnosed 3-centimeter kidney stone was found by her physician. Just a month or so before he had given Linda a clean bill of health. In all fairness to Linda's doctor, kidney stones are not checked for on routine physicals.

Linda's physician was shocked by Betty's accuracy and surgery was scheduled. Another thing noted by Linda's doctor was that Linda's blood pressure medication was underprescribed and needed to be raised. It was dangerously out of control, and had been successfully monitored for years.

Linda is alive today thanks to Betty. In 1996, Betty sent me the following note updating me on her mother's health:

It's been three years since that fateful day. My mother is happy and healthy. Our already close relationship has become even more solidified since the experience. And in that three years' time, I haven't been the same since that angel touched our lives. Its presence is part of my daily existence and guides me with its light and love. Every day, miracles never cease to amaze me. I've grown more spiritual and have a genuine gratitude towards life.

Prior to having this dream, Betty had a rather conventional belief system and would have written such an occurrence off to mere fantasies or anxiety.

This dream did more than save Linda's life. It placed them both on a spiritual path of growth and empowerment.

A Precognitive Dream Wins a Lottery

In the early 1980s I hosted a late-night radio show called "Insights into Parapsychology." Occasionally I conducted a live past life-regression, and had many interesting guests representing various aspects of the field of metaphysics.

One evening, a former patient named Skip called in to update me on his life, and relate his experiences in my office. Skip has a most unique voice, and I had no trouble identifying who he was.

When he spoke on the air, he related to my listeners how he had been to my office the previous year with his life in disarray. Skip was injured on his assembly line job and was retired on disability.

He had marital and financial problems, and his life was falling apart. I worked with him to get him off alcohol and to eliminate his depression. Skip was also trained in the art of using age progression to view his future and reprogram it.

This works through the cleansing mechanisms using the REM cycle as I explained earlier. Skip had made excellent progress with his issues, but there was still one unresolved problem when he left my office.

His future showed him running his own business. To accomplish this goal, Skip was going to have to obtain about $5,000. He liked everything we did, but was still somewhat pessimistic about the likelihood of acquiring the requisite seed money for his new business.

On the air he informed me that he used my age progression technique to "see" a winning lottery number. This vision won him $5,000 in the state lottery. Normally I am pleased to hear about my patient's good fortune, but not on the air with age progression references.

Skip couldn't understand why I preferred that he had told me this story off the air. I informed him that my office would be flooded with calls the following Monday morning about stock picks, horse race selections, and other types of gambling.

My show was heard all over the East Coast up to Canada. When Monday came, I received every possible offer to use my services from blackjack to football bets. This is not what I planned when I developed age progression.

But for Skip I was, and still am, happy that he used his dreams to reprogram his future and positively change his life. He is still married and his business did quite well over the years.

Custom Design Your Future With Your Dreams

Through the use of hypnotic programming, you can actually design your own future through your dreams. This will result in a very special form of empowerment, as you need no longer fear tomorrow, but welcome it with confidence. I have throughout this book shown you that this method is not merely wishful thinking.

It is important to maintain a good attitude when practicing these exercises. There are no dangers, but your success rate will be significantly enhanced if you believe in what you are doing. By acting as if your future goals will be accomplished, more opportunities will avail themselves because you are more open to receive them.

This preknowledge of the future transforms your previous inappropriate beliefs into more positive ones and facilitates the growth of your self-image. Because your brain cannot distinguish between a real experience and one that is imagined, your dreams of the future further reinforce the fact that this destiny is your reality.

The data you will receive are reality based, not fantasy. By readjusting your focus to this new future, you have taken the first step to dreaming your problems away.

There are many advantages to using age progression to train your dreams to see into your future. Among these benefits are:

☆ A feeling of importance is felt, as you now begin to structure your life with specific steps. This also means you are assigning an importance to the project of achieving the success and self-fulfillment that you desire.

☆ The little successes you initially have increase your motivation for additional applications of this technique, and further add to your self-image.

☆ You receive information and ideas that you could not obtain from your conscious mind.

☆ Your confidence in general will increase, as you find yourself no longer worrying about the outcomes of events in your life.

☆ Accept the unusual and expect the unexpected. There are no boundaries or limitations to what your mind can create and accomplish.

Always keep your motives pure. It is not selfish to seek money and possessions. It is only selfish if you do it at someone else's expense or to get back at another person. You may succeed in the short run, but you will hurt yourself and retard your spiritual growth. We are not violating any universal law by using our dreams to access the future. Techniques accomplishing this have been done since ancient times.

To fully appreciate what we are attempting with age progression and precognitive dreams, let us discuss precognitions in more detail.

We all have the potential to experience precognitions. Unfortunately, most of this data is forgotten or repressed by the time we awaken.

The problem with precognition is that the effect appears to occur prior to the cause. We must always remember that we live in a space-time continuum in which neither space nor time exist independently. Because we are simultaneous inhabitants of the world of space and time, cause and effect cannot exist as independent entities. Time is referred to by physicists as the fourth dimension of the space-time continuum. Evolution has limited our physical brain to perceiving only three dimensions. It is no wonder that we find it difficult to understand how precognition can work.

This precognition suggests a very independent nature to our consciousness. It also illustrates how inaccurate and incomplete our previous concepts of time are.

Precognition is awareness of facts and circumstances that cannot be accounted for by science or logic. Anything that can be explained in terms of subconscious knowledge, or by interpreting a known past sequence of events, or by an intelligent assessment of the situation based upon detailed information, cannot be classified as precognition. The subconscious, when relating information concerning your future, treats this data as already occurring.

Many dreams seem to contain fragments of futuristic material, just as they contain fragments from the past. In sleep, our consciousness oscillates rather freely back and forth between what we consider to be the past, present, and future. We seem to be in an eternal now at our deepest level of consciousness in which all past, present, and future events and memories appear to take place all at once. The future is capable of taking many possible final forms. Only when it congeals into the present does it exist as an actuality that we term reality.

The technique I present for initiating precognitive dreams[11] always involves accessing our Higher Self. These cleansing approaches of removing energy blocks (factors that lower the frequency vibration rate of our subconscious mind) incurred in the past can help place us on a far more positive and productive path.

It is best not to contaminate this technique with preconceptions of what the future will be like. This will only hinder your progress. With a little experience and validation that these future events you observed several months ago are now occurring, confidence in this "new you" technique will finally emerge.

The communications from the future may be in the form of a dialogue you hear in your head, just as you hear physically spoken words with your ears. It may be that for you, the contact takes the form of "just knowing" some information came, and recognizing what the information was. It does not have to be in the form of some scene or visualization.

The initial data you receive may not immediately be recognized by you as futuristic material. It is natural to classify the results of every exercise as your imaginings. Eventually, however, you spot some things that, on reflection, look like new ideas that have a different "feel" to them. At that point, you will say to yourself, "Well, I couldn't have made that up because I didn't consciously know the information beforehand."

One concern some people have with receiving precognitive dream information is that they are afraid of violating some universal law. This "forbidden knowledge" principle is a valid one, but not something you need be concerned with. My approach would simply not work if you weren't supposed to obtain this data. As time-tested and successful as my age progression technique is, it cannot allow you to receive knowledge that your Higher Self has determined you are not ready for.

With this background you are now ready for the age progression method to train your subconscious to have precognitive dreams. Try this exercise just prior to falling asleep:

Now listen very carefully. I want you to imagine a bright white light, coming down from above and entering the top of your head, filling your entire body. See it, feel it, and it becomes reality. Now imagine an aura of pure white light emanating from your heart region, again surrounding your entire body, protecting you. See it, feel it, and it becomes a reality. Now only your Higher Self, Masters and Guides, and highly evolved loving entities who mean you well will be able to influence you during this or any other hypnotic session. You are totally protected by this aura of pure white light. Focus carefully on my voice as your subconscious mind's memory bank has memories of all past, present, and future events. This tape will help guide you into the future and the dream of a future event tonight that will facilitate your spiritual growth. Shortly I am going to be counting forward from one to twenty. Near the end of this count, you are going to imagine yourself moving through a tunnel. Near the end of this count, you will perceive the tunnel veering off to the left and to the right. The right represents the past, the left represents the future. On the count of twenty you will perceive yourself in the future. Your subconscious and superconscious mind levels have all the knowledge and information that you desire. Carefully and comfortably feel yourself moving into the future with each count from one to twenty. Listen carefully now.

Number one, feel yourself now moving forward to the future, into this very, very deep and dark tunnel. Two, three, farther and farther and farther into the future. It is a little bit disorienting, but you know you're moving into the future. Four, five, six, seven, eight, nine, it's more stable now and you feel comfortable, you feel almost as if you're floating, as you're rising up and into the future. Ten, eleven, twelve, the tunnel is now getting a little bit lighter and you can perceive a light at the end, another white light just like the white light that is surrounding you. Thirteen, fourteen, fifteen, now you are almost there. Focus carefully. You can perceive a door in front of you in this left tunnel that you are in now. The door will be opened in just a few moments and you will see yourself in the future. The words sleep now and rest will always detach yourself from any scene you are experiencing and allow you to wait further instructions. Sixteen, seventeen, it's very bright now and you are putting your hands on the door. Eighteen, you open the door. Nineteen, you step into this future scene. Twenty, carefully focus on your surroundings, look around you, see what you perceive. Can you perceive yourself? Can you perceive other people around you? Focus on the environment. What does it look like? Carefully focus on this. Use your complete objectivity. Block out any information from the past that might have interfered with the quality of the scene. Use only what your subconscious and superconscious mind level will observe. Now take a few moments, focus carefully on the scene, find out where you are and what you are doing, why are you there. Take a few moments, let the scene manifest itself.

Play New Age music for three minutes.

Now focus very carefully on what year this is. Think for a moment. Numbers will appear before your inner eyes. You will have knowledge of the year that you are in right now. Carefully focus on this year and these numbers. They will appear before you. Use this as an example of other information that you are going to obtain. I want you to perceive this scene completely, carry it through to completion. I want you to perceive exactly where you are, who you are, the name, the date, the place. I want you to carry these scenes to completion, follow them through carefully for the next few moments. The scene will become clear and you will perceive the sequence of what exactly is happening to you.

Play New Age music for three minutes.

You've done very well. Now you are going to move to another event. I want you to focus on a difference in the same future time. Perceive what is going on and why this is important to you. Perceive the year, the environment, the presence of others. Let the information flow.

Play New Age music for three minutes.

As you perceive the details of the next scene, focus in on your purpose. Focus in on what you are learning, what you are unable to learn. Perceive any sequence of events that led up to this situation. Let the information flow surrounding this all-important future event now.

Play New Age music for three minutes.

You have done very well. Now I want you to rise to the superconscious mind level to evaluate this future experience and apply this knowledge to your current life and situations. One, rising up. Two, rising higher. Three, halfway there. Four, almost there, five, you are there. Let your Higher Self assist you in making the most out of this experience. Do this now.

There seems to be an obvious paradox in discussing the concept of the future. We are aware of two types of time. In chronological time, we move forward systematically from day to day, year to year, until we have aged dramatically. Yet we do not *experience* this chronological age until after the fact and we are confused by this concept.

Another form of time is what quantum physics refers to as simultaneous time. This transcendent category is one in which all time occurs simultaneously, so there really is no time at all.

J. B. Priestley elegantly stated this paradox in his book, *Man and Time*:

> *The future can be seen, and because it can be seen, it can be changed. But if it can be seen and yet changed, it is neither solidly there, laid out for us to experience moment after moment, nor is it nonexistent...If it does not exist, it cannot be seen; if it is solidly set and fixed, then it cannot be changed. What is this future that is sufficiently established to be observed and perhaps experienced, and yet allow itself to be altered?*[12]

Other concepts have been proposed to explain how future events tend to be more fixed and unchangeable, as they exist in parallel universes. In these dimensions that exist side-by-side with ours, all of our possible futures are actualized. Although there are theoretically an infinite number of these parallel universes, I detail in my book *Time Travelers from Our Future*, the five major groupings. I detail techniques to show how anyone can perceive these options and program themselves to select their ideal future.[13]

This concept of alternative universes does help explain why many precognitive dreams do not manifest in our reality. The future you dreamt may very well have been a parallel universe whose frequency you are not on. In other words, this event did occur, but not in your world.

My vast experience with progression hypnotherapy since 1977 has shown me that the shorter the interval between the dream and the probable enactment of the event foreseen, the greater the chance that the dream will be played out in waking life unless one is able to avert the outcome by conscious action. Once you learn that you have the natural ability to see into the future in dreams, you can start to experiment with your ability to change that future. This is another mechanism of dreaming your problems away.

16

The Dangers of Waking Sleep

In this chapter we will discuss a rather controversial aspect of our waking life. This is not the same as the conscious dreaming I mentioned in the last chapter. My discussion here concerns something known as *waking sleep.* [1]

G. I. Gurdjieff, the Russian writer, philosopher, and disciple of his fellow countryman P. D. Ouspensky, is well known for the expression, "Man is asleep." His thesis centered around the concept that we tend to understand on an intellectual level in accordance with the habitual functioning of our minds. This results in a reality that is the source of enormous amounts of unnecessary suffering and limitation. The only way we can spiritually grow is to awaken from this habitual state of waking sleep.

P. D. Ouspensky stated the basis of conflict between good and evil is as follows:

> *If a man understands that he is asleep and if he wishes to awake, then everything that helps him to awake will be good and everything that hinders him, everything that prolongs his sleep, will be evil....Those who do not understand that they are asleep...cannot have understanding of good and evil.* [2]

Gurdjieff felt that only at the moment we awaken, not merely to consciousness but also to conscience, could our true spiritual evolution proceed. We must understand that the word "man" includes both sexes, and is used in the context of the era Gurdjieff lived.

We will see in this chapter how all of us have had moments of relative awakening, and how to avoid the many dangers of waking sleep. First, an understanding of what waking sleep consists of is necessary.

Waking sleep is characterized by the following:

1. Being unaware or only partially aware of important, sometimes vital talents, processes, and events within one's own being.

2. Being unaware or only partially aware of important objects, people, and processes in one's immediate environment.

3. Expressing emotional attachment to delusory belief systems, and willingness to defend these false beliefs at any cost.

4. Distorting perceptions of the world in such a way as to subjectively support one's delusory belief systems and daydreams.

5. Walking around in a waking daydream state during which an enormous amount of time is spent in this delusory condition.

The waking sleep results in our living relatively mindlessly instead of in a mindful manner. Dysfunctional behavior characterized by maladaptive thinking, feeling, perception, and action now manifests itself.

Modern studies on mindfulness and mindlessness reveal that we are still asleep. According to Harvard University researcher Ellen Langer:

Individuals can perform seemingly complex tasks with little if any active mental involvement...although people are certainly capable of acting mindfully, they frequently respond in a routinized, mindless way...in much of everyday life, people rely on distinctions drawn in the past; they overly depend on structures of situations representative of the underlying meaning without making new distinctions. This mindlessness holds the world still and prevents an awareness that things could be otherwise...research points to how mindlessly held categories limit human performance

*and even have a negative impact on physical health...in spite of
our awareness of limited information processing, people in general still are far more mindless than psychologists have assumed.*[3]

Langer's work points out that mindlessness is a form of automati-
zation of cognitive functioning and is quite common. She is identifying habits of processing information that are primarily habits,
automatisms that become part of the structure of everyday consciousness. While they often lead to maladaptive behavior and consequent
suffering, they are usually not strongly driven by affective, emotional
forces, like the defense mechanisms.

When we learn to do something, a major source of this
mechanicalness component of our behavior is revealed. For instance,
when we first learn a new task, we must pay clear attention to what we
are doing. We must observe the general situation we are in, the particulars of the challenge to us within that situation, the particulars of
the response we give to the challenge, and how well that response
does or does not help us achieve our goals, as well as other effects it
may create.

Learning to operate a new VCR requires repeated consultation to
the instruction manual in the beginning. Eventually we become expert
at its functioning and lose track of the specific steps of the process.
Langer further points out: "As we repeat a task over and over again,
and become better at it, the individual parts of the task move out of
consciousness. Eventually we come to assume that we *can* do the task
although we no longer know *how* we do it."[4]

These effects take their toll on our consciousness. It may be that
the subtle differences that are not noticed are actually quite important, leading to an inappropriate response that may have quite important consequences. Another possible problem is that we miss what
Gurdjieff calls the "food of impressions"—the stimulation resulting
from actually paying real attention to an apparently familiar situation.
Roboticized, we live a bland mental life of conditioned reactions to
abstractions about abstractions and associations to abstractions—
unsustaining sensory impressions. This process can be halted only by
learning to be in the present and focusing on our senses.

This automatic response paradigm doesn't have to be negative. Reflex
responses absorb less of our conscious awareness than new learning
opportunities. This frees us to engage in other functions. In our VCR
example, we can carry on a conversation while programming the VCR

to record at a certain time. You most certainly don't want to have to relearn how to set your VCR every time you want to set this device to record your favorite program.

Langer uses the term *premature cognitive commitment* to describe forming a mindset when we first encounter an object, person, or situation and then mindlessly clinging to this mindset, allowing it to operate mechanically when we reencounter the same or similar objects, persons, or situations.

A belief in limited resources is also proposed by Langer. She feels we believe our resources are limited, and become fixated by the absolute categories we acknowledge because of this false assumption. We would not need to be so rigid if our resources weren't so limited. An establishment of clear and distinct categories allows us to make rules by which we can allocate these resources.

When we say things repeatedly, such as, "There isn't enough for me!" or "I can't do it!" or "I'm not good enough," we structure our lives to validate these themes. Maintaining the status quo is reinforced as long as we cling to a narrow belief in limited resources. Those who advance by the rigid but arbitrary rules that are set up have a vested self-interest in maintaining the status quo.

Gurdjieff's solution is to carry out ordinary tasks more slowly and mindfully than usual. The insights resulting from this acts to prevent mindlessness from being incorporated in our consciousness.

Our personalities function with contradiction and disparities regularly. For example, in some ways we love our spouse and parents, in other ways we hate them. Sometimes you want something, but you can't have it; you don't want something, but you get it. One part of our being may want to work hard and become rich; another part doesn't like to work and sleeps late. This mechanism results in our suffering.

Gurdjieff stated that if people were suddenly to become conscious of all the contradictory parts of themselves, they would probably go mad. He proposed a concept of *false personality*. He meant that much of what we take to be our selves is not our own free choice but the result of enculturation, socialization, and conditioning processes that may have made us become someone quite contrary to our natural impulses and desires.

Our psyche developed defense mechanisms to prevent this suffering from occurring. The problem is that these defense mechanisms

are the enemy of all therapy in that they do everything possible to see that we resist change. Without change there is no growth and no spiritual evolution.

Lying

All defense mechanisms represent a form of lying. Although most people believe they never lie or do so only infrequently, Gurdjieff was insistent that most people lie most of the time. That they do not consciously know they are lying makes their situation far worse. This subconscious, habitual, and automated lying is the real problem.

We use conscious lying as a defense against social pressure. This often takes the form of a person who swears he or she "didn't do it" to avoid acknowledging their negligence or unethical behavior. This becomes even more serious when the liars so identify with the lie itself that they begin to believe it.

Sometimes we lie and justify it by saying, "Everybody does it; it doesn't mean anything," when something in us knows quite well we have not lived up to our Higher Self.

We discussed defense mechanisms briefly in Chapter 3. One of the most powerful and dangerous of these principles is that of rationalization. In rationalizing, we try to dilute an unacceptable desire or feeling by substituting a plausible reason for the unacceptable motivation.

As with all forms of waking sleep, the solution is one of self-observation. There is always a window of opportunity represented as a moment prior to the rationalization when we have a chance to pinpoint that desire and feeling and deal with it in a functional and empowered manner, rather than by rationalization. By preventing this form of robotic use of this defense mechanism, we can now take a step forward in our mindfulness and arise from our waking sleep.

Denial is another defense mechanism that marshals a strong counterforce that says, "No! I do not want that; I do not feel that way!" There is a strong, violent quality to this direct style of defense. The strength of it, the apparent willfulness involved, makes the user feel alive and determined. You can always detect denial by sensing strong reactions of rejection. Again, self-observation is the key to overcoming this form of waking sleep.

We define repression as a complete blocking of unacceptable desires from our awareness. Repression is best illustrated by burying the memories of rape and molestation incidents deep within the subconscious. It functions to remove the conscious pain of such an incident.

In repression, perceived reality is constructed in badly distorted ways. The desire to know oneself through self-observation may not be sufficient to overcome this block. You may become sensitive to "peculiar" reactions at times, the indirect effects of repression. It may require outside intervention from a therapist to help uncover repressed material. Techniques such as hypnosis can facilitate the recall of this material. I recommend my age regression tape if this is a problem with you. Sometimes self-observation alone is not enough to cope with waking sleep manifestations.

The last defense mechanism we will discuss is sublimation. When you take a desire that was originally attached to an unacceptable object and focus this energy on an approved object, you are practicing sublimation. For instance, a physically aggressive person, knowing that direct violence would cause trouble, might become a very shrewd bargainer in business transactions.

Several patients of mine have reported a chronic history of psychosomatic problems that were resolved following their pursuit of spiritual interests. These individuals had a natural gift for psychic or spiritual work, but had not developed it because it wasn't approved of in their social circles. These psychosomatic illnesses were the result of this sublimation. Teaching these patients hypnosis and superconscious mind taps freed up their psychic potential and allowed them to initiate a special form of self-observation I refer to as *global assessment*, with the aid of their Higher Self.

We can learn from this dangerous state known as waking sleep. For one thing, far too much of our being is invalidated and convoluted in the process of trying to be normal. This simply functions to alienate us from ourselves and from other people, resulting in dysfunctional behavior. The consequences of these actions create unnecessary suffering. This suffering diverts energy that could be used to solve real problems and further our spiritual growth.

The common belief in our culture that a fair amount of suffering is inevitable and normal acts as a further costly defense mechanism that prevents us from questioning ourselves and our culture. Thus, our self-observation capabilities are reduced.

Self-observation is the key to preventing or eliminating waking sleep. The use of the superconscious mind tap and dream techniques presented in this book will assist you both in understanding your ordinary consciousness and waking up. Just think of the growth potential and what we could accomplish both individually and collectively if we could only wake up!

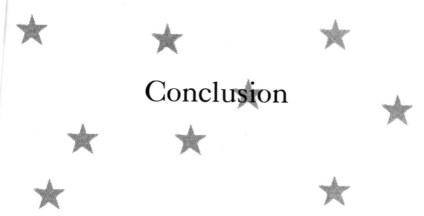

Conclusion

Dreaming is a normal physiological process that is essential for preserving life. In addition to its biological function, our dreams urge us to face the issues that restrict and discourage us, or that limit our inventiveness. They remind us of the responsibility we all have to free up our emotional life. They are, in their own way, a guide to our spiritual growth and liberation from the karmic cycle of rebirth.

Our dreams do not lie. They impart a wisdom that can guide us and make our lives more fulfilling. Whatever our defense mechanisms may display, the truth of a situation is presented honestly in a dream. Sometimes the dream source disguises the message from our subconscious and Higher Self in symbolic form. We only retain a small percent of this version and a distorted form nonetheless. It is easy to miss or confuse this fragmentary sample of a much fuller experience.

I do feel that the dream world is quite real. Dreams are real experiences, and the meaning of the dream lies inside the dream world itself. Dreams are constantly rehearsing us for challenges that lie ahead, and the dreaming mind is not confined to the conventional limits of space and time.

Dream world, as a nonphysical reality into which we travel nightly, is a concept as old as humanity. We all can access this reality and use it to solve problems and grow spiritually.

Every religion has some concept of a nonphysical reality. In Hinduism, there are many levels to the nonphysical dimension. The visions of saints and mystics occur beyond the limits of ordinary human perception. The shamanic journeys into the Upper World and Lower World to retrieve lost souls predates civilization. People have always used their dreams to seek wisdom, guidance, and understanding.

Today a resurgence of interest in these ancient arts is flourishing. In an age of technology, once again we are seeking routes into a dimension where the greatest scientific achievements are transcended by the mechanisms of reality itself.

In our physical reality, our inner states, concepts, and attitudes color our view of the objective reality. In the environment of dreams, subjectivity can totally create the images we see and the events we experience. Dream world has regions that shape themselves according to our thoughts, beliefs, and desires. As we venture more deeply into this dimension, subjectivity plays less of a role and we begin to encounter levels of experience where things do not change to accommodate our individual wishes.

As dream world is encountered, one thing we will notice is a shift in the focus of our consciousness. Whereas the physical senses are the tools of perception during our waking state, more subtle senses come into play in our dreams.

Dreams afford us the opportunity to transcend both time and space, and through inspiration and intuition it assists our growth. We come to know ourselves and grow fuller when we accept the guidance offered by our Higher Self.

Our Higher Self never encourages us through our dreams to pursue paths that will be unfruitful; it never guides in ways that would be detrimental to our greater fulfillment. With our conscious awareness, the choice as to how and what we will accept and act upon is always left to our conscious free will.

Experiencing dream world through the exercises I have presented will change your concept of self, and your concepts regarding the nature of reality. Dream experiences are there for us to learn from. This dimension is a fertile ground in which to plant the seed of investigation and from which to reap the harvest of heightened awareness. It contains clues to our greater nature and lessons in the art of spiritual growth.

We can only know reality insofar as we know ourselves. But knowing ourselves requires more than simply exploring our psychology. An understanding of the true nature of our soul, its past lives, and its future incarnations, greatly adds to our functionality and existential muscle. This undoubtedly involves letting go of our limited conceptions of the nature of self and the nature of reality.

Just as we are equipped with senses that enable us to perceive the physical world, so are we equipped with senses that enable us to perceive the dream environment, the realm of nonphysical reality. This astral plane presents us with a different type of reality, one that we can use to heal ourselves.

When we are involved with our daily, physical lives we are too overwhelmed by the energies of this environment to perceive the subtle reality of the dream world. Some of the more naturally psychic of us attune their consciousness to their subtle senses so that even while awake they perceive aspects of the environment most of us only experience when we sleep. Auras, visions, OBEs, telepathy, and other forms of ESP are but a few examples of the occasional encounters with this subtle reality by individuals who are based in the physical world.

The beautiful thing about dream world is that our consciousness is still functioning. Our defense mechanisms are as asleep as is the physical body, but our subconscious is now able to explore and learn from its perfect counterpart, the Higher Self.

When we use our dreams to shape and guide our lives, this represents a change from within ourselves. Our own desires, not external influences, result in this metamorphosis. This is a true form of psychic empowerment. By learning to control the forces of the universe through our consciousness, we demonstrate the paradigms of the new physics that avers that we create our own reality.

Most of our dreams have the capability of solving our problems, if we only use them properly. Even the mythological themes that characterize many dreams have their therapeutic value. They are a communication from our Higher Self through the subconscious as a way of informing us that something needs to be attended to. This removal of mental, emotional, and spiritual debris will not occur automatically. We must take action.

Joseph Campbell[1] focused on four functions of mythological themes in literature. We can apply these as well to dreams. His first function deals with the conception of the universe as a whole. This cosmological approach assists us in viewing our world in a gestalt, so that the whole is greater than the mere sum of its parts.

His second approach concerns an understanding of the social order and the role we play in it, regardless of the manner in which it was created. Campbell's third function assists our comprehension of our personal ideals and goals. This psychological aspect is part of what I term our "global assessment" mechanism. Last, a metaphysical purpose of these mythological themes exists. This involves a reconciliation of consciousness with the preconditions of its existence. One advantage of this function is that it assists us in reducing guilt from our lives.

Our dreams have always been with us. If we truly seek self-knowledge, we cannot afford to dismiss any experiences, including those we encounter while our bodies sleep. We explore both the nature of reality and the nature of consciousness during our stay in dream world. The realm we venture into is so different from the one that we usually find in our waking life, that from a purely physical perspective, they are unimaginable. While dreaming, we make many determinations about the courses we will pursue in our daily lives. By subtly altering our dreaming focus of consciousness, we can train ourselves to be more alert to these activities as they are occurring, in addition to resolving problems that have compromised our physical life.

We each have a standard of truth that we refer to in judging the reality of the universe before us. Just because something seems at first to be unbelievable is no reason to reject it out of hand. If someone had told our ancestors that some day human beings would walk on the moon, how many of them would have laughed at such a notion?

Since the turn of the century, reputable scientists have proved that it was impossible for heavier-than-air machines to fly, that the bumblebee was an aerodynamic impossibility and couldn't fly, that it was impossible to split the atom, and that interplanetary flight was just a science-fiction fantasy. Yesterday's impossibilities are today's facts. What can we expect tomorrow?

One answer to this question of what tomorrow may bring is an increasing form of empowerment. There are many ways to take charge of our lives and to both heal ourselves and create our own positive reality. Try the methods I have presented in this book. Be open to spiritual growth, and don't be surprised when you dream your problems away.

Chapter Notes

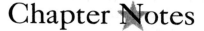

Introduction

1. B. Goldberg, *Past Lives—Future Lives* (New York, N.Y.: Ballantine, 1988).

Chapter 1

1. N. MacKenzie, *Dreams and Dreaming* (London, England: Bloomsbury Books, 1989).

2. C. G. Jung, *Man and His Symbols* (London, England: Aldus Books, 1964).

3. B. Bruteau, *The Psychic Grid* (Wheaton, Ill.: The Theosophical Pub. House, 1979), p. 145.

4. R. Ornstein and R. F. Thompson, *The Amazing Brain* (Boston, Mass.: Houghton Mifflin, 1984).

5. B. Goldberg, *Astral Voyages: Mastering the Art of Interdimensional Travel* (St. Paul, Minn.: Llewellyn, 1999).

6. R. Hornstein, "I.Q." *The Atlantic*, September (1971): 228.

7. B. Goldberg, *Soul Healing* (St. Paul, Minn.: Llewellyn, 1996).

8. B. Goldberg, *The Search for Grace: The True Story of Murder and Reincarnation* (St. Paul, Minn.: Llewellyn, 1997).

Chapter 2

1. B. Goldberg, *Astral Voyages*, op. cit.

2. Ibid.

3. B. Goldberg, *Soul Healing*, op. cit.

4. A. Bessant and C. W. Leadbeater, *Thought-Forms* (Adyar Madras, India: The Theosophical Pub. House, 1978).

Chapter 3

1. E. Rossi, *Dreams and the Growth of Personality* (New York, N.Y.: Pergamon Press, 1972).

Chapter 4

1. M. Eliade, *Shamanism: Archaic Techniques of Ectasy*, trans. Willard R. Trask (Princeton, N.J.: Bollingen Press, 1972).

2. B. Goldberg, *Astral Voyages*, op cit.

3. A. Avalon, *The Serpent Power: The Secrets of Tantric and Shaktic Yoga* (New York, N.Y.: Dover, 1974).

4. M. Harner, *The Jnaro: People of the Sacred Waterfalls* (Berkeley, Calif.: University of California Press, 1984).

5. D. Ashcroft-Nowicki, *Highways of the Mind: The Art and History of Pathworking* (Wellingborough, England: Aquarian Press, 1987).

6. A. Ross and D. Robins, *The Life and Death of a Druid Prince* (New York, N.Y.: Summit Books, 1989).

7. Artemidorus. *The Interpretation of Dreams: Oneirocritica* Trans. R. J. White. (Park Ridge, N.J.: Noyes Press, 1975).

8. H. Betz, ed. *The Greek Magical Papyri in Translation* (Chicago, Ill.: University of Chicago Press, 1986), I:137.

9. H. C. Agrippa, *Three Books of Occult Philosophy* (1531) trans. James Freake, ed. Donald Tyson (St. Paul, Minn.: Llewellyn, 1993), 403.

10. B. Goldberg, *Soul Healing*, op cit.

Chapter 5

1. R. Noone and D. Holman, *In Search of the Dream People* (New York, N.Y.: Morrow, 1972), 32.

2. J. T. Hart, "Dreams in the Classroom: Experiment and Innovation." *New Directions in Education at the University of California*, *4* (1971), 51–66.

Chapter 6

1. R. N. Walsh and F. Vaughan, *Beyond Ego* (Los Angeles, Calif.: Jeremy P. Tarcher, 1980).

Chapter 7

1. A. C. N. Chen and S. F. Dworkin, University of Washington, paper presented at the American Pain Society meeting, (San Diego, Calif., Sept. 9, 1979).

2. B. Goldberg, *Past Lives-Future Lives*, op. cit.

3. B. Goldberg, *New Age Hypnosis* op. cit.

4. Ibid.

Chapter 8

1. E. Diamond, *The Science of Dreams* (New York, N.Y.: MacFadden Books, 1963).

2. E. Diamond, op, cit.

3. E. Diamond, op. cit.

4. M. Ullman and S. Krippner, "An Experimental Approach to Dreams and Telepathy: II Report of Three Studies." *Amer. J. Psychiatry 126:9* (1970), 1282–1289.

5. B. Goldberg, *Astral Voyages*, op. cit.

6. M. Ullman and S. Kruppner with A. Vaughan, *Dream Telepathy: Experiments in Nocturnal ESP* (Jefferson, N.C.: McFarland, 1989).

7. M. Ullman and C. Limmer, *The Variety of Dream Experience* (New York, N.Y.: Continuum, 1987).

Chapter 10

1. C. Green, *Lucid Dreams* (London, England: Hamilton, 1968), 144.

2. M. Arnold-Foster, *Studies in Dreams* (New York, N.Y.: MacMillan, 1921), 28.

3. O. Fox, *Astral Projection* (New York, N.Y.: University Books, 1962).

4. F. van Eeden, "A Study of Dreams." *Proceedings of the Society for Psychical Research*, 26 (1913), 431–461.

5. Arnold-Forster, op. cit., p. 40.

Chapter 11

1. B. Goldberg, *Astral Voyages*, op cit.

Chapter 12

1. N. MacKenzie, op. cit., p. 135.

2. Ibid.

3 Jack Nicklaus, *Golf My Way* (New York, N.Y.: Simon & Schuster, 1974), 79.

4. R. L. Van de Castle, *Our Dreaming Mind* (New York, N.Y.: Ballantine, 1994).

Chapter 13

1. D. Feinstein and S. Krippner, op. cit.

2. H. Bro, *Dreams in the Life of Prayer* (New York, N.Y.: Harper, 1970).

3. The A.R.E. in Virginia Beach, Virginia, preserves all of Cayce's readings in their library. There are 49,135 pages of verbatim psychic material plus related correspondence. Indexing and cross-indexing make the readings readily accessible for study. Their address is A.R.E., Inc., P.O. Box 656, Virginia Beach, VA 23451.

4. B. Goldberg, *Astral Voyages*, op. cit.

Chapter 15

1. M. Ullman and N. Zimmerman, *Working with Dreams* (Los Angeles, Calif.: Jeremy P. Tarcher, 1979), 313.

2. Daniel 4: 10–16.

3. Ibid.: 27–34.

4. N. MacKenzie, op. cit.

5. M. MacKenzie, op. cit.

6. H. Holzer, *The Psychic Side of Dreams* (St. Paul, Minn.: Llewellyn, 1994).

7. B. Goldberg, *The Search for Grace*, op. cit.

8. H. Holzer, op. cit. p 75.

9. J. W. Dunne, *An Experiment with Time* (London, England: MacMillan, 1927).

10. K. C. Sabin, *ESP and Dream Analysis* (Chicago, Ill.: Regency, 1974).

11. My use of the term precognitive here is merely for convenience. Since we can change these dreams, they technically are warning dreams.

12. J. B. Priestly, *Man and Time* (London, England: Aldus Books, 1964), 258.

13. B. Goldberg, *Time Travelers from Our Future: A Fifth Dimension Odyssey* (Sun Lakes, Ariz.: Book World, Inc., 1999).

Chapter 16

1. G. I. Gurdjieff, *All and Everything* (New York, N.Y.: Dutton, 1964).

2. P. D. Ouspensky, *In Search of the Miraculous* (London, England: Routledge, 1950).

3. E. Langer, "Minding matters: The consequences of mindlessness-mindfulness." *Advances in Experimental Social Psychology*, 22 (1989), 137–172.

4. E. Langer, *Mindfullness* (New York: Addison-Wesley, 1989), p.20.

Conclusion

1. J. Campbell, *Hero with a Thousand Faces* (Princeton, N.J.: Princeton University Press, 1968).

Bibliography

Adelson, J. "Creativity and the Dream," *Merrill Palmer Quarterly*, 1960, 6, 92–97.

Arnold-Forster, M. *Studies in Dreams*. New York, N.Y.: MacMillan, 1921.

Artemidorus, *The Interpretation of Dreams: Oneirocritica*. Trans. R. J. White. Park Ridge, N.J.: Noyes Press, 1975.

Ashcroft-Nowicki, D. *Highways of the Mind: The Art of History and Pathworking*. Wellingborough, England: Aquarian Press, 1987.

Avalon, A. *The Serpent Power: The Secrets of Tantric and Shaktic Yoga*. New York, N.Y.: Dover, 1974.

Bessant, Anne and Leadbeater, C. W. *Thought Forms*. Adyar Madras, India: Quest Books, 1978.

Betz, H. *The Greek Magical Papyri in Translation*. Chicago, Ill.: University of Chicago Press, 1986.

Bro, H. *Dreams in the Life of Prayer*. New York, N.Y.: Harper, 1970.

Bruteau, B. *The Psychic Grid*. Wheaton, Ill.: The Theosophical Pub. House, 1979.

Campbell, J. *Hero with a Thousand Faces*. Princeton, N.J.: Princeton University Press, 1968.

D'Andrade, R. "Anthropological Studies of Dreams," in F. Hsu (ed.) *Psychological Anthropology*. Homewood, Ill.: Dorsey Press, 1961.

Dement, W. *Some Must Watch While Some Must Sleep*. Stanford, Conn.: Stanford Alumni Association, 1972.

Diamond, E. *The Science of Dreams*. New York, N.Y.: MacFadden Books, 1963.

Domhoff, W. *The Mystique of Dreams. A Search for Utopia through Senoi Dream Theory*. Berkeley, Calif.: University of California Press, 1985.

Dunne, J. W. *An Experiment with Time*. London, England: MacMillan, 1927.

Eliade, M. *Shamanism: Archaic Techniques of Ecstasy*. Trans. Willard R. Trask. Princeton, N.J.: Bollinger Press, 1972.

Evans-Wentz, W. Y. *The Tibetan Book of the Dead*. New York, N.Y.: Oxford University Press, 1960.

Feinstein, D. and Krippner S. *Personal Mythology*. Los Angeles, Calif.: Jeremy P. Tarcher, 1988.

Fenton, W. N. *The Iroquois Eagle Dance: An Offshoot of the Calumet Dance*. Washington, D.C.: Bureau of American Ethnology, 1953.

Fox, O. *Astral Projection*. New York, N.Y.: Oxford University Press, 1962.

Garfield, P. "Keeping a longitudinal dream record." *Psychotherapy: Theory, Research and Practice*, 1973, *01* (*3*), 223-228.

Goldberg, Bruce. *Past Lives-Future Lives.* New York: Ballantine Books, 1988.

———. *Soul Healing*. St. Paul, Minn.: Llewellyn Pub., 1997.

———. *Astral Voyages: Mastering the Art of Interdimensional Travel*. St. Paul, Minn.: Llewellyn Pub., 1999.

———. *Protected by the Light: The Complete Book of Psychic Self—Defense*. St. Paul, Minn.: Llewellyn Pub., 1998.

———. *Self-Hypnosis: Easy Ways to Hypnotize Your Problems Away.* Franklin Lakes, N.J.: New Page Books, 2001.

———. *Custom Design Your Own Destiny.* Salt Lake City, Utah: Millennial Mind Pub., 2000.

———. *Peaceful Transition: The Art of Conscious Dying and the Liberation of the Soul.* St. Paul, Minn.: Llewellyn Pub., 1997.

———. *The Search for Grace: The True Story of Murder and Reincarnation.* St. Paul, Minn.: Llewellyn Pub., 1997.

———. *Look Younger, Live Longer Naturally: Add 25 to 50 Quality Years to Your Life*. St. Paul, Minn.: Llewellyn, 1998.

———. *Time Travelers from Our Future: A Fifth Dimension Odyssey*. Sun Lakes, Ariz.: Book World, Inc. 1999.

———. *New Age Hypnosis*. St. Paul, Minn.: Llewellyn, 1998.

———. *Unleash Your Psychic Powers*. New York, N.Y.: Sterling Pub. Co., Inc. 1997.

———. "Slowing down the aging process through the use of altered states of consciousness: A review of the medical literature." *Psychology—A Journal of Human Behavior*, 1995, *32* (2), 19–22.

———. "Regression and Progression in Past Life Therapy." *National Guild of Hypnotists Newsletter*, 1994, Jan./Feb., 1,10.

———. "Quantum Physics and its application to past life regression and future life progression hypnotherapy." *Journal of Regression Therapy.* 1993, 7 (*1*), 89–93.

————. "Depression: a past life cause." *National Guild of Hypnotists Newsletter*, 1993, Oct./Nov., 7, 14.

————. "The clinical use of hypnotic regression and progression in hypnotherapy." *Psychology—A Journal of Human Behavior*, 1990, *27* (*1*), 43–48.

————. "Your problem may come from your future: a case study." *Journal of Regression Therapy*, 1990, *4* (*2*), 21–29.

————. "The treatment of cancer through hypnosis." *Psychology—A Journal of Human Behavior*, 1985, *3* (*4*), 36–39.

————. "Hypnosis and the immune response." *International Journal of Psychosomatics*, 1985, *32* (*3*), 34–36.

————. "Treating dental phobias through past life therapy: a case report." *Journal of the Maryland State Dental Association*, 1984, *27* (*3*), 137–139.

Green, C. *Lucid Dreams*. London, England: Hamilton, 1968.

Gurdjieff, G. I. *All and Everything*. New York, N.Y.: Dutton, 1964.

Hall, C. and Nordby, V. *The Individual and His Dreams*. New York, N.Y.: Signet Books, 1972.

Harner, M. *The Jivaro: People of the Sacred Waterfalls*. Berkeley, Calif.: University of California Press, 1984.

Hart, J. T. "Dreams in the classroom: Experiment and innovation." *New Directions in Education at the University of California*, 1971, *4*, 51–66.

Heron, W. "The Pathology of Boredom." *Scientific American*, Jan., 1957.

Hicks, D. "A slow and orderly dying." *Human Behavior*, March 1975.

Holzer, H. *The Psychic Side of Dreams*. St. Paul, Minn.: Llewellyn, 1994.

Hornstein, R. "I.Q." *The Atlantic*, September 1971, 228.

Hultkranz, A. *Conceptions of the Soul among the North American Indians*. Stockholm, Sweden: Ethnographical Museum of Sweden, 1953.

Jung, C. G. *Man and his Symbols*. London, England: Aldous books, 1964.

Kinsey, A. *Sexual Behavior in the Human Male*. Philadelphia, Pa.: Saunders, 1948.

Langer, E. "Minding Matters. The consequence of mindlessness-mindfulness." *Advances in Experimental Social Psychology*, 1989, *22*, 137–172.

————. *Mindfulness*. New York, N.Y.: Addison-Wesley, 1989.

MacKenzie, N. *Dreams and Dreaming*. London, England: Bloomsbury Books, 1989.

Maslow, A. H. *Self-Esteem and Sexuality in Women*, in M. F. DeMartino (ed.), *Sexual Behavior and Personality Characteristics* New York, N.Y.: Grove Press, 1963.

Noone, R. and Holman, D. *In Search of the Dream People*. New York, N.Y.: Morrow, 1972.

Ornstein, R. and Thompson, R. F. *The Amazing Brain*. Boston, Mass.: Houghton Mifflin, 1984.

Ouspensky, P. D. *In Search of the Miraculous*. London, England: Routledge, 1950.

Priestley, J. B. *Man and Time*. London, England: Aldus Books, 1964.

Ross, A. and Robins, D. *The Life and Death of a Druid Prince*. New York: Summit Books, 1989.

Rossi, E. *Dreams and the Growth of Personality*. New York, N.Y.: Pergamon Press, 1972.

Sabin, K. C. *ESP and Dream Analysis*. Chicago, Ill.: Regency, 1974.

Stevenson, R. L. *Memories and Portraits, Random Memories, Memories of Himself*. New York, N.Y.: Scribner, 1925.

Ullman, M. and Krippner, S. "An Experimental Approach to Dreams and Telepathy: II Report of Three Studies." *American Journal of Psychiatry*, 1970, *126 (9)*, 1282–1289.

Ullman, M., Krippner, S. and Vaughan, A. *Dream Telepathy Experiments in Nocturnal ESP*. Jefferson, N. C.: McFarland, 1989.

Ullman, M. and Limmer, C. *The Variety of Dream Experience*. New York, N.Y.: Continuum, 1987.

Ullman, Montague and Zimmerman, N. *Working with Dreams*. Los Angeles, Calif.: Jeremy P. Tarcher, 1979.

Van de Castle, R. L. *The Psychology of Dreaming*. New York: General Learning Press, 1971.

———. *Our Dreaming Mind*. New York, N.Y.: Ballantine, 1994.

Van Eeden, F. "A study of dreams." *Proceedings of the Society for Psychical Research*, 1913, *26*, 431–461.

Walsh, R. N. and Vaughan, F. *Beyond Ego*. Los Angeles, Calif.: Jeremy P. Tarcher, 1980.

Winokur, S. G. G. and Pfeiffer, E. "Nocturnal Orgasm in Women," *AMA Archives of General Psychiatry*, 1959, *1*, 180–184.

Index

About the Author

Dr. Bruce Goldberg holds a B.A. degree in biology and chemistry, is a doctor of dental surgery, and has a M.S. degree in counseling psychology. He retired from dentistry in 1989, and has concentrated on his hypnotherapy practice in Los Angeles. Dr. Goldberg was trained by the American Society of Clinical Hypnosis in his techniques and clinical applications of hypnosis.

Dr. Goldberg has been interviewed on the *Sally, Donahue, Oprah, Leeza, Joan Rivers, The Other Side, Regis and Kathie Lee, Tom Snyder, Jerry Springer, Jenny Jones*, and *Montel Williams* shows as well as by *CNN,* and *CBS* news.

Through lectures, television, and radio appearances, and magazine and newspaper articles, including interviews in *Time*, the *Los Angeles Times*, and the *Washington Post*, he has conducted more than 35,000 past-life regressions and future-life progressions since 1974, helping thousands of patients empower themselves through these techniques. His cassette tapes teach people self-hypnosis and guide them into past and future lives and time travel. He gives lectures and seminars on hypnosis, regression and progression therapy, time travel, and conscious dying; he is also a consultant to corporations, attorneys, and the local and network media.

His first edition of *The Search for Grace* was made into a television movie by CBS. His third book, the award-winning *Soul Healing*, is a classic on alternative medicine and psychic empowerment. *Past Lives-Future Lives* is Dr. Goldberg's international bestseller and is the first book written on future lives (progression hypnotherapy).

For information on self-hypnosis tapes, speaking engagements, or private sessions, Dr. Goldberg can be contacted directly by writing to:

Bruce Goldberg, D.D.S., M.S.
4300 Natoma Avenue
Woodland Hills, CA 91364
Telephone (800) KARMA-4-U or (800) 527-6248
Fax: (818) 704-9189
email: karma4u@webtv.net
Web Site: *www.drbrucegoldberg.com*
Please include a self-addressed, stamped envelope with your letter.

Other Books by Dr. Bruce Goldberg

Past Lives-Future Lives

Soul Healing

The Search for Grace: The True Story of Murder and Reincarnation

Peaceful Transition: The Art of Conscious Dying and the Liberation of the Soul

New Age Hypnosis

Secrets of Self-Hypnosis

Unleash Your Psychic Powers

Look Younger and Live Longer: Add 25 to 50 Quality Years to Your Life, Naturally

Protected by the Light: The Complete Book of Psychic Self-Defense

Time Travelers from Our Future: A Fifth Dimension Odyssey

Astral Voyages: Mastering the Art of Interdimensional Travel

Custom Design Your Own Destiny

Self-Hypnosis: Easy Ways to Hypnotize Your Problems Away